"Are you going to try to seduce me?"
Ellen whispered, her throat tight with
uncertainty.

"Do you want me to?" David asked, his own voice a husky rasp.

"Yes, I do believe I do."

It was a struggle to keep his composure. "Then I guess I will."

"You *guess?* If you want me, *really* want me, you've got to tell me, David. I need to *hear* you say so."

Her face was strained and white beneath the pier light, and he knew it cost the earth for her to say these things.

Lifting her onto the hood of the car, he let her feel the heat of his arousal. Towering above her, aching with passion, he was incredulous at her doubt, and put it off to her blindness. But even if he'd never told her, hadn't she noticed how he could hardly keep his hands to himself?

Dear Reader,

It's that time of year again—when every woman's thoughts turn to love—and we have all kinds of romantic gifts for you! We begin with the latest from reader favorite Allison Leigh, *Secretly Married,* in which she concludes her popular TURNABOUT miniseries. A woman who was sure she was divorced finds out there's the little matter of her not-so-ex-husband's signing the papers, so off she goes to Turnabout— the island that can turn your life around—to get her divorce. Or does she?

Our gripping MERLYN COUNTY MIDWIVES miniseries continues with Gina Wilkins's *Countdown to Baby.* A woman interested only in baby-making—or so she thinks—may be finding happily-ever-after *and* her little bundle of joy, with the town's most eligible bachelor. LOGAN'S LEGACY, our new Silhouette continuity, is introduced in *The Virgin's Makeover* by Judy Duarte, in which a plain-Jane adoptee is transformed in time to find her inner beauty…and, just possibly, her biological family. Look for the next installment in this series coming next month. Shirley Hailstock's *Love on Call* tells the story of two secretive emergency-room doctors who find temptation—not to mention danger—in each other. In *Down from the Mountain* by Barbara Gale, two disabled people—a woman without sight, and a scarred man—nonetheless find each other a perfect match. And Arlene James continues THE RICHEST GALS IN TEXAS with *Fortune Finds Florist.* A sudden windfall turns complicated when a wealthy small-town florist forms a business relationship—for starters—with a younger man who has more than finance on his mind.

So Happy Valentine's Day, and don't forget to join us next month, for six special romances, all from Silhouette Special Edition.

Sincerely,

Gail Chasan
Senior Editor

Please address questions and book requests to:
Silhouette Reader Service
U.S.: 3010 Walden Ave., P.O. Box 1325, Buffalo, NY 14269
Canadian: P.O. Box 609, Fort Erie, Ont. L2A 5X3

Down from the Mountain

BARBARA GALE

SPECIAL EDITION

Published by Silhouette Books

America's Publisher of Contemporary Romance

For Jonah, who sat beside me
during so much of the writing of this book.

 SILHOUETTE BOOKS

ISBN 0-373-24595-5

DOWN FROM THE MOUNTAIN

Books by Barbara Gale

Silhouette Special Edition

The Ambassador's Vow #1500
Down from the Mountain #1595

BARBARA GALE

is a native New Yorker. Married for over thirty years, she, her husband and their three children divide their time between Brooklyn and Hobart, New York. Ms. Gale has always been fascinated by the implications of outside factors, including race, on relationships. She knows that love is as powerful as romance readers believe it is.

She loves to hear from readers. Write to her at P.O. Box 150792, Brooklyn, New York 11215-0792 or visit her Web site at www.barbaragale.com.

Dear Reader,

It is an honor to introduce two very special people blindsided by life.

Having lost her vision early on in childhood, Ellen Candler has lived most of her life sequestered on a Montana mountainside. Facially scarred in an auto accident, David Hartwell is a forest ranger who patrols the New York State Adirondack Park in solitary isolation. Feeling their differences keenly, they have each, in their own separate ways, withdrawn from the world. When circumstance obliges them to spend three months together, they are confronted with hard choices. They can remain sequestered in their comfortable but lonely worlds, or they can challenge themselves, confront their demons and struggle toward a greater happiness.

Perhaps Ellen and David will offer you the comfort of their own story, as you carve out your own destiny.

Much good fortune,

Barbara Gale

Chapter One

David softened his death grip on the steering wheel, wincing as he rubbed his pounding temple. He hoped the rental agency didn't inspect its cars too closely because countless deep ruts had kept him bouncing as he careened up the rough Montana mountainside. Forced to reduce his speed to five miles an hour, it was all he could do to take it slow and not bottom out on the isolated dirt road, dusty with July heat. Peering through the windshield, he tried to recall where the potholes were, but he'd been gone too long, and the light was fading, getting on to twilight.

Still, the evergreens were as tall as he remembered, casting the same deep canopy of shade that had made him so uneasy as a child. Even now, twenty years later, and he a grown man, they seemed ominous and forbidding. Interesting how the lush evergreen forests of upstate New York, where he now lived, didn't make him feel this way at all. Another mile up the mountain, a darting jackrabbit or two, and a house—a veritable mansion—finally came into view.

His childhood home.

David shivered, surprised that after all these years it could still affect him so, this dark pile of brick that belonged on some lonely moor in England, not sculpted into the side of an obscure mountain in the Midwest. Well, he thought as he sighed, no one ever denied that the law was a lucrative profession, and his father had certainly been a most successful lawyer. All this was history; now John Hartwell was dead. Hard to believe, that. John had thought he would go on forever, had warned everybody he would, joked about it all the time, although it had never seemed funny to David.

And leave it to dear old dad to have the last laugh, David thought wryly, the way he'd up and died during the first vacation David had allowed himself in years. A vacation that forestry headquarters had practically forced upon him, insisting that it wasn't healthy for a lone man to take on so much. Finding himself scuba diving in Antigua, sipping margaritas, dozing on a hot, sandy beach— things he'd never done before—David had thought maybe they'd been right. So it was frustrating to get a telegram insisting he fly home, until he realized that it was for his father's funeral. To settle John's estate, as it turned out, because it had taken so long for headquarters to track him down that he'd missed the actual burial.

But he was home, now, staring up at the towering, grand house that John had built, homage to a beloved wife who hadn't lived long enough to enjoy it. Mullioned windows, elaborate turrets, opulent gardens... David shrugged away memories that haunted him still. It was all so long ago, but now...

Now he was stalling, he realized ruefully. Taking a deep

breath, he forced himself to climb from the Jeep and, sailor-like, hoist his duffel bag over his shoulder. He was about to mount the wide slate steps when the great oak doors of the house swung wide and a reed-thin, red-haired woman appeared on the threshold.

Wine-red hair and long legs. A good combination, David decided. Young, but not so very. Twenty-five, maybe thirty. Grief-stricken, if the deep lines around her mouth were any indication. But when she raised her head in welcome, it seemed to him that, through the haze of the late-day sun, a burnished halo surrounded her face, and he felt an odd stirring. She had touched something so long buried that he couldn't put a name to it, but he must have sighed because although her glance fell on him, she took a quick step back.

"I'm sorry. I didn't mean to frighten you," he apologized as he reached the top stair, his dark eyes searching as they scanned her pale face. Black, sooty lashes made a natural frame for the young woman's troubled eyes. Green eyes, very nearly luminescent. Uncanny how they almost looked right through you.

It was his face, of course, or rather, the road map it had become, compliments of a drunk driver twenty long years ago, that scared her. It always happened, and in just this way. One look at his scars, the little girls clammed up, and whoever this woman was, she was certainly no different, the way she looked every which way *but.* He watched her fidget, her flushed face an easy read as she searched for words. Embarrassment was a common response from strangers, though David had never understood it. Shock, yes, even horror and repulsion, he could fathom, but what the hell did people have to be *embarrassed* about? They were his scars, after all.

Her voice, when she found it, was almost convincing

as she denied his accusation. "I'm not frightened," she protested. "That is, unless you're not who I think you are. But you *are* David Hartwell, aren't you?"

He bowed his head in mock salute although he was careful to keep his voice polite. "Yes, ma'am. The prodigal son returned home."

"I'm so glad. We've been expecting you every day since— Well, ever since your father passed away. Welcome home, Mr. Hartwell, though I am very sorry to greet you under the circumstance."

David said nothing as she stood aside to let him pass, his face unreadable as he stepped past the threshold of his childhood home for the first time in more than a decade. Probably as big as his entire cabin back in New York, was his first thought as he surveyed the vestibule. But how John loved the finer things in life. Certainly it was reflected in the design of his home. Quiet colors, subtle lines, but everything realized in a way that could only be called palatial—the long refectory table, the gilt mirror above it, the fresh flowers gracing it. Why, the table was probably three hundred years old, the mirror was definitely Louis XIV, and the flowers were...orchids! What in heaven's name had John meant, coming to live in Montana and building such a house?

"Not much changed that I can see," David observed ruefully as he maneuvered his duffel bag past the young woman's slight figure.

She was curious, but her mouth quirked with humor. "You don't think so? John liked to shop but he hated change, so everything he bought stayed where it landed. Oh, now and then the odd piece was moved, but overall, I'd say you're probably right," she agreed brightly. "Of course, he had a very keen eye."

"No disastrous purchases?" David asked, openly amused. "Not once? *Never?*"

The young woman laughed and he admired the sparkle in her eyes, even if it was fleeting. "If you only knew how he researched every purchase!"

"Like this was his private museum?"

"John Hartwell was downright obsessed! I teased him about it all the time and everyone told him that he should have been a curator, but he always said that if he'd have been a curator, he wouldn't have been able to afford his expensive taste! He was an authority on Flemish art, you know. Museums from all over the world called him every day and they always deferred to his opinion! All yours, now," she said with a vague sweep of her hand.

Amused but unmoved, David shook his head. "This stuff would be very out of place where I live. Best contact the local museum."

"Oh! I thought— Well, that's your decision, of course," she said, the light leaving her eyes. "I'll be glad to help you, whatever you decide."

"Now, ma'am, please don't let's get all sentimental," David frowned. "They're just antiques. There's no *real* buried treasure here."

Although David spoke courteously, beneath his polite manners the young woman was sorry to hear an underlying tone of impatience. She had hoped… It would have been nice for John's son to have shown an interest in preserving his father's collection. No matter how small, it was a museum quality assemblage. But what she hoped didn't matter. She couldn't blame him for his lack of interest, even if it weighed heavily on her heart.

"You're right," she agreed softly, trying to hide her disappointment. "It's just a bunch of antiques. But still, John would have wanted you to claim *something* for yourself. He has some beautiful figurines in the library that might interest you."

"Look, ma'am, how about you pick something out for me? You seem to be pretty well-acquainted with his collection."

"Me? Oh, no, I couldn't do that!"

"Yes, you could."

"No, I couldn't, really," she insisted firmly. "It's too personal a decision."

"You think I'm behaving boorishly." David sighed, sensing that her strong conviction was a part of her character. "I had hoped my dad had made arrangements for his collection. He knew I wasn't interested in antiques."

"Maybe he had some idea that you'd think differently, once you returned to Montana. He loved Montana and he thought you did, too. He always believed you would return, on a permanent basis. Maybe that's why he made no plans. Maybe he was waiting for you."

David countered coldly, angry at the wave of guilt that flooded him. "He shouldn't have been waiting, and well he knew it."

Her face clouded with confusion. "But John said you had unfinished business here."

"I did once, but that was a long time ago and things have changed since then. Once I left—once I made the break—I couldn't bring myself to return. My dad knew that."

"But you're here now."

"A little late, don't you think, for whatever he intended?"

"Late for the funeral, perhaps," she agreed softly. "But not too late to return home. Like I said, John always believed you would, one day."

"As I said, I'm too late," David reminded her, weary

of their argument. But noting the shadow of sorrow in her eyes, he was sorry to have been so abrupt. Although they had no history to claim, it was nothing short of rude to behave so badly. It wasn't her fault if she had no idea of the extent of his grief. And his regrets were legion.

"Look here, ma'am," David said, his voice carefully neutral. "I don't mean to come off coldhearted, but I'm not too good with words. I guess I'm still a little shell-shocked at how fast everything is happening, but I did love my father and I'd be grateful if you'd cut me some slack."

The young woman turned away. It was clear that John's son would not be consoled. "Of course, Mr. Hartwell, I can do that," she said quietly.

"And please call me David, my friends call me David and— Oh, hey, don't do that!" David begged, horrified to see a tear roll down her cheek. "I didn't intend to hurt your feelings!"

"He was good to me, you know," she explained as she brushed away her tears.

"No, I don't know, though I guessed as much. I don't know who you are, remember?"

"We were friends, John and I."

We were friends. Was that her idea of an introduction? Once again David was struck by the unreal quality of the situation, how changed everything seemed but was not, the presence of this stranger, how she refused to meet his eyes. Unless…

He stepped to one side. She didn't stir.

He thrust his body the other way. No response.

Holding his breath, he placed his face in hers, but she didn't flinch. Another inch and it would have been an interesting moment. Well, at least now he knew why his ravaged face didn't offend her.

"How long have you been blind?"

"You noticed. I wondered. Or were you trying to be polite and not say anything?"

"*Polite* is not a word commonly associated with me," David laughed matter-of-factly. "But were you seriously trying to hide your blindness?"

Her smile was lopsided but she said nothing.

"Oh, come on, did you honestly think I'd miss it?" he asked with heavy irony, trying to ignore the faint scent of gardenia that teased his nostrils now that they stood so close.

"Of course not!" the thin girl laughed lightly. "It's just that I prefer my blindness to be observed as late as possible. When people realize I'm blind, it sort of complicates things."

"Yeah, I'll bet," David said, disbelieving.

But she took him seriously, and David watched, fascinated by the way her mobile face registered the smile in his voice. She might be blind but her eyes were a myriad of emotions. He didn't even know her name, but the weirdest feeling came over him, that he would never tire of watching the play of emotions on the face of this lovely, sad woman.

Generally she was resentful of this situation, of having to explain herself, but something told her that it was very important that this man understand her, from the first. So she steeled herself, took a deep breath and tried to speak patiently. "Look, people tend to build whole cloth out of the fact that I'm sightless. I hate when that happens. I'm just someone who had a run of bad luck, who, for a very short time, was very sick, as a child. My blindness was the result."

"And how did you end up here on an isolated mountain

in the middle of Montana, in a museum of a mansion, with a seventy-five-year-old man?''

"Oh, that was my *good* luck!"

David clasped her chin gently, the better to look into her eyes to measure the truth of her words.

"But it's true!" she insisted proudly, and he believed her.

"Then what does that make me?"

"The prodigal son, didn't you say?"

David dropped his hand at that dash of cold water. "Well, hell, just look what happened to *him,* wasting his inheritance, crawling home with his tail between his legs."

"True," she laughed softly as she shut the door behind them, "but then, it was never *only* about money, was it?"

David turned slowly on his heel as she fiddled with the locks, his eyes half slits as he circled the huge foyer and tried to absorb all the old feelings that came surging back. Half a lifetime's worth, he thought absently as he remembered how many times he'd been scolded as a child for sliding down the banister's irresistible, gleaming curve.

"You'll be wanting your old room back, I expect," he heard the young woman say. "I've had it aired—not that it needed doing, of course. Our housekeeper is a tyrant, you know."

"No, ma'am, I have no idea how demanding *your* housekeeper is," he said, surprised back to earth by a vague surge of territoriality. But, after all, it was his home.

With the acute hearing of the blind, she blushed to hear his irritation. Awkwardly she cleared her throat. "I guess you're wondering who I am, since we've never met."

She was brave, he gave her that. "Actually, I thought *you* were the housekeeper, but I have a hunch you're going to tell me otherwise."

"Yes, I guess I should explain. It's like, well, your father sort of adopted me. Not legally," she hurried to explain, "but he took me in, oh, it's been quite a while, now. You could say that John was sort of my guardian. My name is Ellen Candler," she announced, her hand thrust forward.

Staring down at her small hand, David hesitated, then clasped it in his own with casual politeness.

"Oh, you work outdoors!" Ellen cried, surprised by his calluses.

"Very good, Miss Candler," David said with a faint smile. "I'm a forest ranger, back east."

"Yes, I remember now. You live in New York and work up in the Adirondacks. John told me."

Abruptly, David dropped her hand. "I daresay he did." Her apparent intimacy with his father struck an uncomfortable chord. Honed to a cordial detachment with the rest of the world, David had long since learned to keep his own counsel. But that didn't stop him from wondering about the *exact* definition of *guardian*.

Oblivious to David's turmoil, Ellen chugged along. "You must be very tired after that drive, Mr. Hartwell, um, David, not to mention your long plane ride. Would you like to rest or would you prefer your dinner first?"

"If you don't mind, ma'am, I'd just like to take my bag upstairs and maybe think about food a little later."

"Of course, whatever you wish," Ellen agreed softly, hearing his shoes tap the marble tile as he mounted the steps. "Oh, and Mr. Hartwell—David—"

Ellen heard him pause. "I really am so sorry for…that John…your father…I really am sorry for your loss."

Half turning, David stared down at Ellen, her upturned face a delicate shadow in the early evening light. "Thank you, Miss Candler. I'm sorry for your loss, also." He watched as her green eyes misted over with his quiet words.

"Thank you," she said softly. "John was very good to me."

"Yes, well…" David left off, unsure what to say. He was grateful when she walked away, disappearing through a side door. Taking the steps slowly, he studied the winding staircase, trailing a light hand along its polished banister. Reaching the upstairs landing, he fought an impulse to throw his leg over the handrail and hurtle back down to the ground floor. Older and wiser, his long stride guided him down the familiar hall to his bedroom. His hand on the doorknob, he entered cautiously, but Ellen Candler was right. It felt as though he'd been gone hours, instead of ten years, thanks to the vigilance of that efficient housekeeper. No doubt his father had given strict orders to have his room kept in readiness. Still, it was creepy to think that a stranger had been rooting among his possessions, lifting things, peeking into drawers, glancing through his books. But it was what he himself did now, feeling like an outsider as he discovered the treasures of his childhood. A battered copy of *The Catcher in the Rye,* his bottle top collection, pristine baseball cards still encased in their slender plastic cases.

Noticing his frowning reflection in a nearby mirror, David leaned in for a closer look. Silky, raven hair drooped across his forehead, skirting the long-lashed blue eyes his unruly hair tried to hide, balanced against a fine straight nose. The Black Irish lineage of his ancestors stared back beneath a thick and unforgiving brow, eclipsed by a violent network of lines that mapped the entire right side of his face.

He might have grown to be amazingly handsome, but he never thought about that anymore. Nearly fifteen years ago a cruel automobile accident had sent him flying through the windshield of a car and ended that possibility. The finest plastic surgeons in the country had done everything they could for the young teenager. The slim hope that modern medicine now offered with its newly developed techniques wasn't remotely tempting to the man that child had become. David simply refused to endure any more skin grafting—and the excruciating pain that went with it—to effect only the slightest chance of change. Even now his right eye ached—nerve damage that no amount of surgery would ever repair. His raging headache he attributed to jet lag.

He hardly noticed his scars anymore, they had become such an integral part of him. On the other hand, rubbing his stubbly, hard jaw, he realized that he desperately needed a shave, and a shower wouldn't hurt any, either. Stripping down to the buff, David soon had the bathroom steaming, his calloused hands lathering a hard, lean body toughened by eight years in forestry service. But he was tired, and the hot shower too soothing because, when he finished shaving, he collapsed on his bed, jet lag winning out.

Four hours later he woke to darkness outside his bedroom window. Switching on the low bedside light, he saw that someone had left a tall glass of orange juice, some hard cheese and a plate of biscuits. The redoubtable Miss Ellen, he guessed wryly as he gratefully devoured the cookies. Many thanks, ma'am, he silently saluted with the icy glass. And I do hope you enjoyed the view, he grinned as he glanced down at his naked body.

Oh, but she would not have, he reminded himself with a twinge of guilt for his foolish thoughts.

Half an hour later, dressed in chinos and a light summer sweater, David sauntered into the library. He frowned as he paused by the bar. Fortification? But before he could pour himself a drink, a faint rustle distracted him. He glanced in the direction of the fireplace, where a fire had been lit against the evening chill.

Nestled on the sofa, a book resting in her lap, Ellen Candler faced the fire. "David?"

"Yes, ma'am, it's me," he answered promptly.

She really was lovely, he thought, her pale skin glowing in the firelight, her red hair a golden waterfall burnished by the fire. How on earth had she managed to live here these past ten years, and he never heard a word of her existence? How careful the old man had been, to never mention her. How strange.

"Up kind of late, aren't you? I was thinking of a drink. Care to join me?"

"I…um…" Ellen flushed, feeling foolish at her inexplicable attack of shyness. But David's deep voice was so devoid of emotion, she wasn't sure how to respond.

"Don't feel obliged. I don't mind drinking alone," David said briskly as he splashed some bourbon into a glass and settled on the sofa. "By the way, thanks for that midnight snack I found beside my bed. I fell asleep, just as you predicted."

"You had a very long day. When you didn't show for dinner, I understood, but I thought you might want something when you woke."

"You were right absolutely right. Those biscuits didn't last a minute." Tossing off half the bourbon, David rested an arm along the back of the sofa and stretched his feet toward the fire. Looking around the library, he could see that nothing much had changed here, either, aside from the presence of the young woman. Sitting beside her, David enjoyed the unexpected pleasure of perfume suddenly wafting to his nostrils. A flowery concoction, delicate and faint. Gardenias again. He hadn't smelled perfume in years and discovered that he missed it. Wrapped in its elusive magic, he turned his head her way, wanting more.

"Is it hard to master Braille?" he asked, glancing at the spine of her book.

"Not if you want to read," Ellen smiled, unaware of the captivating picture she made.

"What's it called?" David teased, running his fingers over the dots and dashes. "I don't know Braille."

"The Return of the Native."

"Never read it."

"I love Thomas Hardy and— Oh, I never thought!"

David laughed even though it was something only half his face could do. Somehow, though, because Ellen could not see his distortions, he felt freer to emote. "Please, don't apologize! There is an irony here that is irresistible! After all, I am a native returning home, too, in my own way."

"Yes, well," she said uncertainly, "as long as you understand that I meant nothing by it. I'm plowing my way through all Hardy's books."

"Jude the Obscure, too?"

"Jude the Obscure, too!" she admitted. "Hey, I thought you just said you'd never read Thomas Hardy."

"I never said I hadn't read old Thom Hardy, I just said I'd never read *The Return of the Native.*"

"Oh. Well, it's my favorite."

"Then I'll put it on my list of books to read. Brilliant *and* beautiful! Seeing you now, I understand why my father kept you under wraps." He was glad he could openly admire her, she certainly was a pretty little thing. More than pretty, quite beautiful, actually, even if she did look drawn and tired. John had shown good taste, but how on earth had he had the nerve to rob such a cradle? He watched as she played with her book, her face an easy read as she searched to uphold her end of conversation. Failing miserably, she gulped her silence like a fish and he supposed she was grieving, which would make conversation even more difficult. Theirs even more so. He wondered, too, how she felt about his father.

"Did you love my father?" The words were out of his mouth before he could stop them. Even David was shocked to hear the tactless question floating on the air. But he couldn't bring himself to retract it. Something wicked in him wanted to know. No one who knew him would believe the way he was acting, behaving like a fool, barely in control of a conversation he'd never meant to begin.

"Sorry, Miss Candler. That was unkind, even for me. Maybe I'm more upset than I want to admit. I guess I'm not quite sure how to treat you, although I sure don't wish to quarrel with you. As my father's mistress, I know how much respect is due you."

"His mistress?" Ellen gasped. "Oh, how *could* you think that? John Hartwell was the kindest, most generous man who ever lived, and he would have never...never— Oh, you dreadful man! How could you think such an awful thing?"

David's face grew hot in the face of his mistake. "Hey, I just assumed...your living here all these years. You're so beautiful, I just figured... Hell, why else would anyone who looked like you want to hide away on the top of a mountain?"

Ellen scrambled to her feet, fumbling for her cane. "I'll tell you how it is, Mr. David Hartwell," she exclaimed. "I was born here in Montana. My parents were attorneys down in Floweree and very good friends with your father. They were going about county business when they were

killed in a plane crash, six years ago. I was seventeen—
an only child of only children—about to be fostered when
John heard and intervened." How to explain the kindness
of an old man to a young girl? Taking her in at an age
when most men were planning their retirement, asking
nothing in return except some decent dinner conversation.
Surely he had given more than he received, but how to
explain that to David? Her words sounded inadequate,
even to her own ears.

"Took you in, you mean?" he asked uncertainly,
amazed at his father's generosity.

"Took me in," she repeated proudly. "A grief-stricken
teenager who also happened to be blind. Quite a handful
for a man about to settle into his senior years, don't you
think? Young as I was, I knew that. I knew the generosity
of his act. The day I walked through his front door, I
vowed never to make him regret his decision, and he
never did!"

David stared into her grass-green eyes, shiny with
tears—or was it anger? It didn't matter. The look she harbored was unforgiving. "Look here, Ellen, I didn't
know."

Ellen's body language was her answer to the apology
in his voice. She was rigid, her breathing shallow, her
voice arctic and impersonal, when finally she spoke. "My
cane, please. I thought I left it near the fireplace."

He found it at once, a beautifully carved mahogany
staff inlaid with mother-of-pearl. He'd bet anything it was
an antique, and a gift from his father, but he didn't dare
ask.

"Thank you," she said coldly. "Now, if you'll point
me toward the door, I seem to have lost my bearings."

Turning her in the direction she requested, David's fingers clasped Ellen's shoulders, his touch light. But her

stiff resistance made him want to shake her. "Listen, Miss Candler, I'm only trying to understand how things were. There was a lot of distance between my father and me, and now I'm here, I'm beginning to see it was greater than I thought. I mean, look how it is for me! He never even mentioned you, for Pete's sake! Don't you think there's something odd in that?"

He must have touched a chord because he felt her ease up, ever so slightly. "I suppose," she admitted slowly.

"Yes, you had best!" David agreed with mock severity. "I don't suppose you have any idea why he kept your presence a secret from me?"

"None whatsoever!" A thin chill clung to Ellen's words. "I didn't even know he had. I always assumed you knew about me. After all, he talked about *you!*"

"And you never thought it strange that we never met?"

Ellen frowned. "Of course I did, but after a while I just figured you were busy and couldn't be bothered with an old man and a blind, adolescent girl."

"I would never be so unkind!"

"How could I know that?"

"Why would you not? Did John portray me as some sort of monster?"

"A monster?" she repeated, vaguely amused.

And in that instant, in the innocence of her smile, David knew that Ellen knew nothing about his scars, that his father had been kinder than expected, and he was grateful. Although he had long learned to live with his disfigurement, regret was an old wound that never fully healed. Ordinarily he was philosophical about those things beyond his reach, but something about Ellen had touched him, and for all she confused him, she seemed a gentle, straightforward soul. And then, certainly she was a great beauty, and he was a great respecter of beauty, he himself so badly maimed.

She sighed so charmingly he wished they could call a truce and begin again. But then, he wished many things that were never going to happen, and wishing had made him a bitter man. So he shrugged away his curiosity and bartered her ignorance for a rare moment of peace, when he could pretend for an hour that he was normal and uncut. He cupped her cheek, watched as she blushed, and was grateful that, for once, it had nothing to do with revulsion. "I give you my word, Ellen Candler, that for as long as I know you, I will never willfully cause you pain."

Since she couldn't see the sincerity in his eyes, her only gauge was the sound of David's voice. She stepped back, hoping she was out of range of his touch. She wasn't sure she *wanted* his protection, wasn't sure if this knight's armor was all that shiny, even if he *was* John's son.

"Harry Gold, your father's attorney, will be here tomorrow. He said he had important things to say about John's will."

Perceiving that Ellen was trying to create a physical distance, David was careful not to trail her. "I know Harry quite well. He helped my father to raise me, after my mother died."

"That's good. Then you have someone you can trust. And now, Mr. Hartwell," Ellen sighed, unable to fight the heaviness in her heart, "if you don't mind, I'm very tired and I'd like to go to bed."

Not daring to argue with the sadness in her eyes, David watched as Ellen left, her path unerring as she headed for the door. The tables turned so swiftly, he was helpless to do anything but stare as she closed the door behind her.

He stood lost in thought until the night chill finally roused him. Throwing a fresh log on the fire, he found the decanter of bourbon and retrieved his glass. It would be a long night and he had no other friends.

Chapter Two

Harry Gold, attorney for the late John Hartwell, arrived promptly at ten o'clock the next morning. The witching hour for lawyers, Ellen mused as she made her way to the library. As far away as the hall, her sensitive nose picked up the aromatic scent of an expensive cigar that always seemed to be in the air when Harry was around. Harry would probably die with a Havana clenched between his teeth. Turning the doorknob, she tensed involuntarily. Cigar smoke may have disguised any scent of David Hartwell she might recognize, but when he cleared his throat, she knew he was in the room. Her red curls severely anchored by tortoiseshell combs, her stiff spine sent an unmistakable message as she entered the library.

To David, looking up as he pored over some papers, Ellen looked every inch a queen as she glided across the room. Damned if she wasn't intent on behaving like one, too, he grinned as he watched her raise her elegant chin and purse her dainty pink lips against any threat of conversation. From him! Harry Gold was another matter altogether. He watched as Harry hurried to her side, whispering his condolences, positioning a chair for her, assuring her comfort. Feeling slighted, David pulled his chair alongside Ellen's and sat so heavily the chair squeaked in protest. By the way she frowned, he guessed that Ellen would have liked to protest, too, and it gave him bad-tempered satisfaction. But if he were honest, his temper had more to do with the hangover he had given himself than anything Ellen had done. Still, he felt as though he'd just won a small skirmish in a larger battle. What that battle was about, he had no idea, only that he and Ellen were its main combatants—its only combatants—and that she was fully engaged, too. Well, let the hostilities begin, he thought bitterly as he gave the go-ahead to Harry Gold.

"For the record, David, my condolences. Unfortunate business, eh? So sudden—John's passing, I mean. You should have been told that he was ill but he refused to tell you. Kept saying he'd bounce back. He didn't want you to think that you must come home, not if you didn't want to."

"Harry, we all knew it was for the best I left Montana. Better for me, better for my father."

Harry shook his head, his mouth a melancholy twist. "We knew *you* believed that, David, but we never could figure out how to persuade you otherwise."

"Too many memories," David explained with shrug. "You know that better than most. There were some things I had to do alone. Make my own way, on my own terms."

"Ah, well, what's done is done. Shall I start with the pensions and endowments? There are quite a few."

"Perhaps we might skip over them," David suggested.

"After all, we're among friends, aren't we, and I'm sure my dad wouldn't have wanted us to drag this out. The endowments are probably everything they should be, especially since you drew them up. Don't you agree, Ellen?"

If she didn't understand his words, she surely understood his meaning when David covered her hand with his own. "Of course," she agreed quickly, startled by the unexpected contact.

"Good," he said softly, his hand hovering over hers. "Please, continue, then, Harry. We won't say another word."

"Well, then. In aid of cutting to the chase..." Throwing down the papers he was holding, Harry leaned back in his chair, his fingers a temple over his vast belly as he fastened his eyes on the ceiling. "John Hartwell has left the bulk of his estate to you both—*equally.*"

"Everything left is to be split down the middle. My guess is about two million each. With certain stipulations," he warned as he lowered his eyes to face his audience of two. *"Certain ironclad stipulations,"* he added ominously.

This time it was Ellen who reached for the hand that had late imprisoned hers, her sightless eyes wide with surprise. David stared at the long, delicate fingers that curled around his hard knuckles, his mouth a tight slash that pulled at his scars. He watched her green eyes fill with tears, her lips quivering as she spoke.

"David, I had no idea, you must believe that! I mean, I knew he was leaving me something, he'd told me so. But two million dollars! I'll sign it back over to you immediately. I only need a very little to tide me over. You're his son, after all. I don't deserve this."

Harry reshuffled his papers and peered over his glasses.

"I think, young miss, that perhaps I ought to finish before either of you makes any decisions. These ironclad stipulations, you see…'' he explained, almost apologetic. "The situation is such that—I'm sorry, David, but this is the case—that you, 'said David Hartwell, is required, in order to meet the terms of the will, to attend to the well-being of one Miss Ellen Candler, for the next four months…'''

"Excuse me?"

'''…twenty-four hours a day,''' Harry continued, his voice becoming sharper and sterner, '''seven days a week, until such time—deemed by her doctors, in writing—as no longer essential to her well-being.' John has left behind for you, David, a sealed letter explaining his reasons. But in essence, if you refuse—or in the unlikely event that Ellen declines your help—'' Harry concluded solemnly ''—the entire estate is to be signed over to charity—pensions and endowments included."

"Why, that's blackmail!" David swore, jumping to his feet.

"Oh, John, what have you done?" Ellen whispered, her shoulders drooping.

David rose to his full height and glared down at Harry. "You can't be serious!" he hissed. "Are we talking *living together? Co-habitating?* As in *man and wife?*"

Harry looked up, amused for the first time that morning. "Really, David, I think John intended something a little bit more…brotherly."

"Dammit, Harry, you'd better talk quickly or some cat hospital is going to be very happy tomorrow!"

"Very well, David. Ellen is scheduled for eye surgery in early October. She needs someone to care for her till then. John needed someone he could trust absolutely, and you're it! And just in case you're thinking to hell with it,

Ellen needs the money desperately, even if you don't. Surgery is a very expensive proposition, exceedingly so, in her case, and Ellen has never been able to buy insurance. Preexisting condition, or some such nonsense. Anyway, no insurance company would take her on. So, as I said, my boy, *you're it!*''

The room was silent as everyone digested Harry's words. David felt murderous, although he knew he couldn't blame Harry. His father was the sole author of this misdeed, and David knew that no one, not even Harry, had ever been able to sway John Hartwell once his mind was made up.

"Damn!" The sound of David's fist resounded through the room as it came crashing down on the desk.

"Mr. Gold," Ellen begged, her hands twisting in her lap, "surely you can see for yourself that this won't do. There must be some way around it. John couldn't have meant…he must have known that David wouldn't…'' Words failed her, but David knew what she meant.

"Ellen's right," David agreed coldly. "I'm not fit to live with. You know that better most, Harry." Unconsciously he rubbed his scarred cheek, a gesture not lost on Harry Gold. But the gesture was futile. Harry's hands were tied.

"I really am sorry," he clucked sympathetically as he shuffled to his feet, "but there's nothing I can do, absolutely nothing. It's an airtight will. Unfortunately you both have only until tomorrow noon to decide what to do. That's another stipulation of the will. John didn't want things dragged out. I'll return at twelve for your decision.''

Walking toward the door, he paused by David's side, placing a sympathetic hand on the young man's shoulder. "I'm terribly sorry, son. Believe me when I say I tried my best to talk your father out of this. But you know John. He refused to reconsider—said something about cats and canaries. His letter is on the desk, there. Maybe it will explain things better. I certainly do hope so.''

Stunned, neither Ellen nor David spoke for some time after Harry left. Ellen was a million miles away, while David perched on the edge of the desk, staring hard at the woman who had him trapped. It was Ellen who spoke first.

''I'm sorry, David, I really am. I had no idea. It's kind of spooky the way John is trying to control your life almost from his grave.''

''What about yours?''

''I know, it's crazy.''

''Do you at least know what's in his letter?''

''No, I do not, but he was very thorough.''

''That he was.''

''And I might as well tell you now that he knew he was dying, for well over a year.''

''You're joking! Harry said Dad knew he was ill, but not dying! And certainly not for a year!''

''I wish I were joking,'' Ellen said sadly. ''Maybe that will go a little way toward explaining his behavior. I begged him to tell you how sick he was. We had quite an argument over it, more than one, but he refused—the only thing he ever refused me. I even tried to call you myself, one morning, but he walked in while I was dialing and became absolutely livid. He insisted I hang up, and swore me to secrecy right then and there. He certainly knew how to tie up loose ends, though, and I guess I was one of them. I just wish he'd asked me what *I* wanted. He could be a little autocratic at times.''

''A little?'' David snorted as he rose to his feet. ''Now there's an understatement!''

Ellen took a deep breath, courage fighting with her instinct to run. Courage won out, but the cost was high. John Hartwell's high-handedness, coupled with David's resentment, was upsetting. The way Harry Gold had kept apologizing to David had really begun to grate! Hey, what about her? she'd wanted to shout. Didn't she rate the same consideration? What on earth was so special about David Hartwell, that everyone should feel sorry for *him?* After all, *she* was the one who was going to undergo surgery! If anyone should complain...

She stopped short, shocked by her display of self-pity. If she didn't watch out, she was going to begin to sound like an off-key singer in a honky-tonk bar. Still, David Hartwell was so bitter, Ellen had to wonder, and not for the first time, exactly what had happened to him. It was awful, that much she knew, but only because of certain allusions John Hartwell had made about David, not because of anything specific John had told her. When pressed, John had always blown her off, and now, here David was, raising the same red flag to any and all trespassers who dared to cross the same line his own father had so carefully drawn. It was enormously irritating.

"You know, John hasn't asked you to do all that much, just help me out for a couple of months. Does my blindness make you uncomfortable? People sometimes do have that reaction. Being handicapped is not a popular venue."

David's silence was awful.

"Yes, well, perhaps we need a break," she decided, fiddling nervously with her cane. "I know we have an important decision to make, but this whole thing has been a big surprise to both of us. I know *I* certainly need time to sort things out. John was very good to me, but this... I need to try and figure out what he meant."

"The answer may be in this envelope," David said, forcing himself to speak as Ellen rose to her feet.

"I'm sure it is," she agreed with a tight smile, "but you must read it first, alone. It's what John wanted, or it would have had both our names on the envelope."

A curious brooding filled David's heart as he watched her escape to the safety of her rooms. How much had she known? How hard had Harry Gold really fought this will? How much had John laughed? He hardly knew what he was doing as he opened his father's letter.

Greetings, my son, from your dying father,

Now, I ask you, how's that for an opening? I trust it got your attention, something I wasn't very good at doing in real life. My truest regret is that we won't have time to make our peace—we would have, you know. I believe that with all my heart—because if you're reading this, then the worst has happened—but you've come home.

The car accident you suffered as a boy left a void you never allowed me to fill. Well, I am going to fill it now. However you have rewritten history is the quarrel of a young child, but suffice it to say—to the wounded man that poor, scarred boy has become—I leave my most valued possession. You're the only one to whom I can entrust the well-being of Ellen Candler. She needs you, although she would never admit to it and I know you will protect her with your life. In return, she will give you back yours. I only wish I could be there to enjoy the fireworks.

Your loving father,
John

David stared down at the letter crumpled in his fist. *Got me!* Just as he knew he would. He closed his eyes and massaged his brow, fighting the onslaught of a headache. This was no time for a headache, not when he needed his wits about him—for Ellen's sake, if nothing else. Even if it was she who had unwittingly opened the old wounds of that *poor, scarred schoolboy! Wounded man!* Let's not forget *that* part! But hey, he could be forgiven a lot of sins for what happened one night, twenty long years ago! And the personal cost to him—well, hell, only his damned face—and all semblance of normal life! And if anybody doubted that, they just had to watch people gawk when he walked down the street, or went to a museum, or entered a restaurant, or…or looked in a goddamned mirror and saw what *he* saw every goddamned day of his tormented life!

Two million dollars and a blind girl!

Fireworks? David shook his head sadly. More like murder in the first degree—and who'd be holding the smoking gun was anybody's guess.

Ellen kept to her room that afternoon, perhaps unable to summon the energy to go another round with him. Relieved by her disappearance, David decided to hike the three miles to the summit of the mountain. If he stayed in that mausoleum one minute longer, he thought he would go crazy. It made his skin crawl. Too many memories haunted the place. Every turn he made, he expected to see his father and every room he entered, he looked for his mother, his beautiful mother, always ready to laugh, always ready to stop what she was doing and gather him up in her soft, perfumed arms. Almost as if she had known their time together would be short. Sometimes he thought that when she'd died, she'd taken his laughter with her. His father's, too. Laughter, perfume, hugs and kisses—all the soft, sweet things in life that her two grieving menfolk never managed to make up for.

It was dark, nine-thirty, when he finally returned to the house. The housekeeper met him at the door.

"Miss Ellen asked me to tell you that she had a headache and would see you in the morning. She took a dinner tray in her room. I thought you would like the same."

David's windblown hair almost hid his scars, but they couldn't disguise the tired lines that pulled his mouth taut. Still, he managed a faint smile. "Dinner and a headache? Sounds fine to me."

Hurrying upstairs, he paused by Ellen's door and almost knocked, but a glance down at his stained jeans and muddy work boots changed his mind. When he finished showering, his dinner tray was waiting in his room, the aroma of beef stew and freshly baked rolls reminding him how hungry he was. He was so famished, he ate in his bath towel, downed the entire jug of iced tea and practically licked the dessert plate clean. Feeling more human, he threw on a pair of cutoffs and made his way down the hall to Ellen's bedroom. He knocked lightly, but when there was no answer, he turned the knob.

The room was dark but a sliver of moonlight let him see exactly where everything was, including Ellen. Huddled beneath a silvery sheet, she was sound asleep. Her red hair curling around her delicate face, a hand tucked beneath her cheek, she was a vision he thought existed only in fairy tales. Annoyed with himself for being so fanciful, he nudged her awake more roughly than he meant. And when she woke with a start, he cursed himself for a fool, for not realizing how sensitive she must be to touch.

"Whoa, Nellie! It's only me, David." He caught her just before she toppled off the bed in panic.

Ellen relaxed as David's voice began to register in her clouded mind. Rubbing sleep from her eyes, she remembered she wasn't dressed and covered herself, but not before David got an eyeful. One beautiful lady, he thought, and sighed wearily as he released her.

Scurrying back against the headboard, Ellen pulled the bedding around her. No one invaded her privacy, it was a cardinal rule. If she didn't answer a knock at her door, it was understood by the household that she didn't wish to be disturbed. David's invasion—although she dimly understood he was unaware of his trespass—made her want to rage and cry at the same time. It reminded her of her vulnerability on about a thousand different levels. Still, she didn't want to start an argument with him in the middle of the night, and her in a flimsy nightgown, to boot. Maybe *he'd* seen hundreds of half-naked women and would find her modesty laughable, but it wasn't anything *she* was used to. So she struggled to remain calm, trying to find him with her sightless eyes.

David understood immediately. ''I'm here, to your right. We have to talk.''

''Now? In the middle of the night?''

''Sorry, but I wasn't watching the clock. Unfortunately, Harry Gold is. And I wanted to know why you disappeared today.''

''Why *I* disappeared? What about you? You made yourself pretty scarce, too!'' Ellen sniffed.

''True.'' He couldn't help the faint smile that tugged at his mouth. Her indignation was charming, but in giving him the cold shoulder, Ellen had unintentionally given him another wonderful eyeful. Scanning the smooth sweep of her elegant shoulder, the delicate curve of her spine, the satin sheen of her skin in the moonlight, he thought it was ironic that he'd been asked to protect the one woman in the world who might need protecting from him. Having not seriously looked at a woman in years, he was susceptible to a pretty face. A few years back, when he'd still harbored hopes of a normal life, he'd fallen hard for a little blonde from Lake George. It had been a complete disaster. Although the girl had been willing to see him, her parents had come down on him as if he were a freak. It was his last attempt at a normal relationship. The enchantment of romance would never be his. If it happened sometimes that the grief that lingered challenged the thin veneer of his pride, like now... Well, he thanked God that Ellen couldn't see his fists clenched at his side, see how dry his lips had become, see how hard he strove to speak.

"Look, lady," he finally rasped, trying to sound as normal as possible, "let's not equivocate. Harry needs our decision by noon. What's it going to be?"

"That's up to you, isn't it?" Ellen reminded him, impatience coloring her voice.

"What's that supposed to mean?"

"That I'm at your mercy, for goodness' sake! Either you agree to help me, or you don't, but I certainly can't win an argument over this. I can't force you, can I?" she exclaimed.

In the face of such odds, David admired her spunk. "True enough. Okay, then. This operation of yours. What's it all about?"

Ellen didn't know how to answer. How did she explain the chance of a lifetime—or at least, the hope of one? How could she describe what successful surgery would mean to her? How could she describe its failure? It served no purpose. Since David had no idea what it meant to be handicapped, she wasn't sure she could find the right words to explain it. In the end, she decided not to try, to just stick to the facts. He wasn't stupid, just ornery. He'd figure the rest out for himself.

"There's a doctor in Baltimore named Charles Gleason. Have you ever heard of him? He's been doing a great deal of research on my type of eye condition, using laser beams. He's had success—in varying degrees—returning sight to the blind. It gets him a lot of press coverage. And guess what?" she laughed, though there was no humor in the sound. "It seems his father was a friend of your father's from their college days. When John read about this research, and found out who was doing it, he begged— well, maybe ordered is a better word—the famous Dr. Gleason to examine me, to see whether I was a viable candidate for his research. I had nothing to lose, you see."

She shivered, but David knew she wasn't cold because he heard the resignation in her voice. Disturbed, he paced the room. For the first time he noticed how carefully the furniture skirted the walls. In deference to her blindness, he supposed. Come to think of it, most of the house was set up like that, even if it was a fancy mansion. Was this what his father intended for him to do the next two months? Keep Ellen out of harm's way; wrap her in cotton wool until the big day?

Baby-sit, for chrissake?

"Go on," he prompted her while he tried to get comfortable on a delicate lady's chair never meant for his bulk. "The operation?"

Ellen jumped, startled by the sudden force of David's deep resonant voice, so how unlike his father's light lilt. In her world, so heavily invested in sound, David's husky voice was mesmerizing. She could have listened to him speak for hours, he cut right through to her senses. Too bad the rest of him came with that great voice. Even now she could detect the irritation he tried so unsuccessfully to hide.

"Right," she sighed. "Dr. Gleason. Well, there's not much else to tell. No one could refuse John Hartwell once he'd made up his mind, and he convinced Charles to take me on."

"Charles?" David frowned.

"Dr. Gleason insists that I call him Charles," Ellen said lightly. "He says it's more friendly-like."

I'll just bet, David swore to himself as he stared at the rise and fall of Ellen's breasts in the watery moonlight.

"Be that as it may, there was quite a waiting list and I couldn't be scheduled for surgery until this fall, October fourth, to be exact. It's been a long wait, well over a year, and something tells me John knew he wouldn't be there. Now that I think about it, that would explain his curious will, wouldn't it?" she said thoughtfully.

David didn't answer. He was still mulling over *Charles.*

"Anyway," Ellen continued, reining in her sorrow, "I need to be in Baltimore a day or two prior to the operation, for a battery of tests. I can stay in a hotel, but I obviously can't negotiate Baltimore alone. I need an escort and I guess John thought you were the best candidate." She shrugged helplessly. "I'm sorry."

David was incredulous at her casual apology. "Sorry? What do *you* have to be sorry about? You've just inherited two million dollars. That's a helluva lot of seeing-eye dogs!"

Ellen's mouth twisted wryly. "You don't mince words, do you, Mr. Hartwell? I'm simply trying to say that I'm sorry you've been assigned this distasteful job, I'm sorry that you're being blackmailed for your share of your rightful inheritance, and I'm sure sorry that I can't do something about it. But like I said, you don't have to help me."

"Oh, sure, right, like I have a choice. I just walk away and live with my conscience for the rest of my life, knowing that I blew your opportunity to live a normal life!"

"I know," Ellen agreed sadly. "It's blackmail, any way you look at it. I just hope you believe that I had no hand in the matter." She waited for his assurance, but wasn't surprised when it wasn't forthcoming. A hex on the strong, silent type, she swore silently, and tried another tack.

"Would it help if I said I wouldn't be too much trouble?"

His skeptical laugh ruffled her feathers.

"I'm perfectly able to care for myself," she continued. "I can even cook, once I know where everything is...sort of."

David's silence was unnerving until it occurred to Ellen that she was looking at the situation solely from her point of view. "Oh, you're afraid I'm going to invade your privacy! Oh, don't be," she begged. "I'll be the original invisible woman. Women!" she gasped. "Oh! You're afraid I'll be in the way of you and your...er...women friends." She blushed hotly.

"Dammit all!"

"Oh, I won't be," Ellen hurried on, ignoring David's groans now that she understood the situation. "Do you have a girlfriend? I know you're not married, but a girlfriend, yes, I can see how that might concern you. Well, don't you worry. I'll explain everything to her. And when you want to be alone, I'll stay here in my room. You won't hear a peep out of me."

"For heaven's sake, Ellen, stop babbling! Just stop!" David sprang from his chair. Frantic, he made a decision.

"Get dressed. We're leaving in an hour."

"What?" she gasped, jerking upright.

"I didn't hear anything in my father's will that indicated that we had to stay in Montana."

"I just assumed...I thought...I can't! This is my home!"

"So what? It's mine, too. And I hate it! So, like I said, Miss Candler, we're leaving in an hour. I just ate, and I slept away half the afternoon on top of this bloody mountain. I'm set to drive."

"But I have to pack. It will take me time."

"You have plenty of time. I've got to make some phone calls. Sixty minutes should do it."

"An hour?" Ellen protested. "I can hardly dress in that time, much less pack!"

"Look, sweetheart, you're a millionaire now. If you forget anything, you can buy it by the gross."

"I won't go! I can't! That's all there is to it!" Her arms folded on her chest, Ellen was a study in rebellion, but David Hartwell was unimpressed.

"Listen, lady, my father wasn't the only bastard in the family," he swore, giving a sharp tug to her blanket. With a screech, Ellen scrambled to conceal herself, but David's breath was the only thing to warm her as his massive hands grasped her waist.

"I'll be back in an hour, princess, so you might want to put on some clothes. Personally, I have no objection to your traveling as you are, but the airline might."

"O-oh, you...you...monster! I won't go!"

David's hands tightened at her use of the word *monster*, even though he knew her choice of words was merely unfortunate. "Oh, you'll go, sweetheart, make no mistake, because I'll carry you stark-naked and screaming out of this mausoleum, if need be!"

"You snake! You wouldn't dare!"

David shrugged, his voice unsympathetic. "It's time to come down from the mountain, Ellen."

Time for both of us, if only you knew.

Chapter Three

The storm broke about thirty minutes after they left. Ellen could hear the rain pounding on the car's roof, falling harder and growing louder as the miles flew by, while an ominous rumble of thunder trailed them. She wished David would pull over and let the storm ride itself out, but he did not, and after the embarrassing scene of their departure, she didn't dare ask him anything.

She hadn't been ready. She'd had just enough time to shower and dress before he'd returned. But he did give her the extra time she needed, even helped her to gather her belongings. Then he had scooped her up and bounded down the stairs, stationing her on the bottom step and ordering her not to move. A sudden cold draft had told her that he had gone outside, the distant slam of a car door said that he was loading up their gear. Then he was back, bringing the cool night air with him.

"It's chilly outside. I'd forgotten how cool the nights

were here in Montana, even in the summer." Draping a heavy sweater over her shoulders, David thrust her cane in her hand. "I've put your purse in the car," he said, his voice fading as he strode to the door.

Glowering, Ellen shrugged and let the sweater fall to the floor. "I told you I didn't want to go."

David came back and stood silently, looking down at the little woman trying to face off with him. A part of him admired her bravura, but only a part of him. Hands in his pockets, a frown across his face, he tried to decide what to do.

The mountain air on his clothing was sweet and moist, and Ellen thought she could almost smell the night. She could feel him towering over her, his breath ruffling her hair. Was he trying to intimidate her with his size? "Didn't you hear me?" she snapped, with a stomp of her foot. "For the millionth time, I don't want to go!"

"Yes, I heard you! Every time!" David told her crisply. Retrieving her sweater, he tied it tightly in place.

"But I didn't pack enough," she wailed. "I haven't even got a pair of socks in my bag!"

"This country's full of malls, and you have enough plastic in your wallet to buy out most of them!"

"You've been spying on me!"

"Just wanted to be sure you had your driver's license," he mocked.

"I don't want to go with you!"

"Pretend."

Ellen's eyes filled. "I'm afraid."

David reached out to her in a gesture meant to comfort, that surprised him no less than she. Their foreheads touching, his black waves tangled with her red curls, his voice was soothing, but insistent. "I know, Ellen. I know that you're afraid. That's why you *must* leave. But I'm the gun hired to protect you, remember?''

''You won't. You don't *really* care what happens to me. You're just doing it for the money!''

His wide thumbs scraping away her tears, David cupped her ashen face with his large, calloused hands. His mouth didn't quite brush hers as he searched her stricken, blind eyes and tried to promise with words what she could not read in his eyes. ''Ellen Candler, nothing, but nothing, is going to happen to you! This is going to be the most boring trip of your life. I'll be with you every moment of the day. *Every move you make.* You think you're sick of me now?'' he teased. ''See how you feel in a week. Maybe you're right. In a way, I'm being paid to do a job, but I'll be good at it, don't you worry.''

She didn't believe him. He could tell by the way she was breathing, by the way her hands fluttered, that she was starting to panic. Cursing beneath his breath, David hurried her out into the night. Sweet Jesus, she felt so good in his arms, her delicate frame quivering while he fumbled with the handle. He practically threw her into the car and gunned the engine, to hell with the potholes that had thrown him on his way up.

He felt possessed. The minute he'd laid eyes on Ellen, he'd known she spelled trouble. Only two days and she was taking over his mind, seeping under his skin—her silly tears, her flashing temper, her shy smile. Even her damned perfume was starting to cling to his clothes. He rubbed his pitted cheek to remind himself why he couldn't have her. Rage was the only safe thing to feel and if he tried, it wouldn't be so hard to accomplish. All he had to do was look in the mirror.

Ellen wasn't sure if that was a snarl she heard, but whatever it was made her burrow deeper into her seat.

She knew David was deeply upset, but so much of what she said and did angered him. If only he knew how desperate she was. Desperate not to be buried by walls she herself had built and was terrified to tear down.

They drove in silence until Ellen fell asleep and David was finally able to relax. He never realized a body could curl so comfortably across a bench seat—in her sleep, she had made a pillow of his thigh—but she was such a tiny thing, come to think of it. Heading south, he drove another hour, a protective hand on her shoulder. Toward five or so, Ellen stirred and stretched.

"Hey, watch it, princess, that's my driving arm you're poking. Unless you want to take over the wheel," he joked.

Blushing, Ellen rose and tried to finger-comb her hair.

"So, exactly what are the politics of teasing a blind person? Is it a no-no, or what?"

"Jokes would be a novelty." She smiled in a sleepy haze.

"I just wanted to be sure. Wouldn't want you to report me to the American Institute of the Blind, or worse, the Civil Liberties Union. And stop playing with your hair. You look fine, and besides—no pun intended—there's no one here to see, except me. And I don't count, right?"

"I suppose not," she agreed vaguely, not wishing to quarrel. Unable to see the pain in David's eyes. "Where are we?"

"A mile or so out of Floweree, your old hometown, didn't you say? I'm looking for a gas station. We need to fill up and I'd guess you could use the stretch."

"Where are we going?"

"To Great Falls, to the airport. We're not that far."

Waiting for Ellen to protest, David was surprised when she didn't. He couldn't know that Ellen had never flown before and was trying to quell a sudden rise of hysteria. But she wasn't about to say so. She didn't want to give him any more ammunition for the faultfinding campaign he seemed to be waging. They finished the drive to the airport in silence, but she couldn't know how many times he glanced her way.

"Two one-way tickets to Albany, New York," she heard him say when, having returned the rental car, they had made their way to the airport lobby. Then, with an hour to kill before boarding, David guided Ellen to a nearby restaurant that had just opened its doors. In the rosy morning light of dawn, the strain of traveling was having a pronounced effect on Ellen, and he suspected that the bombardment of strange noises on her ears was also taking its toll. Her lips were white and a web of worry lines had appeared near her eyes. Putting his arm around her shoulders, he pulled her into the safety net of his arms. When a noisy lunch trolley rattled by and she buried her face in his jacket, he knew she was near the end of her rope.

"Take it easy, kid. I'm right here," he whispered.

"I know," she said, raising her head even while her shoulders sagged beneath his hand.

"Hey, you okay?" he asked, alarmed at her pallor. "You're not going to faint on me, are you?"

"A cup of tea is definitely in order." She smiled wanly.

David was glad Ellen couldn't see the waitress stare as she led them to a booth. The woman didn't know who to stare at first, the beautiful blind girl clutching a fancy wooden cane, or her heavily cloaked companion. If she'd seen his scars, she would have positively gawked, but David's face, when he ordered breakfast, was carefully hidden by his public persona, sunglasses and a huge felt hat. Though he had lots of hats and tons of sunglasses, his biggest regret was his inability to grow a beard. It would have been such a help, but unfortunately his scars hindered an even growth of facial hair along the right side of his face.

The couple made small talk, desultory and polite, while they waited for their order. David figured Ellen needed time to calm down, catch her breath and get her bearings. He had a hunch she didn't get out much. And then, they both recognized a mutual cease-fire when they saw one. Besides, he could hardly believe his good fortune, sharing a table with a woman and not having to worry about his appearance.

And Ellen wasn't just any woman, she was a goddess. The sun rising across the tarmac painted a golden spray across her porcelain face and turned her hair to a Titian halo. David felt like a kid with a box of Cracker Jack, and he'd steeled himself against the revulsion of strangers too many times not to indulge himself now. And Ellen, having no idea what he looked like, was the bonus prize. No, she didn't know. She would never have been able to hide her knowledge from him, she was such a transparent little thing. Thank God, his father had not revealed his disfigurement. Omitting to tell Ellen about David's horrendous scars was a gift John would never know he gave his son.

David watched though, with no small amusement, as she shredded her paper napkin all over the table. "Nervous?" he asked, covered her fluttering hands with his own.

"How can you tell?" She smiled weakly. "I keep telling myself to trust you to not leave me stranded mid-journey, but—"

"A good idea, trusting me."

"Yes, well…" She made no effort to move her hands,

savoring instead the soothing warmth they shared. She hardly needed to move her fingers to detect his rough, swollen knuckles. "You know, David," she said as she turned his hands in hers and lightly explored his palms, "most people let me see them, through touch. Will you let me touch you sometime? Your face, I mean."

"Hell, no!"

His vehemence surprised her. "Why not? I won't hurt you. I just flick my fingers over your face, like I'm doing to your hands now. It helps me to form an impression of you, gives me something to work with."

"Isn't my lousy temper enough for you to work with?"

"You have something there," Ellen chuckled. "But I'm serious. It's what blind people do."

"I'll think about it," David stalled, unable to come up with a reason for refusing.

"Will you? Do you promise? But you must be very handsome to be so vain," she teased. She was on her second cup of sugary hot tea and feeling calmer.

He paused in the middle of stirring his coffee. "Handsome? Vain?"

"Are you?" she persisted.

"Am I what?"

"Handsome."

"Lady," he laughed harshly, "I'm as ugly as sin. Ask anyone."

Thankfully the huge breakfast they had ordered finally arrived to distract them. The amused waitress looked askance at Ellen's slight build, but said nothing as she placed plate after plate on their table. David didn't say anything, either, as he watched Ellen devour two eggs, a small stack of pancakes and a glass of cold milk. He liked that her appetite was uninhibited and couldn't help wondering if her other appetites were just as hearty.

"It must have cost my father a fortune to feed you," he joked as he pushed his own plate aside. His clumsy attempt to make peace fell flat. Red-faced, Ellen quietly put down her fork and folded her hands. "Hey, sweetheart, I didn't mean to embarrass you. I enjoyed watching you eat. Lots of women pick at their food as if it were a trial."

"For lots of women, it may be. I didn't think I had to worry about my weight. At least, John always used to say I didn't. Do I?" she asked uneasily. "Was he humoring me?"

"Are you fishing for compliments?"

Ellen flushed. "You were the one who made that nasty remark."

"It was a stupid thing to say. I really am sorry."

"Okay, fine, you're forgiven. But why is it that whenever the conversation turns the slightest bit personal, you get hostile? I only asked that question about my weight because it suddenly occurred to me that maybe your father was just being polite. I have some sense of my body, but now that we're talking about it, I realize that the only person who ever gave me any feedback about my shape, or even my looks, was John Hartwell." She touched her cheeks as if she were feeling them for the first time, but when she ran her fingers over her lips, David's mouth went dry. "He told me I was beautiful, but then he would, wouldn't he?"

"Except that he was right," David managed to rasp.

"Beautiful is a powerful word," Ellen retorted doubtfully.

"You forget that I have no stake in the matter."

"Neither did John."

"Well, you are beautiful!" he assured her, but she heard his annoyance and suddenly it was all too much.

"Never mind, David. I don't really care what I look like, I just want to go home. Please take me home," she begged as a tear fell.

David was beside her in a flash, sliding an arm around her waist. "Here, darling, let me guide you." He spoke loudly for the benefit of the waitress bearing down on them with the check and shrugged sheepishly as she placed it on the table. "Newlyweds," he explained lamely as he tossed some bills on the table.

With his firm hand plastered to Ellen's back, he hustled them out to the gate, where their plane was beginning to board. "I have to stow our bags," he told her.

"You mean *your* bags! I only had time to pack the one."

"Whatever," he sighed as he showed her to their seats. "Just give me your word you won't try to escape while I try to find an empty overhead compartment."

"Where would I go?" Ellen asked sadly.

Skeptical, David had no choice but to follow the stewardess up the aisle with his duffel bag.

Ellen slumped down in her seat in despair. This whole situation simply wasn't going to work! David was far too mercurial, kindly one minute, autocratic the next. There must be other options. If she could just make her way home, Harry Gold would figure something out. She'd beg him, bribe him, threaten him somehow, before she spent another day like this. Her mind made up, she grabbed her cane and purse, giving silent thanks to the god of credit cards. Feeling her way along the aisle, she prayed David didn't return too soon. People were so happy to guide her, that she was able to find her way to the exit in moments.

Where David stood, blocking her way. She recognized his distinct male smell seconds before his hands clasped her forearms.

"So much for your word," he hissed, his lips against her ear.

Left no other choice, Ellen took a deep breath and screamed. Well, it's what she would have done, if David hadn't kissed her.

Kissed the breath from her body, erased every sensible thought she had, boldly kissed her smack in the doorway of a 747! And she, all she could think to do was…kiss him back! Lean into him, her body on its own wavelength, desire overwhelming, an active participant to her own seduction.

Everyone laughed and applauded, and Ellen could only imagine how charming David made them seem when finally he released her. His arm ranged around her neck, he nuzzled her hair for their audience as he led her back to their seats. But the grip in which he held her was inviolate.

"I hate you!" she swore as he fastened her seat belt.

"You hate me?" he scoffed. "Well, I can't imagine what it would be like to kiss you, then, if you liked me even a little bit!"

"That's something you'll never know!"

"Won't I?" David laughed as he tightened her belt. "Oh, my dear, *never* say never!" His long hands tunneling through her hair, David slowly dragged her face to his. Skimming her teeth as he ran his tongue around her lips, he knew he was taking advantage of the situation, but the taste of her was an aphrodisiac he couldn't seem to steer clear of. When he raised his head and saw how dazed she was, he couldn't help his satisfied smile. She wanted this, too.

Again he ducked his head, smothering her protest as he took possession of her mouth. But no sweet missive this. His hand locked around her neck, he made her a prisoner of his desire, his tongue thrusting past her teeth. When he felt her mouth soften, he knew he was not mistaken. When he lifted his head, the hot ache he felt was reflected in her wide, green eyes.

"Oh! You...you..."

"Give it a rest, Ellen!" David sternly ordered as he leaned back in his seat and gave a hard, angry tug to his own seat belt.

Crude to the end, Ellen thought in disgust. Her hands opened and closed, itching to strangle him, the edge of violence he brought her to, extraordinary. But she was still reeling from his savage kiss. She had succumbed, yes, but that was because he'd... Overwhelmed her, yes, that was it. She refused to admit to the heady sensation that his lips had aroused, although she thought about nothing else the next hour.

He didn't seem to mind that she refused to speak to him the entire flight, not the way he buried himself in the movie after she declined his offer of headphones. He had been too angry during takeoff to notice her terror, and would have missed it now except that Ellen was chalk-white and her eyes were wide and glassy. "What's the matter?"

"Nothing," she said quietly. "I've just never flown before."

"Dammit, Ellen, why didn't you tell me?"

"After the way you behaved?"

"Oh, hell! Well, how did you and Dad get to Baltimore to see Gleason?"

"We took a train. Look, don't bother yourself now! I'll be fine, just give me a minute."

David could see by the way Ellen was trembling that she was going to be anything but fine, but he didn't know what to do. They were already in the process of landing and would be down any minute. He supposed if she got very sick, a stewardess would have the wherewithal to help, with oxygen maybe, but he hoped that wouldn't be necessary.

"For chrissake, Ellen, do you think that in the future, when you have a problem, you could let me know?" he grumbled as he unbuckled her. Her shaking hands couldn't even manage that.

"Why?" she hissed. "So you can practice a little kindness?" Shoving him away, she tried to stand, but her legs wouldn't support her. Luckily he caught her in time, and she made no protest until he slipped his arms beneath her knees and started to lift her.

"David, stop! I'm blind, not crippled!"

"You're too weak to walk!"

"Please, David, put me down," she pleaded quietly, "don't embarrass me this way. Give me a minute and I'll be okay."

He hesitated, then gently set her down. "All right, then, how about if we just sit here and wait for the other passengers to disembark? Give you a little time to find your land legs."

"Thank you," she sighed, her relief almost palpable as his warm hand covered her cold fingers.

Thirty minutes later they were heading out of Albany in David's dusty blue pickup truck, which he'd left in long-term parking. He could almost feel himself beginning to relax. He had hated to leave the forest preserve. He was always glad when the strange cities that cramped him were only a memory, when he drove back into the mountains, breathed in the pine-scented air and remembered why he chose to live there. But not quite yet. He had one more errand to run, an hour north of Albany, in a tiny hamlet called Queensbury, located at the foot of the Adirondack Park. He headed the truck in that direction.

"Be careful when you get out," David advised Ellen as they pulled up to a small clapboard house. "Might be that Rafe Tellerman is my friend, but he's also the damned laziest guy I know. He hasn't cut the grass in years." With a firm hold on her thin arm, David helped Ellen from the truck and guided her past a rickety screen door desperately in need of oil.

"Rafe, you home?" David bellowed.

"That you, Hartwell?" a male voice called from another room.

Ellen heard a chair scrape, but it was the sudden barking of a dog that captured her attention. Then suddenly there it was, barking ecstatically, and David was laughing—laughing!—apparently the focus of the dog's affection. The man's, too, judging from the way he laughed as he followed the dog into the room.

"Davey, me lad! When did you get back?"

She could almost see the smile on the man's face, he seemed so happy to greet his friend.

"Just this morning," she heard David answer above the dissonance of paws scraping the floor. "Down, Pansy, sit! There's a good girl. Stay!"

"Well, it's good to see you, ranger. And just so you know the worst right away, my mother's madder at you than a hornet!" But the way the stranger was laughing, she guessed it wasn't much of a threat.

"What exactly did I do to make Miss Callie angry? I haven't been around the last few weeks."

"That's just it, friend. You were supposed to show up for dinner, the Friday before you left. Not only didn't you show—oh, don't go slapping your head for my sake!—you also neglected to let her know that your father had passed away. Glen Makker told her when she was searching for your whereabouts."

"You're right, I forgot. Will you tell her that I'm real sorry, that events conspired, etcetera, etcetera?"

"No thanks! That's one you'll have to do yourself."

"Yeah, you're right."

"But seriously, David, we're real sorry about your dad."

"Thank you, Rafe."

"How was the funeral?"

As she stood quietly in the doorway, Ellen listened to their small talk, amazed that anyone held sway over David Hartwell. She hadn't thought about the fact that he had a life beyond the Hartwell manor, that he might have friends who loved him. Lovable was not a word she would have applied to him, not even close. Apparently he kept his rancor reserved just for her.

Lulled by the undertone of their deep male voices, Ellen was startled when Rafe discovered her. Or Pansy, rather, because the dog had ambled over to where she stood and thrust her cold nose on Ellen's knees, causing her to lose her balance and fall.

"Pansy, no!" David shouted. Pushing Pansy aside, David kneeled down beside Ellen, awkwardly sprawled on the floor. "Are you okay?" His voice was rough with anxiety while his hands explored her, checking for bruises.

"Holy cow, David! What's this?" Rafe's voice was tinged with wonder as he took in Ellen's long legs and luscious curves.

"Don't you recognize a girl when you see one?" David asked irritably, his eyes fastened on Ellen. "I'm really, really sorry about this, Ellen. Pansy is as gentle as they come, but I should have warned you—and her. It won't happen again, I promise."

A blush pinked up Ellen's cheeks as she lightly dismissed the accident. "It's all right, David. She just startled me. I haven't been near many dogs."

"Seriously? I would have thought—"

"Well, you thought wrong. Not all blind people have seeing-eye dogs, silly. Or else I've misplaced mine, hmm?"

"Very funny. I'm laughing all over the place," he muttered, rising to his feet with Ellen in tow.

"So am I," chuckled Rafe, nursing his surprise. "You didn't mention you'd brought company."

"Ellen's not company, she was my father's ward. And now she's mine, for a couple of months. I'm taking her up to my place to stay awhile. And she's blind," David added bluntly, "so be careful what you say and do."

"Ah, David Hartwell, tactful as ever," Rafe rebuked him as he pushed his friend aside. "Don't mind him, miss. He has the manners of a goat! My name is Rafael Tellerman and I'm David's best friend. At your service, ma'am."

Ellen held out her hand. "Hello, Mr. Tellerman," she said softly. "I'm Ellen Candler."

"Ah, but you must call me Rafe. Only my students call me Mr. Tellerman—and God knows what else!"

Ellen laughed and her glow caught the men unawares. Rafe looked as though he'd gone straight to heaven, and David knew he had never seen Ellen smile quite that way before. But then, he'd never given her any reason to smile, had he?

"I take it this is your home, Rafe?"

Clasping Ellen's hand, Rafe pressed it to his chest. *"Mi casa es su casa!"*

Disgusted by the nauseating display in front of him, David was quick to intervene. "We're in Queensbury," he explained to Ellen in a clipped voice. "Rafe's been watching Pansy for me. Pansy is my dog. My home is in the park."

"In the park?" Ellen asked, a little puzzled.

"I'm a forest ranger for the DEC—that's the Department of Environmental Conservation. I thought you said my father told you."

"He did. He told me you were a forest ranger, but he didn't go into details."

"So I noticed. Almost like I didn't exist," David muttered.

"But that's the way you wanted it, wasn't it?" Ellen countered cooly but David refused to be baited.

"Well, that's what I am, lady, a forest ranger, and the territory I patrol is the Adirondack Forest Preserve just west of Indian Lake. It's not quite as far as it sounds, and we could conceivably make it home by nightfall, *if* loverboy ever lets go of your hand."

Rafe dropped Ellen's hand abruptly. "Sorry." He grinned, but the tone of his voice told Ellen he wasn't, not in the least. "Ellen, I'm a single, thirty-six-year-old college professor, and tenured, too, so I make a decent living." He laughed, and she could hear the imp in his voice. "I didn't want to leave the transmitting of such important information to my buddy, here. You *are* unattached, aren't you?" he demanded with a sidelong glance at David.

"Of course I am." Ellen smiled.

"Why do you say 'of course?'"

Ellen floundered, unused to such blunt questions. "Well, for one thing I haven't dated much."

Rafe looked shocked. "Well, that's *one thing* that's going to change real soon, you have my word!"

"Mr. Tellerman, are you flirting with me?" Ellen asked curiously.

Gently, Rafe flicked the tip of Ellen's nose. "Why, Miss Candler, yes, I do believe I am. Does it bother you? Do you want me to stop?"

Ellen shrugged. "I don't know. No one ever has before."

"I'll stop if it makes you uncomfortable."

"No, no. I just don't know what to do. Am I supposed to flirt back? I haven't a clue how to do so, if I should."

Rafe laughed. A deep, throaty laugh that was jovial and kind and made Ellen smile when she thought she was bankrupt of laughter. "Miss Candler, you just keep doing what you do naturally and you'll manage just fine!"

Busy adjusting Pansy's collar, David observed all and said nothing, and when he rose to his feet, his anger was carefully masked. So that when Rafe offered to make them sandwiches for the ride home, he was able to decline with civility. If Rafe didn't mind, they had eaten on the plane and he was in a hurry to get on the road.

"But you will be around for my mother's Labor Day barbecue, won't you?" Rafe insisted as he watched David leash his dog.

David shot him a layered look as he guided Ellen to the door. "I suppose if I don't, you'll send Miss Callie out hunting for me?"

"You can be sure of it."

"Well, just so you don't say I didn't warn you, I don't even know that I'll be getting Labor Day off. It's prime vacation time, you know that. The mountains are crawling with tourists already, and I don't think Glen Makker would appreciate giving me any more time off, all things considered.''

"Yes, yes, but surely you can fit in a few hours off that day. If not, then allow me to escort Ellen. You'll love my mother,'' Rafe promised. "Everybody does, even David. He just pretends not to love anything except snakes and dogs. Miss Callie—that's what everyone calls her, including me!—in the way of explaining things, is one of the oldest and most respected matriarchal souls in these parts, and she just also happens to put together the best barbecue in the park. Her sauce is a state secret and she shows it off at her annual Labor Day shindig. Everyone goes! Come on, David, get your act together, old buddy, and show. You'll make him listen, Ellen, won't you?''

"Me?'' Ellen laughed incredulously. "I couldn't make David Hartwell do a thing he didn't want. I have absolutely no influence over him whatsoever, I assure you!''

"Oh, come on,'' Rafe coaxed as he reclaimed her hand and brought it to his lips. "You could make anyone do anything. Try me!''

Ellen smiled, and before she knew it, her palm was lightly kissed. Arm-in-arm, they strolled to David's truck, while David loaded Pansy's supplies onto the pickup bed, right next to their luggage. Rafe laughed even more heartily at the dark look David sent him when he bundled Ellen into the passenger seat.

"Another conquest? You keeping score, I hope?'' David growled as he climbed behind the wheel, having settled Pansy in the rear of the cab.

"Oh, and who was the first?'' Ellen asked impudently as she fastened her seat belt.

Feeling his temperature rise, David wisely said nothing. But as he drove away he heard Rafe laugh loudly.

Chapter Four

The final hour they drove in deadly silence gave David plenty of time to simmer. Ellen kept quiet, refusing to be goaded into the fight she could feel David itching to start.

"Am I getting the silent treatment?" he demanded into the hush that filled the car as they headed toward the outskirts of Longacre. "If I am, I hate to disappoint you, lady, but the silence suits me fine. It's what I'm used to."

The bitterness in David's voice came as a surprise to Ellen. It was disturbing, and she found herself wanting to make peace, but David quickly sensed the change of atmosphere. "Thanks, but no thanks. I don't want your pity!"

"My pity?" Ellen repeated, astonished at the accusation. "What on earth are you talking about? Why should I pity you? Honestly, David, I just don't understand you!"

David cursed himself for a fool but refused to explain.

"You don't have to," he snapped. "It's not part of the deal."

What a jerk she must think him, he sighed as he took the last stretch of road. Well, he certainly did his best to behave like one. It wasn't too difficult, though. The minute he'd laid eyes on her, he knew his life was going to become complicated. Her blindness notwithstanding, even Rafe had fallen under her spell. Well, not him! He'd been around the block, knew a whole lot about handicaps, even if she didn't think he did. All those years spent in hospitals, trying to have his face reconstructed, hadn't left him an easy touch! It took a lot to get *his* sympathy. Not that she tried, he had to admit as he glanced at the figure huddled against the door, chewing on her lip, probably trying not to cry.

And kissing her on the plane! Damn, but that was the worst. Giving in—oh, come on, let's be honest—losing control, was more like it! He simply couldn't stop himself! Falling all over her the moment he got the chance, as if he was drugged or something, now *that* was the truth, if he really wanted to be honest.

An hour later, after being jarred at every turn along a dirt road that should have been illegal, Ellen was still wondering what it was with these Hartwell men, hiding away on mountains that were better left to bears. David hadn't spoken nearly the entire ride, and even Pansy had been quiet, padding back and forth on the truck's tiny back seat. Her nose out the window to growl at the wind was the only sign of life in the truck. Now she thought about it, not much had changed since Montana. They could have stayed there, for all the difference it made. Even though David had argued otherwise, he made it clear at every opportunity that she was a job he didn't want— and she on her best behavior, for goodness' sake! Every chance he'd got, he cut her down, made her feel small and unwanted, succeeding hugely. If she thought she was lonely in Montana, she had a feeling she was about to ascend new heights! Or was it descend new depths? Things wouldn't be half so bad if...

Things were pretty bad, she sighed as she brushed away an unruly tear. Was this how it was going to be, the next few months—a vacuum of sight and sound? She would have liked to explain to her companion that noise was an essential component of her world, that she needed to hear voices, for instance, to feel grounded, that it made her jittery to not hear anything for long lengths of time. Very often she played the radio just to make sure there were four walls surrounding her. She *watched* television, which she despised, for the same reason—the need to hear the human voice.

Touching was another matter, though, and she jumped when a cold, wet something nuzzled her hair.

"Pansy!" David shouted, and the cold, wet thing was gone.

Not liking to feel defeated, Ellen tried to break through David's shell. Perhaps the way to a man's heart was his dog. "Tell me," she asked lightly, "how did you get Pansy?"

"Why?"

"For goodness' sake, David Hartwell, I'm just trying to make conversation. But hey, don't let me interrupt your thoughts! You're probably on the verge of self-discovery!"

David glared at her sideways, but struggled to keep his temper. He could just imagine the next few months—her endless wants, and he her butler, cook, chauffeur, maid and nurse. Look at the way she egged him on even now, desperate for attention. Trust a woman not to know when to hush. He could spit nails, he was so angry, but what good would it do to say? They were at loggerheads already, and they weren't even at the cabin yet. It cost him everything to be civil, but he tried. "It happens she was beaten and abandoned," he said tightly.

"Yes?"

"Rafe found her a few years back, wandering about in his yard. One leg broken and a cracked rib."

"Oh, how cruel!"

"People can be," he agreed, his voice cold. "She's not too crazy about them, as a rule. Rafe managed to get near her, though, after a few days, and she eventually allowed him to nurse her along. It helped that she was starving. He passed her on to me. That's how Rafe and I met. He'd heard about my living up in the mountains alone and all, and thought I'd like some company."

"Did you?"

"Did I what?"

"Did you want more company, like Rafe thought?"

"Nope."

What a surprise. "But you took her in," Ellen mused.

"Strays are my specialty," he said with another sidelong glance her way. Yeah, she was blushing, all right.

Having effectively shut his passenger up, David returned his attention to the road and they took the last few miles in silence.

"How much longer?"

"Eight more miles, but it gets nasty, so hold on." Hearing Ellen swear, so out of character for the little princess, sent an imperceptible smile to David's lips. He remembered the first time he'd done the road when he first got the job, how sore his butt had been. Maybe Her Highness would want a massage.

"Are we there, yet, or do we have a flat tire?" Ellen

whispered faintly as David finally slowed down and braked, ten minutes later. Falling back against the seat, limp, disheveled and sweaty from the longest day of her life, she suddenly bolted upright. In desperate need of a shower, the most horrific thought went through her mind. "You *do* have running water, don't you? *Hot, running water?*" she demanded, her eyes great green pools of dread.

David smiled wickedly. "*Hot* and *running* water? Lady, this ain't the Hilton. I have running water, sure. There's a stream right behind the house, only this time of year it's sort of...brisk, but shoot, I use it every Thursday like clockwork."

"But I don't like streams," Ellen wailed. "Hot or cold!"

Thinking hard, David scratched his chin. "Yeah, it would be pretty chilly for a delicate thing like yourself, it being a natural spring and all. But hey, you want hot water, you got it! I just remembered, there's a cauldron out back that I was using to skin squirrels—you haven't eaten till you've tasted pan-fried squirrel—but for sure it will clean up real good. For sure. We can boil at least ten, maybe even twenty gallons of water, in that old pot, just enough to cover a dainty thing like yourself. I have a wood-burning stove that's pretty efficient, and I don't mind cutting an extra log or two, for you. It's just a matter of hauling the water up to the house. Yup, we'll make you up a nice little tub in the kitchen, and I'll even scrub your back for free. Should be ready in about three hours. It's the wood-cutting part takes so long, you understand."

Ellen's groan could be heard for miles.

"Oh, come on, lady," David said cheerfully. "You made it this far, don't chicken out on me, now." Grinning broadly, he scratched his chest in satisfaction. He hadn't felt this good in days. Evening up the score with her lady-ship was going to be a real pleasure. Stepping from the truck, he opened the door for Pansy, who joyously leaped to freedom. Then, coming 'round to Ellen's side, he helped her out, but swiftly scooped her up.

"Aren't you ever going to let me walk anywhere?" she asked irritably.

"Sure," David promised. "You're no lightweight, you know. Must weigh a hundred pounds, at least!"

"David!"

"Look, Ellen, I'll say it once and no more," he said on a serious note. "You know that ride you just took, the one that's going to make your tush feel real sore tomorrow? Well, I began clearing the land around the house about a year ago, so the ground is rough, maybe not as rough as the road, but close enough. There are boulders all over the place, and though the main path is fairly level, there are small rocks strewn all over the place, so you need to be extra careful. If that doesn't impress you, maybe the snakes will," he added lightly.

"Snakes? Good Lord!" Ellen swore faintly.

She couldn't see the twinkle in David's eyes as he took the porch steps. His voice was carefully neutral as he continued his warnings. "So no midnight strolls and no af-ternoon walks, either. I'll show you what's safe, and if you want exercise, you'll have to do sit-ups or wait for me to come home and take you out."

"Wait for you?"

"I work for a living, remember?"

"But you're rich now. You don't have to work."

"Some of us have a work ethic. Mine says I've got a job. And not only am I good at it, I actually enjoy it. So, I'll keep my job, if it's all the same to you. And when I'm gone, Ellen, you stick to the porch. It's a big wrap-around, so you'll be okay. And I'm not even asking you to promise, I'm *ordering* you, and you're going to listen. Now, come on in and I'll show you the house.''

At which point, David realized that he was still holding Ellen in his arms. He could have put her down, but the harmless pleasure of clasping her soft form to his was not an easy thing to give up. She wasn't doing a whole lot of protesting, either, he noticed. And maybe she was dying for a bath, but hell, she didn't smell half bad to him. The scent of gardenia was still a faint wisp in her hair. He could have stood that way for quite some time—he hadn't been kidding when he'd said she was a lightweight—but when it occurred to him that he had to find his keys to open the door, he reluctantly gave up his burden. So he was surprised to hear her protest when he stood her on her feet.

"Wait just a darned minute." Ellen frowned, a finger poking at his chest. "What if something should happen to you while you're at work? Bears...or something?''

David's lips quirked but he gave her a dignified answer. "Nothing's happened to me in the past ten years, but if it makes you feel any better, there's a built-in emergency contingency to my job. When the department doesn't hear from me after a certain amount of time, they come looking."

Not satisfied, Ellen tugged at his sleeve. "And what if something should happen to *me* while you're gone?''

"Like what?" he asked dubiously. "Keep to the house and you'll be fine. You're not going to be living here all that long, and Pansy will protect you while you are.''

"But you said before that she hated people!''

"Yeah, well, maybe I exaggerated a little. Nonetheless, she's a born hunter so she keeps the periphery of the house pretty much free of roaming animals. If you hear her barking, I recommend you get your butt back in the house and lock the door.''

"Will she hunt me?''

"Are you serious?'' he snorted.

"I'm blind, remember? I have to know these things. I can't make the same kind of judgment calls you do.''

"Sorry, I forgot.''

Ellen was incredulous. "You forgot? You forgot I was blind?''

"I just did.'' How to tell her that he didn't care if she were blind, that her attraction went beyond that. That to a man cursed with his ravaged face, her blindness was a blessing, that to hold her in his arms as he just had—and not see her flinch—was as close to heaven as he was ever going to get.

"Well, maybe you're right. I'll register your visit with the department, and if you should need help—and I do mean only the direst emergency, Ellen!—they would be here in minutes. It's regulations, anyway. And maybe we'll set something up with some friends of mine, just to be on the safe side. Will that make you feel safer?''

"Your carrying a cell phone would make me feel safer!''

"What? You've got to be kidding.''

"Nope—'' she shook her head slowly ''—I'm not kidding. Then I'd feel like you were only a call away. I know I sound like a commercial, but please, will you do it?''

He didn't like it. A noose was tightening around his neck. But when her eyes misted over, he reluctantly agreed. Although the department issued cell phones, he hardly ever remembered to take his. He would now, for her sake, since she insisted. And at that very moment, as if to prove Ellen's vulnerability, Pansy came bounding out of the woods and up onto the porch, nearly tumbling

Ellen to the ground in an overly enthusiastic display of affection.

"Down, Pansy, down!" David commanded, and Pansy obeyed instantly, flattening herself down on the porch, her tail wagging furiously.

Ellen was terrified until she realized that Pansy had backed her into the safety net of David's arms. Swiftly she burrowed beneath his jacket to find a warm, protective haven from harm.

"For chrissake, the dumb mutt thinks she just did something wonderful."

It certainly felt that way to Ellen, suddenly finding herself snuggled against David's broad chest. The man was a miracle of stone, every plane chiseled to perfection beneath her sensitive fingers, the arms that held her a marvel of granite, only warm, and inviting. And he smelled so good, a pure male scent that invaded her senses. A curiosity to know more about his body flared in her but she tamped it down quickly. "I suppose I'm safe now?" she asked, her voice muffled but calm. Safer in David's arms than anywhere else she could think of.

"Oh, sure. Sorry," David apologized to the delicious, warm body tucked beneath his chin. "Sorry about all this. I never saw Pansy do such a thing before, attacking you twice in one day. Wait till Rafe hears."

"David, you apologize more than anybody I've ever met." Ellen smiled as he dropped his arms.

"You're mad at me for apologizing? When you never miss an opportunity to tell me how rude I am?"

"This is different. You're apologizing for…it's not the same…oh, forget it!" Her thoughts becoming more garbled with every word she spoke. He probably had a girlfriend, anyway.

David's eyes narrowed thoughtfully, but he said nothing as he guided Ellen into the house. Left alone on the porch, Pansy howled as if her best bone had been taken away, but David adamantly refused to allow her inside. Pansy needed training in a major way before she could be trusted around Ellen.

As for Ellen, he ordered her to stay put on the sofa while he unloaded the truck. She obeyed, but only because she was tired. Alert to every sound, she stretched out on the couch and tried to get her bearings. Rustling leaves told her that the cabin was nestled close to the woods, and a myriad of chirping birds confirmed that. The fly that landed on her nose told her that the house could probably use some screens, while the humming motor of the refrigerator helped her locate the kitchen. The rumble of her stomach soon made her try to find it. David found her with her nose in the icebox when he came in a few minutes later, loaded down with luggage.

"Hey, I thought I told you to sit still," he snapped as he dropped the bags on the kitchen floor.

"Oh, stop it, David, please! I'm blind, not handicapped. I mean—oh, look what I found," she cried, holding up a brown bottle. "Soda! Is it drinkable? Where's the can opener? I'm parched."

"Ellen—"

"David," she said gently, "please stop giving me orders! Guiding me about, picking me up, telling me to stay put! I know you mean it kindly, but sometimes you act just like an old mother hen!"

"Well, all right, then," he relented, staring at the bottle of dark ale that she held aloft. "Here you are, Your Majesty." Placing a bottle opener in Ellen's hand, he ignored the smug look on her face. He watched, trying not to laugh as she opened the bottle, sent him a mock salute and took a hefty swill. A split second later, beer came spraying from her mouth.

"Like your beer a little lighter, do you?" he inquired innocently as he wiped her chin with a dish towel. "I myself am quite partial to that stout you just wasted. And who's going to clean it up, I hate to think. Who's going to clean *you* up is much more pleasant to contemplate."

"Oh, give me the darned towel," Ellen screeched, as he started dabbing at her dress. "You could have told me, you know."

"Well, I did try," he reminded her smoothly, "but you wouldn't let me. You were busy being a queen."

"And you are a knave!" she retorted. "Just look at me. I reek from beer and my dress is ruined. Oh, for a bathtub! But no, you had to trick me into coming east—to live in the boondocks!"

"Trick you?" David flushed.

"You're right! It was no trick," she agreed with cutting sarcasm as she wiped furiously at her dress. "It was kidnapping! I would call the police, but there probably isn't even a phone up here! I'll bet there's no electricity, either, is there?" she asked softly, the full horror of her situation beginning to sink in. "No radio, no television—"

"Ellen—"

"Don't!" She raised her small fist imperiously. "Don't say another word!"

"But—"

"Dear God, what did I do to deserve this?"

"Look, sweetheart, I think you're getting a little hysterical."

Ellen felt her sticky dress and hair and nearly burst into tears. "Hysterical?" she demanded through clenched teeth. "You think this is hysterical, you overgrown lummox? You want to see hysterical, I'll show you hysterical!'' She shut her eyes, took a deep breath—and counted to ten. Ten wouldn't do. She felt her control returning around twenty-five.

"All right,'' she said with icy calm. "Where's that stupid stream?''

"Say what?''

"You told me that a stream ran out back of the house, remember? That you used for bathing. You don't think I'm going to wait three hours for you to boil up water in that filthy cauldron? I need a bath now, so come on, show me the way.''

Women. He could see there was no use arguing, even if it was getting dark. Not that that meant anything to her. And they were both pretty exhausted. His mouth a tight line, David led Ellen out the back door and down the softly sloping hill to the water's edge.

Ellen flicked her fingers in the frigid stream and rose with a shudder. "It's no hot tub, that's for sure. How deep is it?'' she demanded imperiously.

"Not very, it's a stream, maybe six, seven inches, at most. You won't drown,'' he said with cutting sarcasm.

"Small mercies,'' she muttered, and began to undress.

"Hey, wait a minute.'' He tensed, his eyes glued to a bit of white lace that began to reveal itself as she started to unbutton her dress.

Ellen flashed a haughty look in his direction. "I need to bathe. Surely you don't expect me to wash with my clothes on?''

"I…er…I hadn't thought about it.''

"And you didn't expect me to manage this stupid stream by myself, did you?''

"I…um…''

Finished unbuttoning, she began to pull her dress apart, exposing the creamiest bosom David ever had the good luck to chance upon. As she struggled with her clothes, they shimmied deliciously in front of his eyes, a lovely crest of pink above a scallop of silk.

"Ellen," he managed to croak, his mouth was so dry. "Ellen, stop! I was joking," he said quickly. "I have a full working bathroom with lots and lots of hot, running water. I installed the system myself."

Ellen stood there, a tight-lipped statue, and David felt his heart constrict. Judging by the heave of that magnificent bosom, she was pretty mad. He guessed he was in for it now. "Come on, princess, it was just a joke. You were acting so high and mighty, calling this place the boondocks. Hey, this is my home! You made it sound like being here was a fate worse than death. You wouldn't listen. And, dammit, Ellen, I didn't kidnap you!"

Ellen rebuttoned her dress so slowly, David thought he'd die a quick death before she was done, he'd never seen anything so erotic. He'd also never seen anybody angrier. "Look, I'm sorry. It was a lousy joke and I'll never do anything like it again." Getting on to twilight, he couldn't see her eyes, so very gently, he took her chin to be sure she was listening. "You have my word."

Jerking free of his hold, Ellen's mouth was a mulish line as she decided what to do. She supposed if she were honest, he was right. She had made some very insulting remarks about his home! On the other hand, she wasn't entirely to blame. He'd led her on, for sure! And the nerve of him to let her undress like that, as if she were a stripper! But she didn't want war any more than he. They'd only been here an hour, but they were already at each other's throats. What would the next ten weeks be like, if they couldn't make do for sixty minutes?

David held his breath as he watched Ellen think the situation out. Lousy at arguing, he was worse at making up. In certain ways, men sure were less complicated. Women were something else, though. At this rate he would get in a lot of practice apologizing. Why, if Ellen played her cards right, he thought wryly, she'd have him apologizing for things he didn't even do! But he knew whose fault *this* one was. "How about I put together some dinner while you take a hot bath?" he asked softly, his hand cautiously reaching out to hers.

Ellen looked away, shivering slightly at his tenuous touch. Well, he was trying. An hour ago she wouldn't have expected as much.

When they returned to the house, Ellen opted for dinner first, knowing they both were starved. Dinner was a hasty affair of sandwiches, both of them far too tired for anything more elaborate. But the cheese was real New York State cheddar, and the tea he brewed was hot and sweet. When they were done, David gave her a brief tour of the cabin and showed her to the bedroom.

"But this is your room," Ellen protested.

"How did you know?" he asked in surprise.

"By the smell, silly. Blind people are super aware of smells."

"I *smell?* Do I *smell? How* do I smell? Do I smell *bad?*"

"Calm down!" Ellen laughed. "Everyone has an odor. You just smell more than most," she added impishly.

"No kidding? Exactly what do I smell like?"

The panic in David's voice was irresistible. "Well… like a man…I guess."

"Come on, Ellen, that's no answer!"

"I was only teasing! You smell fine, David, outdoorsy and healthy. No girly colognes or aftershave. John always wore—" Ellen stopped but it was too late. If she could see, she couldn't have known any more clearly that she had just spoiled their truce. Not that David *said* anything, but she could tell by the way his fingers tightened on her arm that all the complicated feelings he harbored for his father had just resurfaced.

"I'll just gather up some of my things while you shower," he said quietly.

"David," Ellen protested, "I don't want to turn you out of your room."

"What do you want me to do—stay?" he asked irritably.

Inwardly, Ellen cringed at the harsh tone David assumed, but not as much as she once might. She was beginning to realize that he used it to defend himself, such as when he was hurt, as he was now. "I meant that I would be glad to sleep on the couch," she said slowly.

"Somehow I don't think that's a good idea."

"But if it's good enough for you…"

"Waking to a half-naked woman in my living room, every morning, for the next few months, is not my idea of a good time!"

"Oh."

"Right," he said curtly as he watched understanding dawn on her face. "In any case, I won't be sleeping on the couch. There's a daybed I never use in the alcove next to the bedroom. I'll be fine."

"Well, let me sleep there, then. A daybed is much too narrow for a man your size."

"Now, how would you be knowing my size?"

Ellen didn't want to remind David how she knew, but the fact was, the way he'd held her in his arms on the airplane had told her a great many things, including his size. He must be pretty tired not to remember why she would. It made it easy to skirt his question. "David, I'm exhausted and I want to go to bed, so please, let's not argue. Just let me sleep in the alcove. I'd be uncomfortable knowing you'd upset your home for me. I'll be fine, really I will, as long as it's warm. I notice it's gotten a bit chilly since we arrived. Just give me a soft pillow and a thick blanket and I'll be asleep in seconds. Besides, I do better in small quarters. It's easier for me to remember where everything is situated.''

Unconvinced, David still had to admit that four months on a daybed that was four or five inches too short for him was not something he relished. ''All right, we'll try it for one night.''

Ellen nodded at her small victory as he led her to the shower. Some ten minutes later she peeked around the bathroom door and jumped when his voice rumbled close to her ear.

''Are you looking for this?'' Thrusting a huge terry-cloth bathrobe in her hands, David smiled as she quickly disappeared. But not before he got a glimpse of soft, moist skin and damp, red curls. Cursing, he vowed to guard against unexpected encounters with her all-too-female body. Perhaps a quick discreet visit to his widow friend was in order. But he dismissed the idea out of hand. Somehow it wasn't appealing.

When Ellen reappeared a few minutes later, his T-shirt dangling to her knees, she heard him snort.

''What's the problem?''

''Nothing. The shirt's too big, is all.'' He had to steel himself against the tug he felt as he led her to the tiny sleeping alcove, where he sat her on the narrow bed. ''Look, if you need me...''

''Just whistle?'' she asked brightly.

''Yeah, sure,'' David drawled as he pulled the blankets back and watched Ellen settle beneath.

''David, you know what your trouble is?''

"You're not going to disappoint me and keep it a secret, are you?"

"Nope." Ellen grinned. "Your trouble is, *you're* too sensitive."

David laughed, but it was short and humorless. Sensitive. Yeah, that's precisely what he was—right across his pants zipper. "Go to bed, Miss Candler."

"Good night, Mr. Hartwell. Are you going to bed now, too?"

"I'll be right next door, lady," he sighed, and closed the door with a light, sharp click, pretty sure that he wasn't going to get a wink's worth of sleep.

Chapter Five

Ellen meant it when she said she was tired. David must have checked on her five times, that night—just to be sure—before he finally found her stirring in a half slumber.

"Are we getting up anytime soon, ma'am? Cook's already made a second pot of coffee."

Ellen smiled the innocent, sweet smile of someone not quite awake, stretched her long, sinuous body and burrowed back under the covers.

Quickly, David closed the door before she caught him staring, only to remember that it didn't matter. He could stare till kingdom come and Ellen wouldn't know. Well, it was the ethics of it, he scolded himself. All the same, he wondered whether ethics might not someday loose out to plain, unadulterated lust.

He figured Ellen didn't need any more help finding her way to the bathroom when, moments later, he heard the shower running. Twenty minutes later she was tapping toward the kitchen with her cane and he was secretly pleased at her seeming independence. When she appeared at the doorway, he decided not to lead her to the kitchen table. If she was going to succeed in getting around after he returned to work, Ellen's training began then and there.

"Over here, miss. Five steps straight ahead, three to the right."

Ellen did as he said and met his chest, head-on.

"Good morning," he laughed.

His playfulness was a surprise but Ellen said nothing, only laughed and rubbed her nose. Breathing in the fancy scent of her expensive shampoo, David shared her laughter, born of his budding admiration for her intrepid nature.

He had lain awake half the night, thinking about it.

Ellen had been through a lot the past two days, and on the whole, had handled the changes with something akin to grace. No one knew better than he what a royal bastard he'd been throughout. He wished he could explain his behavior, if only to himself! Even now, he appreciated how she didn't hold a grudge, just thanked him quietly when he showed her to her seat and placed a mug of coffee to her right.

"Oatmeal? Do I really smell oatmeal?" Ellen chuckled when the scent of steamy milk and porridge reached her nostrils.

"The lumberjack special," David grunted as he set a bowl of cereal down directly in front of her and placed her hand over the sugar bowl. Watching how Ellen carefully memorized its shape pleased him. Although he wouldn't admit to it, he was worried sick about leaving her alone when he returned to work and had even toyed with the idea of hiring a housekeeper. The thought of having another intruder in the house was abhorrent, but if it had to be, he'd do it. But seeing her commit to memory the sugar bowl, and having observed her other methods of retention, he thought perhaps that Ellen might not be as helpless as he feared. "Sausage and toast is on a plate above your left hand. It will be exactly there again tomorrow, along with the sugar bowl and oatmeal."

Amazed, Ellen turned her head in the direction of his voice. Perhaps he wasn't the insensitive clod she'd tagged him. "Any chance of getting some fresh eggs around these parts?" she chuckled. But her smile fell at his next words.

"Ellen, I'm going back to work in two days."

"What? So soon? But we've just arrived!"

"I must. My boss called this morning and gave me the word. Even if it is nearing the end of the season, it's still summertime and there are hundreds—thousands, really!—of tourists camped all over the place, half of them in my territory. I was only on a brief vacation when my dad died, and they couldn't refuse me the additional week, but the party's over, sweetheart."

Sweetheart. An endearment Ellen heard him let slip before. What difference did it make if it was just an empty phrase, if it softened his tone. *An empty phrase.* That reminded her... She hesitated to bother him, but it had been on her mind since they'd left Montana.

"David, I was wondering. If you didn't mind, I would like to have my housekeeper ship me some stuff I left behind." She blushed to remember the speed of their departure and hoped he didn't notice. "My computer, in particular. It's especially geared to my needs and I have a lot of stuff on my hard drive that can't be replaced."

"What do you need a computer for? Expensive little toys. Oh, but I forgot—you're rich now!"

"You make it sound like a sin. Are you forgetting that you are, too?"

"Maybe, but that's a pretty recent event, in case *you've* forgotten. In general, I work for my living."

"So do I," she snapped. "I happen to be a writer! And I definitely need my computer to do that."

"Well, well! Do tell!"

"No, I don't think I will." Ellen frowned into her coffee. "The simplest conversation seems to be beyond you, David Hartwell, and why I thought today was going to be any different, I don't know. Every conversation we have is filled with innuendo or criticism. It's positively exhausting talking to you. You've spoiled my breakfast, the way you're so quick to lose your temper."

As if to prove her words, David slammed down his mug. "Have your damned housekeeper mail any damned thing you like," he told her curtly, the screen door slamming loudly as he left.

David Hartwell, how would you like to be drawn and quartered? Ellen seethed. Or maybe a cement necklace...or strychnine in your tea...or—

"I'm sorry, Ellen. Write me off as a jerk, but I didn't mean to loose my temper."

David had returned so quietly that Ellen hadn't heard his footsteps. She pursed her lips unforgivingly and folded her hands primly on the table.

David tapped her softly on the shoulder. "Ellen, did you hear? I apologized."

"Apologizing is something you do hourly, Mr. Hartwell."

"Yeah, so I noticed."

"It's only a matter of time before you say something else equally boorish."

"I know—I mean I won't—I promise!"

"A worthless promise," she said bitterly.

David took a deep breath. "Well, I promise to *try* not to do it again. How's that?"

"Oh, David!"

"Come on, Ellen, this is hard stuff for me. A woman hankering for attention at breakfast is a little hard on my nerves. I'm a loner, always have been. Silk panties drying in the bathroom, it's an outright shock to my solar system. Perfume in the air is a positive nightmare. You have to be patient."

"I wasn't *hankering!*"

"Oh, really? Well, what do you call it when... You're right, you weren't hankering." It was probably the other way 'round.

David spent the rest of the morning teaching Ellen the layout of the cabin. It was going to be difficult for her to remember everything all at once, but David took the precaution of pushing aside as much furniture as was feasible, so that her path was as clear as possible. But after lunch, when she begged to go outside, he readily agreed. He, too, was desperate for air. Maneuvering her lithe body around the cabin had been a lot more physical than he'd expected. Guiding her hands along appliances, aiming her feet in the right direction, steering her shoulders through doorways, not exactly hard work, except that as the hours flew by, all he wanted was to steer her into his bed. She had a slim, wild beauty that was beguiling. He was very careful to keep that bedroom door closed.

Going outside turned into a joint venture with Pansy, but David took advantage of the opportunity to work with Ellen and the dog. Together they walked up and down the porch, Ellen clutching at a makeshift harness that David had attached to Pansy's collar. It didn't take long before they both agreed that Pansy was beginning to have an understanding of Ellen's fragility. They worked until Ellen refused to take another step in the scorching afternoon sun.

"All right," David relented, and led her to a wicker swing. "I guess you deserve a reward. Stay here and I'll get us something cold to drink."

"No beer!" she laughed as she slipped off her sandals and propped her feet on the porch railing. "But maybe some cookies?" she begged sweetly.

David drank in the sight of the enticing long legs stretched in front of him. She made a pretty picture in the black shorts he'd lent her, even if she'd needed string to hold them up. That thin trail of sweat down her purple T-shirt made for a very interesting design—and couldn't disguise the fact that she was braless. She was also half asleep when he returned with a tray.

"Mmm, I do believe I smell cookies," she sniffed when he sat beside her, the tray balanced on his lap.

"Vanilla wafers," she said approvingly with a lazy smile, sharing them with Pansy even if David didn't think it was a good idea.

"You love it here, don't you?" she murmured in between cookies, not really asking as much as guessing. Her head resting on the back of the swing, she could hear the crickets and birds at play. "And you never get lonely, do you?"

"I do, a little."

"I was lonely in Montana," she confided, but didn't elaborate. After a while, she dozed.

David had to grab the glass from Ellen's hand before it shattered on the ground. Stretched beside her, his hefty legs propped alongside hers, he made a mental note to pick up some plastic cups, maybe some unbreakable dishes, too. And wondered why she'd been lonely, on that mountain, in Montana.

He had no objection when her head dropped to his shoulder, having fallen into a light doze himself. It was Pansy who startled them both awake with her loud barking. It was dinnertime. Her stomach said so. How dared they sleep through her dinner? Laughing, they made their way in the house, a little shy in this uncharted zone of civility. With profuse apologies to Pansy, who graciously forgave them the instant they presented her with a pan of kibbles, David began to cook their dinner while Ellen showered.

Another noose around his neck, he thought as he rinsed vegetables, even if it didn't seem as tight as the last one.

After dinner David insisted that Ellen make one more dry run of the house. It went well, until they got to the stove. Stopping there, he took her by the shoulders and refused to release her until she gave him her word she wouldn't cook, not even boil water for tea. She promised, but feeling humiliated, she stormed off to bed, lashing out at anything that came in the path of her cane. But David knew that this time she would keep her word.

"David, I've got to get to a drugstore for some personal things. And clothes. I have no clothes, remember," Ellen announced the next morning.

"Look, can't you hold out until the barbecue? It's only a couple of weeks."

"Sorry, I can't."

If Ellen couldn't see, she could almost feel his face grow hot with understanding. "Oh, of course. I didn't think. Well, then I guess we'll have to make a trip to town."

The ride to Longacre was eleven miles before he pulled

up to the town's general store. There was nothing special about Longacre, New York, just that it was quiet and clean, had no crime to speak of and boasted a fairly decent diner. He would like to have stopped there to grab some lunch, but knew that everyone in the diner would go bug-eyed at the sight of Ellen. He'd never get away without answering at least four hundred questions. A quick trip to the supermarket would be a lot less painful.

"Hey, can't a person get some service around here?" he called as he led Ellen into an old-fashioned mercantile store complete with glass jars of gumdrops and licorice and barley sugar lollipops crowding the old oak counter. Helping himself to a few gumdrops, he gave one to Ellen. She hadn't eaten a gumdrop in years and popped it in her mouth. Watching her lick the sugar from her fingers, David grew restless, but the sound of footsteps kept him from running out the door.

"Hold your horses. I'm coming, I'm coming!" a sweet, musical voice called. "O-oh, David, you're back?" the voice cried.

"In the flesh, Patty." He smiled and endured the way she threw her arms around his neck.

"Oh, David, we heard about your father and I can't tell you how sorry we all are. Glen told us. We wanted to send flowers but Chuck said we couldn't be sure you were there and then no one would know who had sent them and— Did you make the funeral in time?"

Although she tried to be discreet, letting her hands explore the cluttered counter, Ellen was all ears. If David wasn't going to reveal things about himself, his friend seemed awfully willing to, and she was perfectly willing to listen.

"Glen Makker looked all over the state for you, until it finally occurred to him to call here. We were the ones who told him where you were, David, and I hope you didn't mind. When he told you to take a vacation, he didn't think you'd go to Antigua!''

''It's all right, Patty.'' David sighed and dragged Ellen forward before Patty could tell the rest of his life story. His scowl dared Patty to say another word when her brow rose at the sight of the pretty girl at his side. Not much of a worry, though, because Patty's mouth was hanging open.

''You'll catch flies if you don't shut your mouth,'' he whispered. Then, more loudly, ''This here is my father's ward, Ellen Candler. Ellen, this is Patricia Carmichael. She owns this store we're patronizing—or trying to, if she'd ever stop talking!''

''Hey, David, I'm in no hurry. I don't mind setting a spell. Why, I could even get us a pot of coffee. Just baked a fresh batch of cookies last night.''

David looked down at the tiny powerhouse in awe. ''Patty, so help me, I don't know how Chuck gets a word in edgewise with you gabbing all the time!''

''Never mind, sugar, he manages. Chuck says I have the true makings of a politician! Now, about those cookies—''

''Patty!''

''Okay, okay, okay! Just thought I'd—'' Patty swung back to Ellen, held out her hand, then took a deep breath and adjusted her smile. ''Well, blow me down! You're blind! And here I was wondering why you haven't said a word and figured you for shy.''

Ellen smiled and held out her hand in the direction of Patty's voice. ''Pleased to meet you, Patricia.''

Patty turned red with embarrassment as she looked to David for an explanation. But he just leaned against the counter, his arms folded across his chest, a crooked smile on his face. Returning her look with his own rascally gleam, she understood that she was on her own.

Apologies were not Patty's forte. Indignity was more in her line. ''Well, I'm sure I haven't met that many blind people, that's all! None, actually, now that I come to think about it. How many have you met, Mr. Hartwell, hmm? So you'll have to forgive both of us, Miss Candler. Me for my ignorance and David Hartwell for his lack of manners!''

Ellen waved her apology away. ''There's nothing to forgive.''

David straightened abruptly. ''Well, that's good, then. Now that you ladies are bosom buddies, I think I'll take myself down the road and pick up some stuff at the supermarket. I'll be back in thirty minutes, so don't waste time.''

''Hey, wait just a gosh darn minute!'' Patty cried as David started walking toward the door.

''Ellen will explain everything,'' he said, his blue eyes wary. He wasn't used to answering questions about his personal life and he could see that Ellen's presence was a tantalizing cipher to Patty. He couldn't get out the door fast enough.

Bells tinkling as the screen door closed told Ellen that David was gone and she blushed for his bad manners. Patty herself gave David's back a narrow, thoughtful glance before she turned back to Ellen. She had thought her to be about seventeen when David first introduced them, but staring openly now, she could see that Ellen was a bit older than that. And beautiful. Maybe the most beautiful woman Patty had ever seen. Those shiny red curls were natural or she'd eat her hat! David's ward, indeed! Only...how sad that those lovely green eyes couldn't see. Her heart went out to the game young woman and gently she reached out to touch Ellen's hand. But when Patty touched her, Ellen jumped. "Well, I guess that's lesson number one," Patty said softly as she stepped back.

"I don't like being touched unexpectedly," Ellen explained with quiet dignity. "It startles me."

"And in your position, it's always a surprise, isn't it?"

"Yes. People with sight don't think about things like that, but people without sight can't make the same calls."

"Like stepping aside?"

Ellen smiled. "You do understand!"

"In some things I'm a fool, but not as big a one as David Hartwell would lead you to think," Patty said proudly. "If you're patient with me, I'll get it right, I promise."

"David never said anything about you, much less that you were a fool!"

"Well, okay, I believe you, but the truth is, though, sometimes I'm not sure that David Hartwell occupies the same planet as the rest of us. But he is right about one thing. I do talk a lot!" Their shared laughter was the seal on a lifelong confederacy.

Feeling a little guilty at abandoning the women, David didn't have the courage to show his face until an hour later when he had finished loading his truck with his hastily purchased groceries. He stalled additional time by stopping at a farm stand and stocking up on an early crop of homegrown tomatoes. In the heat of summer, his favorite vegetable was the plump, crisp string beans straight from the basket. Pacing the pavement in front of Patty's store, he munched on a few while he peered through the window. The way they stood, like schoolgirls bent on sharing some deep secret, he gathered they'd made friends, and denied the streak of jealousy that surprised him as he watched.

"You sure you didn't forget something?" he drawled when Ellen finally emerged, clutching three big shopping bags.

"Hello to you, too," Ellen retorted with a wintry smile, determined not to allow the good mood she and Patty had established be spoiled by David's peevish greeting.

Her arms loaded with more boxes and bags, Patty brought up the rear. "No, siree, she didn't forget a thing. Nothing I had in the store, anyhow," she chuckled as she thrust the lot in David's arms. "When you come back down for Callie Tellerman's barbecue, she'll pick up the stuff I'm going to special order."

"Who said we were going to Miss Callie's barbecue?" But neither woman seemed to hear him.

"Thanks a million for helping me, Patty. David, please pay the lady. It seems she doesn't take plastic." Ellen's face was a study of innocence as she popped a gumdrop in her mouth.

Outrage and surprise flashed through David as he tried to balance Ellen's packages and rummage around for his wallet at the same time. Patty was going to mention that he could put the tab on his house account, but suddenly Longacre's favorite son—its own personal Smokey Bear, the one person *everyone* counted on to keep his wits— was falling apart *over a girl!* Watching him drop his bags, fumble for his car keys, stoop to pick up his lost booty, Patty felt as though she were watching an Abbot and Costello movie. And all the while, he was glaring at Ellen, watching her lick the sugar from her fingers, his face red as a beet, as if he was going to have a heart attack. Wait till Chuck heard about this!

Easing her tired body into the truck, Ellen rolled down

her window and kissed Patty goodbye. As David drove away, she kicked off her shoes and wriggled her toes, and allowed the summer wind to play havoc with her hair. ''Patty has almost everything in that store of hers, doesn't she?''

David didn't answer. It was almost unbearable for him to watch her red curls blow wild, much less speak. His silence didn't faze Ellen one bit. She felt no burdensome bond of involvement. She felt no noose tightening around her neck. She was a young girl out for a ride on a sunny summer day, radiant, delighted with the world.

''You know, I really, really like Patricia. She says most people think that she's a ditz because she dresses funny and has strange ideas. Does she really dress funny? What does she mean by *ditz?* I never heard that word before, but it doesn't sound like something she would be. She sounded…alive…to me. Full of energy! Fun! And look what she gave me.'' Ellen happily waved a thin, gold tube in the air. ''Did you notice my lipstick? I've never owned a lipstick before, it's a fact, do you believe? Is the color right for me? Patty says it makes me look—'' She bit her lip and turned away. Her memory must be failing not to remember the last time she'd asked David how she looked.

But David *had* noticed her red-painted lips the moment she'd walked out of Patty's store. It was a beacon he could have lived without. He thought so then, he thought so now. Helping her into the truck, he'd immediately noticed the smile she'd been trying to hide, had sensed her lighter spirits immediately. Part of him desperately wanted to share the joke, another wanted to kiss that grin off her lips. But a third remembered his cloying responsibility *to his ward,* and that side won out.

As they made the drive home, Ellen tried her best to

ignore her temperamental guardian. Forty-eight hours ago she had been snug in her bed in Montana. Now she was driving down a back road in upstate New York with a perfect stranger, and it might have been fun, even exciting, except that her fellow traveler was so disagreeable. Her first outing into the world in ages and she had the misfortune to be squired by a misogynist. Well, she wouldn't let him spoil her day if she could help it. The self-satisfied smile that kept breaking out was hers to enjoy. And the joke was, it had a lot to do with him!

The truth was, she hadn't needed half of what she'd purchased at Patty Carmichael's, but figured it was a good joke to play on her grouchy companion. After all, it wasn't going to hurt his pocketbook any, and it was good for Patty's business. Meeting Patty had been the best part of her day, her week, probably her whole darn month. She'd made a friend, someone to confide in, someone to share secrets with. And Patty had promised to drive up the mountain and visit her next week, so that they could have that coffee David denied them.

She would tell David about it later, when he was in a *really* rotten mood! Judging by the atmosphere in the car, he was pretty near to boiling. He'd grunted once and sighed twice—heavily! Not a good sign. When she heard him sigh a third time, she recalled her conversation with Patty, how Patty had sworn David's bark was worse than his bite. She had even gone so far as to try to convince Ellen that David Hartwell was one of the sweetest, gentlest men in the Adirondacks! Why his bad mood, Patty couldn't say, but she'd sworn she'd never seen him like this before! *Never!*

Ellen had been incredulous. "We *are* talking about David Hartwell, aren't we?" she'd asked skeptically, and heard Patty laugh. It was a wonderful sound to Ellen's ears. David *never* laughed. Come to think of it, neither had his father, John.

"Yes, we're talking about the same man. That giant out yonder, pounding the pavement."

"Oh, is David here already?" Ellen had asked, and began to gather up her things. "I guess I should go, then."

"Hey, slow down, honey! It won't kill him to wait a minute or two. It's good for a man to know his place. Believe me, they get even on Super Bowl Sunday. Anyway, he looks too scared to come in and get you. Is he afraid of you, by any chance?"

"Me?" Ellen had laughed, incredulous at the idea. "On the contrary."

"Oh, really," Patty had said. "Then please explain to dumb little ole me why he's out there peeking in, checking his watch every ten seconds and not haulin' his butt in here to fetch you home?"

"I wouldn't know," Ellen had said, wide-eyed with worry. "But I don't think fear enters into it. I can't imagine David being afraid of anything, or anyone."

"True. He is six foot two, you know, and almost as broad."

"No, Patty," Ellen had reminded her gently, "I don't know how tall David is." But she'd left out the part about how *broad* she knew him to be, or she'd have to explain about being kissed into oblivion once or twice by *that giant.* "Actually, I don't know anything about what David looks like because he won't let me touch him." She had explained how blind people liked to touch faces so they could get a handle on their friends, and how David Hartwell had emphatically refused her request.

"Oh," Patty had said.

Ellen thought she detected a certain tension in Patty's voice, but unsure, she continued on.

''David can be so mean. In any case, he doesn't care what I think.''

''Maybe he can't let himself care,'' Patty had suggested.

''For goodness' sake, why not?''

''Well…'' Patty had hesitated. ''Maybe he thinks he's in a no-win situation.''

Ellen was bewildered. ''What on earth are you talking about, Patty?''

''Oh, Ellen, you know how men are when you invade their territory. He *has* been living alone for years. It's probably driving him crazy, the thought of having you around the next four months. I mean, the idea of having *anyone* around would probably send David up the wall,'' she'd hastily added.

Ellen hadn't known what to say, but she'd decided that since Patty knew David a whole lot better than she did, she'd take her word for it. ''Okay, whatever you say. But it sure sounds like it's going to be a long summer.''

''Come on,'' Patty had argued, ''surely a smart lady like you will be able to get the better of one lone, grizzly forest ranger!'' Patty had chuckled. But she'd made Ellen feel a whole lot better, and Ellen had left the store her spirits higher than when she had arrived.

The day David returned to work, Ellen slept so late, she was up in time only to wave goodbye. Looking utterly adorable in her new red pajamas, and very forlorn, she looked so pitiful, David almost turned back before he remembered that he was on duty for the next five days, and Ellen *had* to learn to cope. He would stay in the neighborhood, or as close as his patrol allowed, and he would even try to stop by for lunch, but the bottom line was, Ellen simply had to learn how to manage.

David couldn't know it, but today was the first day in

Ellen's entire life that she was spending completely alone. In the past, her parents or a housekeeper or tutors had always been around. When she was living with John Hartwell, a myriad of servants had hovered nearby. Now there was…Pansy. When the sound of the truck was gone, Ellen wiped away her tears—tears she had *not* wanted David to see—and slowly made her way into the kitchen. Sitting at the table, she sipped the tepid coffee David had left for her, but her stomach revolted. Lifting the plate that covered her oatmeal, she wrinkled her nose and offered the bowl to Pansy, who gratefully accepted. Wondering what next, she thrummed her fingers on the table.

She could call Patty. Yes, that was a good idea. But after that, what? One thing she knew, if she didn't get her computer, she'd go bonkers the next few months, the silence was so spooky. Locating the wall phone, she asked an operator to place a call to Montana and was grateful when the housekeeper answered the phone.

"Yes, it's me, Ellen. Yes, I'm fine. How are you? No, Mr. Hartwell isn't here. Why do you ask? Actually, he hasn't been *all* that terrible." She found herself defending him. "In fact, he's been rather…um…nice." Suddenly, Ellen didn't want to hear the housekeeper say anything bad about David. "Listen, I would be very grateful if you sent me some things. Express Mail, if you would. Have Harry Gold arrange it."

She gave the housekeeper her list and got off the phone as soon as politeness allowed. Ugh. Unpleasant woman. She'd need a hot bath to wash away the bad feelings the housekeeper had generated. A good idea at that, to take a long, leisurely bath.

Finding the bathroom was no problem, and Ellen brought along a cup of tea for company—microwaved, as per David's orders! As the bathtub filled, she removed her nightclothes and sat on the tub's edge, sipping the hot, sugary tea—four sugars, and no one around to make a snide comment! Come to think of it, it was kind of nice to be sitting here, sitting at the edge of the tub, nursing a cup of tea, hanging around in the nude. A novelty. A first, in fact! Arching her back in a long stretch, she ran a hand down her torso. Maybe she couldn't see, but skimming her breasts with her palms, she could feel they were a fairly nice shape, soft and firm, all at the same time, assuming that was how they ought to look! Running a hand down her legs, she thought they had a good shape, too, but who was to say? When the tub was full and steeped with some godawful expensive bath salts that Patty Carmichael had insisted she needed, she climbed in and settled to her chin in the delicious hot water.

Ellen's skin was a mottled mass of wrinkles by the time she found the energy to get out. After a brisk rubdown, she dropped her towel and strolled to her sleeping alcove. Perched on the bed, she covered her entire body in a sinful array of lotion and scents, more of Patty's supplies. Delighting in her newfound freedom, she strolled back to the bathroom to comb her hair and clean up after herself. She even dabbed on a little lipstick. Finally dressed in a baby-blue tank top and white overalls that ended mid-thigh— her most popular seller, Patty had promised—Ellen wondered what to do next, until she remembered the bags in the living room, waiting to be unpacked.

That's where David found her, nestled among a mass of cardboard and tissue paper, when he walked through the door at noon. "Hey, there, anybody home? What's for lunch?"

"Oh, David, you came back! I'm *so* glad you're home!" Scrambling to her feet, Ellen wrapped her arms around his waist, surprising them both.

"Sorry," she mumbled apologetically. "I don't usually...I didn't realize...I guess I'm more nervous than I thought."

David smiled, touched by her greeting. "No problem. As greetings go, it was mighty nice. But I'm only here for lunch, mind."

"Just for lunch," she agreed vaguely, rubbing her cheek against his shirt. He smelled so nice, a little sweaty from working under the summer sun, but all outdoors, piney and clean.

"Hey," he asked, a little alarmed at the way she was clinging, "it wasn't all that bad, was it, being alone?" He searched her eyes, ever amazed that she couldn't see, when they seemed so full of light.

The shock of discovery hit her full-force. "It wasn't bad at all. The bathroom probably smells like a brothel from my bath. It's only that it was a first, my being alone, that is."

"Hey, I didn't realize. I'm sorry."

"There you go again, apologizing, when you couldn't even know, because I didn't say. I told you, I enjoyed it. But I'm glad you came home, even if it's only for a little while."

"I won't always be able to, but I thought, this week, just once or twice."

"Yes, just once or twice would be fine." But once or twice would make her happy.

David actually found himself enjoying the way Ellen puttered around the kitchen, fixing their sandwiches, tuna fish with only a little too much mayonnaise, pretty crude crudities and extremely strong coffee. He stayed longer than he intended.

And ignored the noose as it continued to twist stiffly 'round his collar.

Chapter Six

The next morning, Ellen made sure she was up in time to share breakfast with David before he went to work. David wouldn't allow himself to even think how much he enjoyed the sight of her stumbling into the kitchen, her coppery hair tousled, her eyes sleepy, her smile shy. But Pansy wasn't so timid, and put her nose on Ellen's lap the moment Ellen sat. Pansy was becoming so possessive of Ellen, seemed to consider Ellen her private possession, that David was starting to wonder if it was possible to be jealous of a dog.

After he left, Ellen sat on the couch, her hand to the cheek David had awkwardly kissed on his way out the door. A kiss very unlike the brutal kisses they'd shared on the plane ride east. This kiss was a feathery caress, absentminded, almost husbandly, if she dared to think about it like that. Was David Hartwell mellowing? No, not likely. It was probably that he was simply glad to be back home. Yes, that was the more likely explanation. Making peace with her the past two days was no doubt just survival tactics. But hey, she'd take anything. Four months could feel like a lifetime.

Come to think of it, she ought to give Dr. Gleason a call to make sure there was nothing she was forgetting to do before the big day. And to make sure the surgery hadn't been canceled. The very thought made her break out in a cold sweat. For the first time since John had died, Ellen allowed herself to dwell on the operation, allowed all the *what-ifs* to surface. Such as *what if* there wasn't a room for her at the hospital, *what if* she were allergic to anesthesia, *what if* Dr. Gleason broke his hand, *what if* the nurses went on strike…*what if*… Her stomach began to churn and she wished David were there. When he was there, she didn't worry about these things, and if he knew that she did, he knew how to calm her.

Now why on earth had she thought that? Helping her was an anathema to him. He'd said so more than once. But lately, contrary to his words, he *had* been very helpful, more than she'd expected. More than he'd probably expected, she would bet, although she couldn't tell because he was very careful to keep his voice neutral. Still, that farewell kiss, this morning…

That kiss again.

On the other hand, he had been very nice to help her to clean up her mess of boxes and tissue paper last night, when she was sure he'd just wanted to put his feet up and relax. And he had very politely insisted she use the bathroom first at bedtime. And if only she could keep her eyes open long enough, she was sure he was checking up on her, in the middle of the night. The first time, she had thought it was Pansy, but she didn't think so now. Whatever it was that had stroked her cheek, it hadn't been wet or cold.

Dependency thoughts. Ellen shook her head. Not a good idea. No one was going to take care of her anymore, blind or not, so she'd better get used to doing for herself, and fast. John Hartwell was gone, and that was that. And if she were honest, wasn't it just a little bit exciting, after a lifetime of coddling, to finally be on one's own? Weren't those years just a little bit stifling? Never allowed to travel without an escort, doing things at someone else's convenience, never learning the meaning of independence—all with only the kindest intentions, of course. But to be honest, hadn't it all been the *tiniest* bit suffocating? So that David's irritable acquiescence at caring for her actually made for a breath of fresh air, his high expectations a signal for her to grow up.

Yes, make those phone calls yourself, get back to your writing, learn how to make a proper cup of tea.

David was right. Come down from the mountain.

By ten o'clock Ellen was showered and dressed, and her telephone calls had been made. Managing to leave a message for Dr. Gleason, she had been assured by his secretary that he would return her call. Deciding to get domestic—she had never even made a bed before—she fooled around with hers, and found it wasn't all that difficult to flick a sheet. It *seemed* to feel pretty smooth. Perhaps she should try David's bed. If he didn't want her to cook, she could at least share some of the cleaning. Besides, the idea of wandering around in his room was intriguing. But first she'd do the breakfast dishes.

She had a hunch she'd used far too much soap, and guessed they were the cleanest dishes in America by the time she finished what seemed to be a *very* long rinse. Still, it seemed to take forever before she could gather the courage to make her way into David's bedroom. Something told her this was forbidden territory—not that she was going to let *that* stop her, not even when she tripped over his sneakers, first thing, and cursed him for such carelessness. That this was his private domain was irrelevant. But she used her cane more carefully.

His room smelled nice, masculine, like David. Finding her way to the bed, she discovered that it was already made, a revealing sidelight to Mr. Hartwell. She sat on the bed. A firm bed. Well, he'd need one, wouldn't he? A man his size? The thick, goose down blanket was as soft as the bed was hard, and the pillow she tested, as thick and soft as the blanket. A wonderful bed to snuggle into on a chilly night. She shouldn't have been so quick to give it up.

David didn't return for lunch that afternoon, a fact Ellen noticed around one o'clock, when her stomach began to growl. Deciding that tuna fish two days in a row was beyond the call of duty, it was an interesting exploration to find a jar of peanut butter. Recalling most of the kitchen's layout, it took her less than ten minutes to make a sandwich. But she knew a container of milk when she touched one.

After lunch, she and Pansy wandered out onto the porch. Sitting on the steps, she threw sticks for the dog to fetch. When they were bored with that, they sat together in the shade, Ellen cooling off on the porch swing while Pansy sprawled, panting, at her feet. Pansy was beginning to make an excellent companion, and she would bet that Pansy would make an excellent seeing-eye dog, if Ellen had felt the need for one. With the operation at hand, though, it was a moot point, and besides, she was sure that David wouldn't be so quick to give Pansy up, much as he complained about the dog.

She was still sitting on the swing when David drove up around four, having worked through his lunch hour to leave work early. He thought she looked very becoming in an orange tank top, the strap dangling down her shoulder especially beguiling. He also noticed that she was beginning to tan, and made a mental note to pick up a bottle of sunscreen before she got burned. He would apply it personally. The thought made him laugh unexpectedly, and Ellen's ears perked up at the unfamiliar sound.

"You must have had a good day." She smiled.

Embarrassed by his good humor, he frowned. "It wasn't too bad. I fined some clowns for littering."

"That sounds a little harsh. I've never heard of anybody being fined for littering before."

"Well, it was three good ole boys fishing without a permit, and the litter was a dozen beer cans discarded in a public stream."

"Oh."

"Yeah, that's what I said. *Oh.*"

"Uh-oh."

"Yeah, and that's what I *thought.*" He smiled crookedly. And not all he thought. There was something to be said for coming home to a pretty woman, even if the table was bare.

David was soon scraping together a meal while Ellen sat quietly at the kitchen table, a half smile on her lips as she listened to him putter. She was suddenly feeling shy. Remembering how she'd thrown herself at him yesterday, she was reluctant to make any overtures. She'd rather take her cues from him, and he was busy being cordial, but cool.

Actually, David was busy being nervous. Ellen had been working overtime the past few days, trying to be nice, and it was starting to work. She was beginning to break down his defenses. He knew that she was only thinking of him, not wanting to be a burden, but he would have preferred her old feisty self back. She was beginning to tug at his heart, to make him feel things he wasn't sure he wanted to feel. Hell, he still couldn't believe he'd kissed her goodbye this morning, didn't know what on earth had possessed him—and had thought about nothing else the rest of the day. Which was why he'd been in a bad mood when he'd come upon those fishermen. It had been a pleasure to read them the riot act, to slap them with that outrageous fine even if it had been well deserved. Actually, they were lucky to get off so lightly, because he had thought about arresting the jerks.

All because of a kiss.

Well, it wasn't going to happen again. Even if she was the sweetest thing that ever graced his table, sitting there so patiently while she waited for him to say something. And him cooking when he'd rather be doing a hundred other things, all of which involved making love to her. He scratched his chin, his five o'clock shadow, and rubbed his scars. Careful, buddy. Thoughts like that had a habit of ricocheting.

He was polite when he served dinner, remote, his conversation so stilted that Ellen was bewildered. She went over the past twenty-four hours carefully, trying to figure out what she'd said or done to upset him, but there was nothing she could pinpoint. On the contrary, she'd thought they'd been making headway. They had been getting on so well the last day or so, that his withdrawal was hurtful. What had she done? Under the circumstances, it wasn't surprising that she was practically in tears when the telephone rang, its unpleasant shrill making them both jump.

"Hey there, Ellen." Patty Carmichael's cheerful voice

came across the line so loudly that David winced, but Ellen was thrilled to hear a friendly voice.

"Oh, Patty, I'm so glad you called."

Patty heard her unhappiness immediately. "Lover-boy giving you a good time, huh?"

Carefully, David watched Ellen's expression, waiting for her answer.

Ellen blushed. "Well, um…"

"Uh-oh. That's what I thought. Is David close by?"

Grim-faced, he removed Ellen's dinner plate and added it to the pile in the sink, making as much noise as he could.

"Um, yes."

"Okay, gotcha. We'll keep this to yes-or-no questions. But, you know, Ellen, Hunk Man isn't so bad, once you get to know him."

Pressing the phone to her ear, Ellen prayed David couldn't hear Patty's blunt words as he handed her a cup of hot, sugary tea.

"Well, sweetie, are you going to make it till October?"

"Oh, yes! I have to. I will."

"Just asking. You know that Chuck and I would welcome you with open arms."

"Oh, Patty, if I only could. But…I can't."

David stared at her, tight-lipped.

"Why not?"

"Patty—" Ellen cautioned.

"Okay, okay, tell me another time. Still, if you're going to stay there, you can't go on like this. You sound terrible. There's got to be a way to break the ice."

"Well, if there is, I haven't discovered it. I thought I had, but…" Patty couldn't see her helpless shrug, but David did.

"Maybe you're not looking in the right place."

''What do you mean?'' Ellen asked nervously.

''Well, maybe the poor boy needs a bit of shaking up.''

''Do you think so? I thought we were dealing with…er…something…more mature.''

''Ellen, honey, there's nothing more childish than a man in…'' When Patty paused, David almost grabbed the phone from Ellen's hand.

''Than what? What were you going to say?''

''Ach, never mind. I forget.''

David released his breath.

''Well, now, let me think. What would make David sit up and think? Hmm. How about a big, fat kiss on hunk man's mouth?''

David turned a red-hot mix of fury and embarrassment, but Patty was all ears.

''Not possible,'' Ellen confided bleakly.

''*No kidding?* Wow! Golly gee, that man must be made of brick!''

Ellen sighed. ''No, it's me. I just don't have what it takes.''

''Honey-pie, have you looked in the mirror lately?''

''Nooo.''

Patty's laugh was full and throaty and Ellen could almost see her wipe her tears way. ''Sorry, hon', you must get that a lot, huh?''

''No, I don't,'' Ellen declared, smiling through her uncertainty, ''but I love it. It makes me feel like I'm a part of the human race.''

David felt terrible. He'd had no idea how lonely Ellen felt, and he knew he had a lot to do with it.

''Well, let me tell you something, Miss Ellen Candler. You're *too* gorgeous! If anyone's got a problem, it's Mr. High-and-Mighty Hartwell. But don't you worry. Give me a day or two and I'll come up with something. Hey, but

I really called to tell you that a couple of boxes were delivered here this afternoon. I figured anything that came to Longacre by Express Mail must be important. They're from Montana, and they're addressed to you.''

"Oh, thank goodness, I can work again. It's my computer and some odds and ends I had shipped from home. I'll ask David to pick them up.''

"No, wait a minute, I've got a better idea. How about if I bring everything up, tomorrow, after the store closes, and spend the night? I'll run it by Chuck, but I'm sure he won't mind. We can have a regular girls' pajama party. It's been years.''

Ellen looked in the direction of the sink, where she could hear David still washing the dishes. "Years for you, never for me! But maybe I should ask about this. What do you think?''

"Yeah, I guess. Go on. I'll wait.''

Ellen hesitated. "This may not be a good time.''

"Ellen, are you afraid of David?''

"Yes. Yes, I do believe I am,'' she admitted sadly.

David paled. Had he done this to her? The thought made him sick.

Patty, on the other hand, was incredulous. "David Hartwell wouldn't hurt a mosquito! I've told you that a thousand times!''

"Yes, well, I'm no mosquito.''

"Right. Worse, you're a girl! You itch more!'' Patty cackled and went into peals of laughter.

What David wouldn't have given to have his hands around Patricia Carmichael's neck that moment! Too late, he remembered that old saw about eavesdroppers never hearing good of themselves. Wanting desperately to leave, perverseness kept him glued to the kitchen, scrubbing the counter vigorously. He was concentrating so hard, not wanting to miss a word, that Ellen had to call his name twice to ask whether he minded if Patty spent tomorrow night with them. He said yes, that was fine. He would sharpen his machete.

After she said goodbye to Patty, Ellen took Pansy into the living room. Now that she had something to look forward to, she didn't care that David was in one of his moods. But it was only moments before David followed her, handing her the remote phone.

Telephone calls, overnight guests. Only a few days and Ellen was breaking up his peace, and he didn't like it one bit. He didn't like the sound of Dr. Gleason's voice, either. It sounded too young and enthusiastic. And so did Ellen when he handed her the phone.

"Charles! How are you?"

Charles? Boy, did that one kill him!

"Hello, my dear," he heard the doctor say, and felt his hands curl into fists.

A good thing this wasn't a house call.

The next evening, when he pulled up and saw Patty's old Thunderbird parked on the grass, David thought he really was going to lose his sanity. All day long he'd been hoping it was just a bad dream, but no, the little minx had really shown up. Unloading his gear, he cursed a brown streak, but when he strode up the porch steps, he schooled his face to be a little kinder, for Ellen's sake. He buried the disappointment he felt that she wasn't sitting on the swing as usual, hugging her knees while she waited for him park, handing him a cold beer and asking a hundred questions about his day. He'd never asked her to do that, it was just something that had evolved, so why did he feel forsaken? Well, he did! Damn, even Pansy was nowhere to be seen!

Shucking his muddy boots just outside the door, he could hear the women's voices coming from the kitchen, a soft, cottony murmur floating on air redolent with the smell of a warm, yeasty kitchen. Since Ellen had arrived, his cold, barren house had begun to fill with funny noises and curious aromas. With life, David was beginning to realize. The bouquet of life. And not just of food, but of bubble baths, perfume and lotions. With giggly phone calls, lingerie strewn to dry all over the bathroom—expensive *silk* lingerie—womanly things disrupting his household, creating expectations that made him nervous, such as the domestic sounds he heard now that made him think about families, kids...a wife. All the things he couldn't have, never hoped to have, and was beginning to ache for. An intruder in his own home, he snuck into the shower and washed away the mud of the woods. Wearing clean but crumpled shorts and T-shirt, he strolled into the kitchen to surprise the women.

"Ah, the wandering hero returns after a hard day at the mines," Patty greeted him, toeing up to bestow a sisterly kiss on his cheek. When all Ellen did was send him a smile, he was careful to mask his disappointment, even though he knew there was no reason to expect more. Sitting down to the fabulous dish of pot roast Patty set in front of him, even the wonderful steamy smell couldn't dispel his confusion. The more they plied him with fresh-baked bread, the more they coddled him, the more depressed David became because he began to see the wonderful home-cooked meal as a barometer of his personal poverty.

After dinner, needing something to pull him out of his funk, David volunteered to put Ellen's computer together. Hauling the boxes from Patty's car trunk into the living room, he began to sort the lot. The women hung out with him, sipping wine and laughingly giving him plenty of advice, none of which he needed, which they all knew. But no one had ever teased him like this and he enjoyed their easy female banter, good-natured ribbing and slightly flirtatious manner. When he was done, they all took a fresh bottle of wine out onto the porch and lit citronella candles against the dreaded mosquitoes. The scene had a fairy-tale quality that escaped none of them.

"Now I understand why you live up here," Patty whispered as she sprawled on the porch steps and scanned the black night sky.

Her acknowledgment pleased David. "I am hoping that one day Ellen will see them."

"Them?" Ellen asked as she took her favorite spot on the wicker swing.

"The stars," David explained as he settled down beside her.

"Oh. Yes, I would like that, to see stars once again, and the sun, and—oh, just about everything!" She laughed softly and then they all fell silent under the weight of their own personal dreams.

It was a new experience for David to hang out with women, and he was a little gun shy, until he realized it was probably a new experience for Ellen to hang out with anybody at all. In this he was correct, and so in their own way, they took a giant step together, down the towering mountains of seclusion they had separately built for themselves. Under Patty's amiable influence—and that of the wine—they idled the night away, talking about nothing and arguing about everything, laughing low into the sultry night until David rose to his feet, reminding them that he had to get up early.

"I'll take the couch," he announced graciously. "You two can have my bed." A sleepless night on the couch wasn't going to kill him, he decided. Hadn't he already had more than a few, mooning over that redhead?

Patty plopped down on the wicker seat he'd vacated and shot him a mischievous look. "Thanks, chum, don't mind if we do. 'Nighty-night, then, ranger. Ellen and I are now going to have a cozy, girl-talk chat." She laughed at his confusion. "Hey, don't worry, Hartwell, we're not going to talk about you. Why on earth would we do that?" she giggled.

The look he sent her told her that was *exactly* what he thought, would put money on it, in fact, and both girls burst into laughter. It didn't take a genius to realize that David was jealous. It made them stay up longer than they ordinarily would have, maybe drink a little more than they should have, laugh a lot more than was funny, and finally stumble past David's uncomfortable makeshift couch-bed at 2:00 a.m. He listened as they washed up and tumbled into his bed, and listened to their girlish whispers far into the night. The idea of Ellen beneath his featherbed, her hair spread across his pillow, made him miserable, and he was a rag when he got up the next morning. But nobody saw. The girls had slept in.

When he returned that evening, Patty was gone and Ellen was back on the porch swing, handing him a cold beer. But his resentment over her disaffection the night before still lingered and he returned her greeting brusquely. When she caught on, Ellen rose and, without saying a word, disappeared in the house. Ever faithful, Pansy trailed behind, leaving David to roll the cold bottle between his palms, feeling like a heel. It seemed there was no end to the pain he could put her through, and she hadn't done a damned thing to deserve it. Last night had really been a lot of fun, even if her allegiance had been to Patty. Regret came hard upon the heels of enlightenment. He was a jealous bastard, all right. Jealous of Patty and Rafe, jealous of a damned dog, jealous of his dead father, for Pete's sake! Using them to hurt her, using his jealousy to create a barrier between them so that *he* wouldn't get hurt—when she left, as she one day would.

But who was aching more, her or him? When he went inside, Ellen was stationed at her computer. He wanted to apologize, but didn't think she would believe him, and he couldn't face her disbelief just then. The meal he put together was almost inedible, in stark contrast to the divine dinner of the previous night. Ellen excused herself almost immediately and he tried to lose himself in some paperwork. A few minutes later David heard her run a bath— the woman was obsessed with bathing!—and the scent of gardenia blossom found its way into his makeshift study. It pointedly ended all hope of concentrating on anything other than her and, hoping for distraction, he turned on the television, but somehow, every step she took as she made her way from bath to bed was more interesting than whatever was on the screen.

That was the strained pattern of the couple over the next week or so. Relief came in the form of Chuck Carmichael, sent up the mountain one morning by his wife, Patty, to escort Ellen down to Longacre for a couple of days. Ellen left a note, which David promptly tore into a thousand pieces when he arrived home that night.

Look at you, he jeered himself. Bloody woman leaves for a couple of nights and you fall apart. What's going to happen when she leaves for good? Nothing but heartache ahead, chum. Better start working longer hours. Go right to sleep, right after dinner. Maybe stop checking up on her, at night, too. And, hey guy, how about leaving a little earlier for work, *before* she comes in to say good morning, looking like she needs to be tumbled back into bed—preferably yours!

Whatever he told himself, it didn't matter. When Ellen returned a few days later, David couldn't deny his relief that she was back. He was just careful not to let it show in his voice. Sitting on the porch steps as though she'd never been gone, holding out an ice-cold beer to welcome him home, Ellen was easy, telling him that, yes, she'd had a wonderful time, that Chuck and Patty were angels and couldn't do enough for her, and she'd been introduced to practically the whole town, but she was glad to be home.

Home. He heard her say it, let it roll it around his mind, felt it fasten to his heart while he watched her rise to her feet, her sweet hips swinging as she went indoors.

Home. She meant it, too, he thought wryly as he followed her into the house, if the trail she was leaving was any indication. Sandals at the door, a floppy straw bag tossed on the sofa, gumdrops strewn all over the coffee table—she was obviously starting to feel pretty comfortable in the cabin, even if she was a bit messy.

She was bustling about in the kitchen, putting together another one of her gourmet meals of tuna fish when he came in, towel-drying his hair. Singing quietly. Perhaps it was for the best that she had gone down to town a few days, because she had sure come back in a pretty good mood. Maybe he should ride the tide, make peace with her. Wasn't anything better than the silent war they'd been waging before she'd left? Maybe he should he tell her that he liked having her back. But how did he do that?

Fresh from his shower, David smelled wonderful. Ellen could feel his warmth surround her like a cloak. Still, his arrival had startled her and she'd scraped her hand against the rim of the tuna can and cursed softly.

She heard his rare laugh, teasing and warm. "You're

getting to be a regular trooper, judging from your language. Here, let me see.'' His thick mat of chest hair tickled her shoulder as he reached to examine her finger.

''Are you bald?'' she asked impulsively as he soaped up her hand.

''Good grief! What makes you ask that?'' he laughed as he dried her hand with a dish towel.

She spun around so fast he couldn't stop her. ''It's just that I could tell you had a furry chest.''

''You don't like it?''

''I heard somewhere that hairy men were bald. It made me wonder, that's all.'' With lightening motion, she stood on her toes and ran her fingers through his thick, silky hair, exploring the way it brushed his brow and fell to his neck. ''Don't like barbers, hmm?'' she teased gently, laughter crinkling her sightless green eyes.

Then suddenly her hands were on his face, skimming his nose, brushing his lips, grazing his cheeks so lightly that he almost didn't notice—except that he did, and froze. Ellen didn't stop until she reached the top of his head. ''I'm not embarrassing you, am I?''

David had no voice to say, either way.

''Well, you're definitely not bald!'' she announced with an easy chuckle, and as suddenly as she'd touched him, she turned back to finish making dinner. It was over before it began.

David stared. Surely she had felt his scars. She had to be blind— Well, Christ, she *couldn't* have missed them, so why didn't she say something? If she were waiting for him to explain, well, he damned well wasn't going to. She could wait till hell froze over and he wouldn't say a word.

''Ellen?''

''Hmm?'' Nibbling on a slice of tomato, she turned in his direction.

"Come on, Ellen."

"Oh, are you ready for dinner? I'm a little slow tonight, huh?" She held out the salad bowl and when she felt him take it, she reached into the refrigerator to find the vinaigrette and pitcher of iced tea.

She was getting to be real handy around the kitchen, he noticed absently. But still, she should say *something*. Nobody could be that innocent. He tried for a little sternness, hoping to hide his distress. "Ellen!"

"David, I'm moving as fast as I can. If you're so hungry, set the table."

Maybe she was too embarrassed at what she'd found. Maybe she was trying to save face. Ha, that was a good one! Or was it possible that she *hadn't* felt anything, that his scars had no meaning for her, at least, not in the same way they meant for him? After all, if she didn't know color, what would a ragged patch of skin mean?

"Ellen!"

"David, you keep saying *Ellen*. Is there something you want to tell me?"

"Yes. Yes. I've…I've got a day off coming to me, day after next. I thought maybe you'd like to do something."

"But I just got home."

"Oh, right. Well, I meant maybe take in a movie. Oops, sorry. I meant—"

The smile she sent him was forgiving as she slid into her seat. "Thanks, David, I know what you meant. How about a fancy dinner in one of those glitzy, overpriced restaurants? We could dress up. I'll bet you could use a decent meal."

"Well, that sounds fine," he said, pleased by her interest. "Actually, there's a mighty fine inn down in North Creek. If you wanted to get in some shopping, we could make a day of it."

"You mean, if I *must* shop?" she teased.

"Was I that obvious?"

"Yes."

"Right. Well, we'll figure out something." Maybe she *hadn't* noticed his scars.

After dinner, Ellen went straight to her bath. She sank beneath a luxurious bed of soap bubbles and thought about her discovery, of the monkey on David's back. To her sensitive fingertips, trained to read Braille since childhood, reading his scars had been simplicity itself. Hopefully, her trembling hands hadn't given her away as they'd traced the contours of his cheeks and made her discovery, because she had been pretty surprised. She'd known early on that he was hiding something, but a disfigurement hadn't counted among her guesses. Turning in his arms seemed such a natural thing to do at the time. Her hands had risen almost of their own volition to surprise his secret. If only he knew the effort it took not to run her lips along his jaw, to tell him that she didn't care. Wanting to say that if he really wanted to frighten her, he would kiss her—oh, would he, please?—because she was pretty sure that she was falling in love with her ill-tempered guardian. But he hadn't said a word.

Was he so upset that he couldn't speak?

Possibly.

Or had he convinced himself that she didn't know what she was touching?

Possibly.

So many unanswered questions, and they came fast. First and foremost, she had to wonder why Patty hadn't told her about David's face. Chuck, too, of course, yes, and Rafe. For goodness' sake, strangers passing them on the street knew what David looked like! *Everyone* knew what he looked like—except her! Why? Were his friends protecting him? Didn't they trust Ellen not to spurn him? For goodness' sake, why would Ellen, *of all people,* do that? No, it just wasn't possible. Patty knew her better than that. Then why? Was this a test? Were David's friends putting her through some sort of test and awaiting the results? Boy, would that really upset her!

The more Ellen thought about David's scars and the veil of secrecy that surrounded him, the angrier she got. John Hartwell would have called this collusion, she thought, bolting up in dismay. The quick, fluid movement sent her bathwater splashing and her bottle of bath oil crashing onto the bathroom floor.

She heard David's footsteps pause outside the door. "Everything okay?"

"Sure, just peachy," Ellen muttered.

Hearing no answer, David opened the door a crack and glanced in just to make sure Ellen was all right. She was more than all right. She was a fairy-like specter surrounded by a rainbow of bubbles, her glossy damp curls piled high, a becoming flush coloring her damp cheeks. But he couldn't deny her pouting red lips. When he saw the broken bottle, he presumed the source of her sour look.

"Don't worry. Patty sells that kind of stuff by the gallon, doesn't she? We'll pick up another bottle when we go to town." He disappeared, to return a few moments later, loaded down with a dust broom, dustpan and paper towels. Squatting beside the tub, he swept up the broken glass. "Nobody's perfect, you know."

"Oh, *I* know that!"

Hunched on his knees as he swept away the glass, David glanced up at her curiously. "Something wrong?"

"Collusion," she murmured, rolling the word over her tongue.

"What's that?" he asked as he swept the last of the shards of glass into the dustpan.

Ellen turned in the direction of his voice, her voice a husky mix of steam and annoyance. "What are you doing in my tub?"

"Hey, lady, if I were in your tub, you'd know it." David grinned. "As it is, I'm cleaning up your mess."

"Well, do it later," she huffed. "I'm bathing. No need to have a Peeping Tom hanging around."

David stood up, the realization that Ellen was in a bad mood unmistakable. "Peeping Tom, is it?"

"Peeping Tom, it is!"

"Oh, really? And how are you planning to get out from under those pretty bubbles if I don't clear a path for you?"

Ellen sat up, an unexpected sight that gave David enormous pleasure. The lifespan of a bubble was about a second.

"I'll think of something," she said loftily. "You don't have to rub my blindness in my face."

"For Pete's sake, I am not rubbing your blindness into your face. Or are you one of those weirdoes that can walk on hot coals and ground glass?"

"Very funny. I am not amused!"

"Sorry, Your Majesty," David smirked as he pulled down the toilet seat and made himself comfortable. "I'll just sit here quietly while your Royal Highness contemplates her dilemma."

Ellen was furious. "I'll call you when I need you!"

"You need me now," he snapped.

"Do you think so?" she asked sweetly. Faster than fast, with the flat of her palm, Ellen suddenly sent a tidal wave of bathwater and bubbles in his direction.

"Dammit, Ellen!" David jumped, spluttering as he

grabbed for the nearest towel. "What the hell's wrong with you?"

"Nothing that your leaving won't cure!"

"Well, this is one party we're leaving together," he said grimly. David didn't know what in hell had gotten into her but he'd had enough. In one fell swoop he scooped Ellen out of the tub, ignoring the flood the bathwater made. Turning a deaf ear to the shrieks of the woman in his arms, he carefully skirted the mess on the floor and carried his precious bundle to her alcove, where he plopped her down on the bed.

Ellen lay there in shock, half risen on her slender arms, her naked body an absolutely lovely, painful sight to David's parched soul. He would have given the world to lie beside her and take her, half bubble, all woman, even if he was furious with her.

"Don't you *ever* call me a Peeping Tom again," he ordered her gruffly. "When I want to see you, hell, even you'll know I'm looking!"

Enraged, Ellen scrambled to her feet, swaddled her wet body in a blanket and marched after her tormentor.

"Where the hell do you think you're going?" David demanded when he felt her bounce off his back.

"My bed is all wet, now, Mr. Hartwell, thanks to your bullying. I can't sleep on a wet bed, can I?" she challenged, sounding like a shrew even to her own ears. "You have any suggestions?" she asked brightly.

"Yeah, but you're too young," he growled and, slinging Ellen over his shoulder, he marched into his own bedroom and dropped her down on his bed. "Satisfied? And don't get up, again. My back is beginning to hurt."

"And where are you going to sleep?" she asked, suspicion written across her face.

"Not in my own bed, I suppose?" David asked with cutting sarcasm.

"Do you want to?" she asked impulsively, freezing him with her outspoken question.

"Ellen, watch what you're saying," David warned her softly. "I'm a grown man and at a certain point, I stop playing games."

"Oh, really?" Ellen said, staring crossly into the void as she remembered his secret scars. "And when is that, do you suppose?" she called after him as he spun on his heel. But her words hung heavy in the air, unanswered, as she heard him slam the door.

Chapter Seven

Notwithstanding their argument, Ellen thoroughly enjoyed spending the night in David's huge, wonderful bed. She lingered long beneath the covers, the next morning, listening to the raindrops' tattoo on the windows, and Pansy's heavy snoring, as the loyal dog camped on the floor beside the bed. She wondered what David did at work when it rained, and made a mental note to ask him, if he were talking to her when he got home. She had already decided to ignore their argument of last night and to see what he would do, see if he'd try to make peace with her, which she sincerely doubted, given his nasty temper. Emotion was not David's strongest talent! She really did have him over a barrel.

She thought of calling Patty, to tell her that she'd discovered David's secret and to demand from her an explanation for the secrecy. But before she got around to calling, she had a change of heart. She was unsure how much

Patty would want to say, since she hadn't said anything before. There might be reasons Ellen hadn't thought of. Better to think things out a little more, before she jumped the gun and maybe hurt her friends, in passing. Much more rewarding to snuggle back into David's bed and daydream about her tormentor.

But later that day, after a lazy morning and a leisurely shower, Ellen was hard at her computer, where David found her when he came home from work. Shaking his long hair free of rain, he eyed his ward and wondered what kind of mood she was in now. "Had a hard day?"

"Totally exhausting, but I managed." Ellen sighed, smiling to herself. "What do *you* do when it rains, Mr. Forest Ranger, and you don't have to guard the trees from fire?"

So she was playing it cute. Well, he could live with cute. David chucked his heavy work boots into a corner and padded over to her computer.

"'Savoring the warmth of the fire, he watched as Amanda raised her slender, pale arms and covered her—'"

"Good Lord, Ellen! Exactly what kind of books do you write?" David asked, shocked from his toes to his calloused fingertips.

"Sweet, sexy books about men and women falling in love."

"You mean, the mating of cannibals, rather!"

"David Hartwell, what a dreadful thing to say! How cynical."

"Yeah, *cynical,* my middle name."

Hearing his feet shuffling, she grabbed his leg. "Hey, wait a minute. You can't just walk away."

David looked down at Ellen's arm clutching at his trouser. "I guess not."

Ellen flushed and released him abruptly. "I hate when someone walks away from me in the middle of a conversation."

"I stand corrected."

"Good. Now about that remark."

"About cannibals?"

"About love!"

"'Love is nothing save an insatiate thirst to enjoy a greedily desired object!'"

"David Hartwell!"

"Montaigne, actually."

"My goodness! Who clipped your wings?"

David winced. "No one. I just happen not to be a believer in the course of true love. We don't all have to behave like gleeful fools marching to our doom, do we? I mean, I know a lot about lust, and I'd be very happy to prove it, sweetheart, but as for love—" He shrugged, his voice cool, matter-of-fact, distant. "It's for children and books. *Now* may I make us dinner?"

Flabbergasted, Ellen followed him into the kitchen. Stunned by such cynicism, she didn't know what to say. Most of his words could be dismissed as so much nonsense, but the rest... Until that moment she hadn't understood how much pain he was in. Did Patty or any of his other friends suspect the depth of his misery? Surely she wasn't imagining it. The picture of David Hartwell that she had been trying to put together was beginning to flesh out a melancholy image. Toward the end of dinner, she couldn't contain herself.

"David," she blurted, "are you saying that you've never made love?"

David's beer went spraying as he choked on her scandalous words. "For chrissake, Ellen, there's a time and a place!"

"Sorry," she snapped, impatient with his concern for the niceties. "I didn't think."

"Well, *think,* next time," he warned, a touch ironic as he reached for his napkin.

"Okay, okay, but it's only the two of us. I just thought—"

"Of course I've made love to women, lots of women, for Pete's sake. And no complaints, I might add."

"I'm not talking about sex." She bristled. "What I meant was *making love.* Passionate, undying love."

"Passionate, yes. Undying, no. *Undying?* Good Lord, where do you find these words? Do you make them up as you go along, or do you have some sort of writer's code book?"

"O-oh, Mr. Hartwell, I am just so-oo amused at your flippancy."

"Well, Miss Candler, have *you* ever made passionate, undying love?"

"I've never been in love!"

"Well, it's early days yet, for a young chickie like you."

"Early days?"

"Care for me to show you?"

"Show me sex?"

"Show you *passion.* I thought we were talking about *passion.* Long, slow turns around heaven. My mouth on yours, my hands roaming your delectable body, my breath tickling you until you begged me to—"

"Stop!" Ellen shrieked, covering her ears with her hands. "That's vile. I don't know what you're trying to prove, David Hartwell, but it just won't work!"

"I'm just helping you out with your book, sweetheart. I thought it was rather good, myself."

The bitter edge of cynicism in David's voice that Ellen

had never heard before made her gasp. Stumbling past him to the safety of her alcove, she would have locked the door, but there was no lock, so she dove beneath the coverlet instead.

It took David a while, but eventually he followed her. "I apologize a lot to you, don't I, lady?" he said sadly as he perched on the edge of her bed.

"Ellen, are you listening?"

When she made no response, David tugged the blanket down. Funny how she clenched her eyes shut. He took her by the shoulders and shook her gently. "Ellen, open your eyes! I have something to say, and you're going to listen. It's ''fess up' time for David Hartwell."

He ignored her sudden intake of breath, but what he couldn't ignore was the way she clutched at her blanket as though it were a lifeline or something. "Poor blind fool," he said softly. "Don't you get it? I'm so crazy about you, I want you so much that I can hardly think straight."

Brushing a hand across his face, he forced himself to continue. "But I took a vow not to touch you, and if you think I'm doing penance, well, you couldn't be more right. *But I think about you all the time.*"

"Oh, David, how can you say such a thing to me? Do you think I'm so easily played? Do you think that people in love act the way you do?"

"No," he said with raw and angry finality. "I know I'm a fool, and you can treat me like one. I won't retaliate. But I won't let you chance your inheritance over me. You need it too much. With my father's money, you'll be your own woman. You won't have to answer to bastards like me ever again. But I promised to deliver you to Baltimore, and I'm going to keep my end of the bargain. After I hand you over to Dr. Gleason, you'll never hear from me again, but not until then.''

She didn't speak when he rose and left. But she cried a lot after he was gone.

When not a single word had passed between them in three days, David could stand it no longer.

"Get dressed," he ordered Ellen, barging into the alcove on the third morning. Slapping her rump, he looked for a sign of life beneath the covers, unaware of the wonderful dream she was having. In which he played a major role. "Come on, lady, I'm taking you to work with me today."

The dream seemed so distressingly real that Ellen worried David could read her face. But when she heard his announcement, she emerged from her covers, her green eyes bright.

"Really? Do you mean it?" she asked, forgetting their quarrel in the excitement of the prospect of an adventure. It had been a very long, lonely three days, and forest rangers had such romantic jobs. At least she thought so.

"I really mean it," David grunted, secretly relieved that she was talking to him. "Breakfast is on the table, so come on, slowpoke. And wear those boots at the foot of the bed."

"Boots?"

"I picked them up yesterday," he offered casually. "Special hiking boots. You'll need them where we're going."

She scrambled out of bed to meet his chest with her nose.

"Slow down, lady," he said, clasping her soft shoulders. "I'll wait." Smiling to himself as he left her to dress, David wished that he'd thought of this before.

After a breakfast she hardly touched, Ellen stood by the door, impatient to be off. David thought she looked sensational in her new hiking boots, and especially nice in her khaki hiking shorts and that bright sweater. Red socks peeped from her boot tops, but to David her bare legs were the best part of the outfit. When Pansy started whining as they walked to the car, Ellen wondered what he was going to do, but when he called for the dog to follow, she smiled for the first time in days.

They drove down the mountain, Pansy sitting quietly in the truck as they bypassed Longacre and headed north into the heart of the Adirondack Mountains. Having sulked indoors the past few days, Ellen was ecstatic to be out in the fresh air, filling her lungs with the loamy bouquet of the lush mountains blossoming under the cool morning sun. The trail David chose, when they finally arrived at the first site he supervised, was fairly smooth. Modern conveniences abounded in state parks these days, he told her as they hiked up the path. He even knew of parks that sported beaches, game rooms, electricity, water hook-ups and *hot running water!* Why, she herself would be happy to pitch a tent one of these days, he said suggestively. No, not tonight, he teased when he saw the gleam in her eyes. Another time. *Yes, he promised.*

David stopped at two other state park sites over the next few hours. With Ellen's arm tucked safely in his, he chatted up the campers, reminded kids not to play with matches, went over the day's paperwork with his men and gave them their next week's schedule. Each stop they made, Ellen tore his ear off with a hundred questions, but privately, he thought her curiosity did her credit.

Obedient to her master, Pansy trotted beside them and never once left their side, but she received lots of attention from the other rangers every time David stopped at one of their outposts. They in turn cast admiring looks Ellen's way, and waited to be introduced, but David was never forthcoming. Ellen might be innocent of the turmoil she was creating, but not David, who sent his men deep, angry scowls. But one ranger was not so easily intimidated and brazenly strolled up to greet her.

"Mr. Hartwell, sir. I would be grateful, sir, if you would please introduce me to your friend."

"Nope," David snapped as he hunched over his clipboard and made notations.

"I didn't think you would." The young ranger grinned as he smiled at Ellen. "Hello, there, miss. I'd like to introduce myself. I'm David's best friend, Hank Collins."

Ellen smiled and extended her hand. "Hi. I'm Ellen Candler, David's ward. But I thought Rafe Tellerman was David's best friend."

"Well, seems to me David is going to have a lot of best friends, today, seeing as how you're with him." Hank laughed.

"Why, thank you, Mr. Collins. That's very kind of you to say."

"It's true, miss. Are you going to be visiting us long?"

"Eight, ten weeks or so."

"Er, I'm not wishing to seem too forward, miss, but perhaps you would like to be shown about sometime?"

"Fast talking isn't going to get your work done, Mr. Collins." David interrupted him with a glare.

"True enough, sir. Maybe Miss Candler would like to accompany me on my rounds?"

"I'd love to. May I, David?"

"Hell, no! Collins, you ought to know better than to take a civilian on patrol."

Hank's eyes twinkled good-naturedly. "Well, if I didn't, I do now. Miss Candler, then may I please have permission to call on you sometime? Maybe take you out for a root beer float?''

"Oh, yes, that would be nice. Please call."

"I will," he promised. "Real soon, too, miss." That last, a message to David. When Ellen heard Hank drive away, she turned to David with a doubtful look.

"David, why were you being rude to that nice young man?"

"Me, *rude?* I was not being rude! *Rude* is when I punch his lights out! Now, come on, let's get out of here. I'm finished for the day and we have a long drive ahead."

"Where to?"

"It's a surprise," he said defiantly, "so no more questions."

The surprise was that fancy dinner they had talked about, at that fancy inn in North Creek. David had warned Ellen it was a long ride, so it was getting on to twilight before they pulled up to the tiny, unpretentious inn. They were a little too casual in their shorts and sweatshirts, but that wasn't why the maître d' stared when David removed his hat as they were led to their table. Ever sensitive to the public eye, David noticed at once, but he was determined not to let a gaping stranger spoil their meal. Before they sat, he had the waiter move their chairs together so they were able to sit side by side, their backs to the center of the room.

Ellen didn't ask why, and he didn't tell her. She assumed he was trying to place them on easier footing, trying to make up for their horrible fight. In love, she was generous, willing to forgive and forget. Maybe he was even going tell her about his face. Good. Then she could tell him how it didn't concern her, that his shoulder brushing hers was far more important, his knee grazing her thigh far too sexy, his lips an inch from her ear as they talked quietly driving her crazy. She couldn't even begin to remember what their quarrel was about.

The menu was elegant and they both swore they'd never had a better meal when, two hours later, they leaned back, stuffed to the gills. And the wine! David had plied her with such expensive champagne! An extravagance, she argued, but he wouldn't listen, said they only lived once. But, privately, he thought it was worth it to see her smile. Declining coffee, David paid their check and guided them into the evening air.

"Wow!" Ellen caught at the handrail as the cool air hit her face. "I think I drank too much. I feel a bit off balance."

"That's the champagne talking." David smiled. "Here, let me help you." One short step led him to her side and he settled his hands on her hips as she swayed, standing on the step above. "Hey, you okay, sweetheart? I didn't intend for you to get tipsy."

But a dizziness that had little to do with wine threatened to whirl Ellen into oblivion. For the first time in her life she was experiencing the tremulous beginnings of passion. Champagne and David Hartwell were a heady combination. Linking her hands around his neck, going nose-to-nose, Ellen laughed. "Oh, didn't you?" she teased, and brazenly brushed her lips against his. The most exciting sensations were beginning to build. "Yum, you taste delicious."

Surprised, David returned her kiss lightly. "So do you, princess." He knew it was the champagne that was making her suddenly so carefree, but he didn't care.

"Well, Mr. Forest Ranger, what's next?"

"What do you suggest?" None of this was supposed to be happening and he was feeling a little confused.

"I suggest—" she smiled dreamily "—that you kiss

me, Mr. Forest Ranger, *really* kiss me, unless, of course, this spot is too public for a public servant.''

''Lady, Madison Square Garden wouldn't be too public for a kiss from you.'' His lips hovering inches from hers, coaxing and warm, his fingers traced her temple. Their breaths mingled, sweet with champagne, and when their lips brushed, he could feel her shiver.

Brazenly, Ellen snuggled closer, and felt David respond in kind. His arms lashed around her waist, molding her into an intimate embrace that let her know exactly what she was doing to him. Dimly aware that he was behaving outrageously, David only pulled her closer—could they get any closer?—and felt her meet him with an eagerness that was thrilling.

It was easy for Ellen to give herself so freely. She was under the sway of an uncontrollable joy. The heat of David's lips left her mouth burning, sent shockwaves through her body, left her reeling. A wave of passion flowed through her and she hoped that he felt it, too, and hoped, too, that he felt the love she harbored and that determined her course. That she would have him make love to her.

Thank goodness another exiting couple brought them to their senses. Spellbound, Ellen was lost to all propriety.

''Come on, sweetheart, let's get out of here,'' David whispered, ''before someone calls the vice squad.''

Laughing like kids, they made a mad dash to the parking lot. To hell with the past, David decided. *This felt right.* Ellen was his, he couldn't possibly miss her message, and he was going to have her. Finding his keys, he settled her into the truck and drove northwest.

''Part of the surprise,'' he explained, as he helped her from the truck twenty minutes later. ''A co-worker of mine owns a houseboat here on Indian Lake. I've never stayed overnight, but he's always offering it to me, so I decided to take him up on it. I thought you'd like the change and, honest to God, Ellen, I have no ulterior motives. What happened back at the restaurant... I just figured this was better than a mall.''

"Better than shopping?'' Ellen grinned. ''I don't know. *Maybe.*'' Her voice faded as his fingers, a little shaky, rose to stroke her brow. She could hear the waves lapping against the boat, the only noise in the eerie night, sounding lonely.

"Are you going to try to seduce me?'' she whispered, her throat tight with uncertainty.

David's trembling hand fell. ''Do you want me to?'' he asked, his own voice a dry, husky rasp.

"Yes. Yes, I do believe I do.''

It was a struggle to keep his composure. ''Then I guess I will.''

"*You guess?* You sound hesitant. Don't you want to?'' she asked uneasily. ''If you want me, *really* want me, you've got to tell me, David. I need to *hear* you say so.''

Her face was strained and white beneath the pier light, and David knew it cost the earth for Ellen to say these things.

Silly questions.

Lifting her onto the hood of the car, he let her feel the heat of his arousal. Aching with passion, he was incredulous at her doubt, and put it off to her blindness. But even if he'd never told her, hadn't she understood his sloppy restraint, hadn't she noticed how he could hardly keep his hands to himself? With a flare of impatience his mouth covered hers with unapologetic gruffness, and when he released her, she was limp.

"Ellen.''

She raised a hand to cover his mouth before he spoiled the moment with words. "Hush. It was a silly question."

Carefully he caught her hand and led her down the pier. "It was. Come on. It's a tiny one-room houseboat meant for fishermen, so I make no promises."

"Are we safe?" Ellen whispered, suddenly nervous in the face of the blanket of silence that surrounded them.

"If you're expecting bears again, you'll be disappointed." He laughed softly, turning on his flashlight. "Unless they've learned how to swim." Leading her to the tiny houseboat, he guided her inside. "Don't worry, I know the layout. I've been here before."

"With someone else?" Ellen felt her face grow hot. "Ohmygosh, please, don't answer. It's none of my business. I can't believe I said that. It just came out."

Ignoring her apology, David sent her a steely look and made sure it reflected in his voice. "Ellen, I've been here before, to fish, but only to fish. Some of the best trout in the county is swimming in Indian Lake. Do you understand what I mean?"

"Yes," she whispered, wanting to die of embarrassment.

"Good. Then come over here and sit down on the couch while I turn on some lights and find blankets. Are you cold?"

"I guess." She meekly agreed and curled up on the sofa.

David soon had the generator going, creating just enough light to shed romantic a glow, but not enough to warm the cabin much. "It's still a bit chilly, don't you think?"

"I guess."

He looked over his shoulder and felt his dreams for the night slipping away. "Ellen?"

"Hmm?"

"You're falling asleep on me, aren't you?" He sighed.

Ellen didn't lift an eyebrow when, an hour later, the cabin warm and toasty, David shifted her to the bed. But the next morning, she woke with a throbbing headache.

"A hangover," she muttered in disgust. "My first romantic weekend ever and I have a hangover!"

David took one look at her green face and went to find some aspirin. She had burrowed under the blankets by the time he returned, her favorite position, he was beginning to believe. Knowing this was his fault, he felt guilty as hell. If he hadn't plied her with champagne, none of this would have happened, and maybe something better might have! He felt terrible even when she swore she felt better later that afternoon.

"Did I spoil your plans?" she asked as she tenderly lowered herself into a chair.

"Ever fished?" he asked ruefully as he handed her a rod.

The ride home was awkward, neither sure what had happened, and neither sure where to go from there. To make matters worse, there were three messages from Hank Collins on David's phone machine.

"Hello, Miss Candler. Remember me? We met this morning… Hi there, Miss Ellen. Still not home? …Ellen, please call."

David wondered if he could get Collins fired on grounds of…insubordination?

But there was no legal way he could prevent the young man from driving up the road the next day, armed with a bouquet of hothouse roses, a huge box of chocolates and an eager smile. It was a good thing David wasn't there to see, having already left for work. Hank swept up the porch, Pansy's ecstatic barking bringing Ellen to the screen door.

"Please don't be afraid, Miss Candler," he called as he balanced his gifts. "It's Hank Collins. Remember me?"

Ellen smiled. "Of course I do, Hank. Welcome, and please call me Ellen. I got your messages, in case you're wondering, but David and I were away, so I haven't had a chance to return any calls."

"No need to now," he said, walking up the porch steps. "Since I couldn't get hold of you, I thought I'd drive over and see if there was any problem. It's my day off, so I was hoping maybe you'd like to go for a ride, get a soda in town, maybe. Sure is hot. Good day for a soda."

"Oh, I don't know. David's not here and I don't know what he'd say."

"Look, I want to be honest. Word is he's just your guardian or something, but if there's anything I should know about—"

"I would tell you," she finished for him. "Let me leave a note, in case we run late."

Pansy sat on the deck, anticipating a car ride, but Ellen ordered her to stay. Pansy wasn't happy, but she obeyed, although her low growl followed them down the road.

David was growling, too, when he stormed into the Longacre diner two hours later. The way he strode right up to their booth, everyone in the diner perked up.

"Lady, where the hell have you been?" he demanded on a black wave of anger, his face smack-dab in Ellen's. "Anybody give you permission to leave the cabin?"

Not bothering to wait for her answer, he turned on Hank Collins, his eyes dangerous slits. "You touch her, Collins? Because if you did, I'll kill you now, straight out, and save your mama a whole lot of medical expense.''

Everyone in the diner turned to watch, mindful that the situation didn't take an ugly turn. Ellen and Hank were so shocked by David's angry accusations that they didn't know what to say. Hank Collins was the first to find his voice.

''Hey, Mr. Hartwell, sir, take it easy. I just took Miss Ellen for a spin in my new pickup. Uh, poor choice of words, huh?'' He grinned sheepishly when he saw David flush. ''Come on, David, you know I just got a new truck. No need to get all riled up.''

David burned. But so did Ellen as she rose to her feet, her momentary shock recast as anger. ''David Hartwell, how dare you speak to us like this? We are just sitting here, peaceful-like, having root beer floats. Any fool can see that! Besides, I'm not some child to be chastised for going out without permission, and I'm not your private possession to be ordered about, without a by-your-leave! You apologize to Mr. Collins, and to me, right now, do you hear?'' She thought it might be a little dramatic, but she stomped her foot for effect.

Everyone in the diner relaxed. If the little lady was going to take on their favorite son, things were going to be okay.

Unimpressed, David met Ellen head-on, his face literally in hers. ''I'll apologize to Mr. Collins when hell freezes over! And I'll do with *you* exactly as I choose! You seem to be forgetting something, sweetheart. You're under my jurisdiction. I *do* own you—lock, stock, and barrel, until October.''

''Why, you coarse, uncouth, vulgar, overbearing lummox!'' She turned in Hank's direction, the picture of injured womankind. "I assure you, Mr. Collins, that Mr. Hartwell is deliberately misleading you!"

Hank Collins scratched his head. "Well, that's as may be, ma'am, but if you would just explain, seeing how David does seem a might perturbed. I own to being a little confused, myself, and I sure don't want to be accused of poaching on another man's territory, you understand."

Under the circumstance, Ellen thought she was pretty calm. It was a toss-up, after all, which one to kill first. "First of all, Mr. Collins, I am not some…some duck…to be…*poached,* as you so crudely put it! Secondly, I am Mr. Hartwell's ward. Do you understand the word *ward,* Mr. Collins? Until October, when he escorts me to Baltimore for eye surgery!"

Everyone in the diner sighed with relief and even David smiled, but it was humorless. "That's not how it seemed the other night, princess."

Everyone within hearing distance squirmed with delight.

"You were right friendly the other night, princess," David carefully elaborated, his voice low and husky as he leaned forward, his lips a breath away from Ellen's. "*Right friendly,* as I recall."

Ellen clenched her fists, ready to attack.

The diner patrons waited with bated breath.

And Hank Collins figured that one and one still made two. Sliding from the booth, he grabbed his hat. "Miss Candler, if you'll excuse me, it seems to me that you and David have some things to talk about. Mr. Hartwell, sir." He tipped his hat and hurried out the door.

David nodded, but his eyes were fastened on Ellen. Her mouth was scrunched up as if she was ready to read him the riot act, never mind who was listening. Come to think of it… But scanning the diner, it seemed that no one had paid them any mind. The other patrons either had their heads bent, were busy eating or reading the local rag. Thank goodness, or this whole business would be all over town by nightfall.

"Let's go home, Ellen," he said quietly.

Her lips jutting out in a truly rebellious manner, David watched Ellen sit and fold her arms across her chest.

"Ellen, I'm dead tired. I worked all day and then just spent the last hour running around the mountain, scared witless that something terrible had happened to you."

"I thought there were no bears!"

David ignored her sarcasm. "I never said that. There certainly are black bears hereabouts. Look, sweetheart, I just want to go home, have dinner and go to bed."

The diners shuddered with delight.

"Sweet dreams," she said dryly.

Christ. "And what will you do if I leave you here? Hitchhike?"

"There's such a thing as car service."

"Not up here, there isn't. This ain't New York City, darlin'."

"Then I'll stay at Patty Carmichael's. She'll be glad to have me."

"But I want you home where you belong!"

Everyone in the diner took a deep, collective breath.

Ellen's eyes glowed emerald with combative fervor. "You lay a hand on me, Mr. Forest Ranger, and I'll claw your eyeballs out! I've had about as much of you as I can take!"

David looked down at the tiny terror so game to take him on and sighed. Slumping into the booth, he motioned for the waitress. "Mary, I'll have the roast beef platter, with extra gravy, a side of mashed and a slice of blueberry pie for dessert. And bring me some coffee when you get a chance, please. You want anything, Ellen? I think this is going to be dinner.''

Her chin was high as it could get without getting a crick.

''Bring the lady the same.''

Ellen vowed not to touch a bite, but when Mary brought their plates, it smelled so good her mouth began to water.

David knew she wasn't going to speak to him anytime soon, and wasn't sure if he blamed her, but he didn't think that was reason enough to starve. ''Come on, Ellen, eat something, because I'm sure as hell not going to start cooking when we get home. It's a damned waste of food, and anyway, if you don't eat, Mary will be insulted. Leastwise, her husband will. He's a notorious sensitive cook. Please.''

It could have been the way he'd said *please* or the fact that he even said it, but David didn't care. He was just relieved when Ellen picked up her fork. The truth was, though, Ellen was just plain hungry.

They ate in silence and Ellen did justice to her dinner, and even had some berry pie. They left the diner peaceably, but when they got outside, much to his dismay, she refused to get in the truck and started walking down the street, instead.

''Hey, where you going?'' David called as he watched her sashay off.

''I need some air,'' Ellen said tersely, her cane tapping evenly as she marched away.

Cursing low, David followed in her footsteps, and Pansy, who had been patiently waiting on the sidewalk, trotted behind the parade. But when David tried to take her elbow, Ellen shrugged him off. ''Don't touch me, you scoundrel!''

''Just like old times, hmm?''

Ignoring her protector, Ellen kept walking, but David dogged her every step. When she reached a curb, he was there to help her, even if she refused to acknowledge him. With such fine legs and shapely thighs, it was no hardship for him to follow her, and they walked so for twenty minutes before their dialogue recommenced.

"Ellen, I know you're mad, but please, could we continue this discussion at home?" David's words floated on the empty air. "You want me to apologize, don't you? Well, I won't. You can walk all the way to China and I won't."

That didn't seem to scare her, because she just kept walking.

"Look, some of us may be able to sleep late, but some of us have got to work tomorrow."

More silence.

"Dammit, Ellen! This is all your fault! If you'd just left me a lousy note, none of this would have happened!"

That stopped her dead in her tracks. "I *did* leave you a note!"

"Where? I didn't see any damned note."

"Well, then—" she smiled sweetly "—maybe you should go home and look harder!"

"You're damned right! I will!" Ignoring her loud protests, David grabbed Ellen's cane, threw her over his shoulder and strode back to the truck.

He took the street in a long, easy stride, nodding affably to everyone he passed. Everyone he passed stopped to smile at the young couple's tomfoolery, and Ellen's lovely, long legs wriggling beneath David's arms was not a hardship to watch. It was the consensus of the ladies' auxiliary, which met that evening in the church basement, that it was about time young David had found himself a wife. Pansy, too, was excited by all the commotion, even if her mistress didn't seem so enthusiastic.

As a matter of fact, her mistress was boiling mad. "You Neanderthal!" she shrieked, pounding on David's back. "The first thing you do, you don't get your way, is resort to bullying!"

"While you, on the other hand, have perfected the womanly art of being reasonable!"

"I am not unreasonable!"

"I'm not a bully!"

"God," she cried as he lifted her into the truck, "I didn't think it was possible to dislike someone as much as I dislike you! If you don't think this behavior isn't violent, I don't know what is!"

"Then let me show you!" Arching her body into his, David swept Ellen into his arms and buried his hands in her hair.

"No," she whispered, feeling his breath upon her face. By the time he was through kissing her, Ellen's mouth was throbbing. When he set her aside, they were two fire-breathing dragons gasping for breath.

Another silent ride home.

Chapter Eight

Ellen climbed into bed when they got home and fell asleep immediately, the easy sleep of angels and children. David, on the other hand, stayed awake long into the night, pacing, sitting, standing, pausing by her bed to stare down at Ellen. To wonder why she'd been sent to torment him, when his life was already living hell, forgiving him every cruel remark he'd ever made, every sneer, every growl—*everything.*

But would she forgive him his face? He doubted it. He sincerely doubted it. Ellen, as was her right, made certain assumptions about people, and foremost was that they were normal-looking. Now, he wasn't just scarred, *he was disfigured,* and she had a right to know. But to touch him was to know, and to know was to despise. He didn't know if he could bear that. And God help him, he just couldn't find the words to explain to her his situation. So wouldn't it be a sin to take her, and not to let her know? Thank the Lord nothing had happened at that boathouse. Her falling asleep on him was the left hand of God. He wouldn't have been able to face himself—or her—the next morning, if anything had.

Ellen, on the other hand, wanted David to love her. Waking the next morning to a terrific headache, she gave herself a long talking to about that very subject. If she'd been silly enough to hope to change his mind, well, after what had happened yesterday, it was pretty clear that he was never going to accept her as a lover. Something always held him back, he counted too many strikes against them. If his face was one of them, well, how could she dodge that when she wasn't even supposed to know? Fact was, she shouldn't waste time wanting what she couldn't have. John Hartwell had been telling her that most of her life. After all, she had a good career, money enough to ease her way, good friends, and the best of blessings, the gift of sight in a few short weeks! This silly urge to cry would pass in time.

But—fool in love—she found it intolerable that David wasn't the slightest bit apologetic. And fool in love, she felt compelled to say so. Words were her life's blood, after all.

"Perhaps you think I have no pride," she began slowly, halfway through breakfast. "After yesterday, after that silly scene in the diner…and afterward…you're probably right. But I have to admit to a certain curiosity as to how *you* feel about what happened."

Her tone said it all. If there were two things David knew from it, number one was that Ellen wasn't at *all* interested in how he felt! The other was that only a man with suicidal tendencies would dare open his mouth at that moment.

"I myself am confused," he heard her continue right on cue. "But—"

Why was there always a *but* with women?

"I wish to apologize if *I* embarrassed you in any way."

Right! About the last thing Ellen sounded was *apologetic.*

"Naturally, you probably have your own thoughts on the subject…"

He did not.

"…and I understand that."

She did not.

"But I wanted you to know that I understand you were simply worried about me. I didn't want you to fret on *that* account. I thought maybe you'd like to know that, since we have to be in each other's company a few more weeks."

"Ellen, please!"

But Ellen was just getting warmed up. "*Do* let me finish, please, David. You see, it's tough when you're handicapped—blind, anyway. *You're always the last to know things.*"

What the hell did that mean?

"Especially with the opposite sex. Not that I'm any sort of social butterfly, you understand. My social skills are nil, to be perfectly honest, so it's not always easy for me to detect *the nuances.* And we all know what a premium you put on *honesty!*" she added coldly.

"Ellen, please!"

"Of course," she said, pointedly ignoring the panic in his voice, "I'll bet you have all the girls bowled over, they're just knocking down your door, so I can't imagine what I was thinking, anyway, trying to get in line, expecting a man like *you* to want anything to do with a girl like *me!*"

David winced, her ridicule a knife that scored him, which she intended, he knew. If there was ever a good time to speak up, it was now, but he would die a slow death before that happened. He might have a few college degrees under his belt, but *she* was the genius with words, and brother, was she on a roll! Besides, what would he say? *How do you feel about freaks?*

But Ellen wasn't buying into his silence. She wasn't interested in a rebuttal, anyway. "What you do have to know is that I am fully aware of how good you've been to me in all *other* matters—bringing me to Longacre, letting me come live with you, shepherding me about. I have no rights, I shouldn't have expected things to— Well, I have no rights. Our few moments out of time don't count for anything, I understand that now. I really must learn not to read into things." She laughed bitterly. "You must forgive that I did. It's my way, of necessity."

David opened his mouth to mount a defense, but nothing came out. The way she looked, her eyes suddenly lifeless. He saw her shrug, a move anyone else might have missed, it was so faint, except he was attuned to her every movement. Miserable, the muscle in his cheek throbbing, he turned away, knowing he'd just watched her expectations die.

With only Pansy for comic relief, and Patty's telephone calls, the next three weeks passed in chilling silence. Two cats couldn't have stalked each other—*oh, so politely*—better than Ellen Candler and David Hartwell. But the day finally arrived when David helped Ellen pack her bags and load them into the truck. It was time to head for Baltimore.

They left Longacre around six in the morning, for the drive was about six to eight hours to Maryland, depending on traffic, and they didn't want to hurry. They grabbed

lunch on the outskirts of Philadelphia but neither wanted
to linger, so they were back in the car in thirty minutes,
and arrived in Baltimore around two in the afternoon. Deciding that only the best was good enough for Ellen, David had booked them a suite in the very exclusive Harbor
Court Hotel, overlooking the Inner Harbor. He promised
her that one day he would bring her back to see for herself
the magnificent view. With her own eyes, too, she would
see for herself the hotel's famous, soaring grand staircase
that they walked. For now, she would have to rely on his
eyes to describe its elegance, describe as well as their
stylish suite and four-poster bed. While she unpacked, David called down to make sure they had dinner reservations
for Hamptons, which he'd read somewhere was one of the
best restaurants in the country. He was determined to
make this a wonderland weekend for Ellen, even if they
were barely speaking.

Before dinner, though, they headed over to Dr. Gleason's office where Ellen had an appointment for a prelim-
inary checkup. Charles Gleason personally came out to
greet them when his nurse informed him of their arrival.
Tall and every bit as handsome as David had feared, Dr.
Gleason gave Ellen the royal treatment. To David, he graciously extended his million-watt smile. David was unmoved by Gleason's charm. He paced the waiting room
for an hour, not in a very good mood when Ellen finally
came out, Dr. Gleason's arm draped across her shoulders.

"Now, you take good care of this little girl." He smiled
at David. "She's invaluable to me. I'm going to put her
pretty picture in my next book."

"Fiction or nonfiction?" David asked innocently, and
felt Ellen squeeze his arm.

"Funny you should mention that. I've been thinking of
writing a novel lately. I've got a really good plot going

in my head. A murder mystery.'' Gleason grinned. ''All right then, Ellen, until tomorrow.''

Ellen smiled faintly and tucked her arm in David's. She didn't care just then if David didn't like all the leaning she was doing. He was warm and he was strong and he was her pillar. She let him lead her to the elevator bank, unable to see his opinion of snot-nosed doctors and their fancy offices.

''Well?''

''Well, what?''

''What did you think of Dr. Gleason? Seems to me you two didn't exactly hit it off, what with you being snippy and his talk of murder.''

I can't stand men who call twenty-five-year-old women *girls*. Beyond that, I hated his guts. ''I had no opinion,'' David lied. ''And I wasn't being *snippy*. I don't even know what that means!''

The elevator arrived, saving them the trouble of further conversation, but he could see as he led her in, that Ellen was a million miles away. ''Anything wrong? You all set for tomorrow? Did Gleason deliver you some bad news?''

''No, no, not at all. I'm going to be admitted tomorrow. The surgery is scheduled…'' She was so nervous she could hardly say the word. ''It's the day after next.''

''Good. Get it over with.'' Looking at her pale face, David made an effort to be kinder. ''Hey, lady,'' he said softly, chucking her chin, ''how about a nice meal, maybe some music? I read the local rag while the doc was checking you out and I think I've got the lowdown on this town.''

''That sounds nice,'' she agreed, but it was halfhearted and she didn't bother to disguise the tremor in her voice.

Now that they were in Baltimore, David guessed rightly that reality was setting in and Ellen was probably terrified.

It brought back to mind all the times he'd been admitted to hospitals, when he was undergoing surgery, and how his stomach learned to heave at the sweet, cloying smell that permeated hospital halls. All for nothing, certainly not for the better.

They went back to the hotel. While Ellen showered, David catnapped. Not meaning to fall asleep, somehow he did. She was sitting cross-legged on the bed, by his side, when he woke, her wet curls a shiny riot of color in the lamplight.

He sat up quickly. "What's wrong?"

"Nothing. I want company, that's all. A warm body. Yours is the only one available." She smiled weakly.

He fell back in relief. She had just taken ten years off his life. "C'mere." Tugging Ellen down into his arms, he cradled her against his chest, daring to stroke her silky hair. "Big day getting you down?"

She nodded, unable to speak.

"Hey, it's okay, go ahead and cry, you'll feel better," he advised her softly. "Believe me when I tell you I know what I'm talking about. Want to know how many operations I've had? Six!"

"Six?" Ellen sniffled. "Why?"

"Oh, this and that."

"This and that?" Ellen echoed, disbelieving.

David brushed her questions aside. "It doesn't matter why. I'll tell you another time. It was all so long ago. But the thing I remember best is my dad was always there when I woke up, holding a pint of chocolate ice cream. You like chocolate ice cream?" he asked, his lips moving on her hair in the most unconscious way.

"Oh, yes." Ellen gave him a watery giggle. "And strawberry, and vanilla—French vanilla's the best."

"That's my girl! You choose one, I'll have it in hand,"

he promised, trying to ignore the way she wound herself around his body through her vale of tears. It would have been heartless, almost cruel, to move away. Maybe this was fortune's way of giving him a second chance. Maybe this once, he should take it. Tasting her salty tears, kissing her seemed the most natural thing, loving her seemed the logical next step. He pressed his forehead to her brow. "Are you sure?"

"I'm sure," she whispered. "Never more so. I want you beyond wanting. Make love to me, David."

The sun went down as they made love, gentle, leisurely, heart-stopping love, so that they didn't know where the one began and the other left off. She was a siren luring him effortlessly with her adoration, so that loving her was the easiest thing David had ever done, and to hell with the shadows looming on their path. She was artless, but so eager, it was a joy to please her. She loved it all, never wanted to leave that bed, and told him so.

Seeking sanctuary between her pale, lush breasts, David found salvation. Her body was his temple and he explored curves that were pure velvet, his whiskery cheek pillowed the softest belly, the breasts he stroked seemed made for his hands. The heady bouquet of her skin beneath the light perfume she favored was an intoxicating combination. Every inch of her was a honeyed gift.

"Open your mouth for me, Ellen," he whispered, and she parted like a flower, soft, pink, lush and sweet, a wellspring of sensation. He nipped, tugged, rimmed her lips with his tongue, coaxing her to respond so that their kiss became a mutual exploration. It was as if all the things they could never put into words became the expression of their kiss, their bodies the translators of their emotions. He pressed hard, she went soft, he receded, she followed, a fast study.

Ellen had given him so much the past few months, but she had absolutely no idea what she gave him now. When she shared her body with him, he wanted to make this the best loving she'd ever had, the kind she would always remember. So he nestled down between her legs to lie between her thighs, and when she tried to push him away, he refused.

Carefully he inched his way, her woman-scent drawing him toward the center of her sexuality. Instinctively, her body arched and, turning his face into the curly mass at the apex of her thighs, David thought it would be a nice place to die. His first tentative touch with his hand made her jump, but he persisted through her resistance, his fingers rimming her hidden folds. When he felt her shudder, he guessed he was doing it right. When she cried out, he was sure. He probed every inch of her and, pushing further along, searched for the core that would soon receive him. He took his time, and she did, too, letting him duel for her orgasm, but they were a mutual force in the final instant. He held her while she collapsed, a puddle of warm, loving, satisfied woman who could barely muster a word.

"Oh!"

"Oh?" David smiled. "Is that all you can say? After all my hard work?"

"Thank you?" She grinned.

"You're welcome." He laughed, and it occurred to Ellen that she had never heard him laugh so readily. Mustering her energy, she rolled over onto his body and matched him, length for length.

"You're like a rock, you know?" she told him thoughtfully, her cheek resting on the hard planes of his chest while her palms explored the granite contours of his arms. Running her hands down his bare hips to trace his muscular thighs, she marveled at their physical difference, and how the two of them yet seemed to make a whole. The feel of his chest hair beneath her fingers was a teasing joy, his hard physique subdued beneath her soft form, exhilarating. Well, not *quite* subdued, she thought, smiling to herself. Could she make him understand her elation? When his hands cupped her bottom and lingered there, caressing her softly, she thought that she must try. Her lips pressed to his chest, she smiled when his furry hair tickled her nose, but grew serious when her lips studied his flat nipples.

"Isn't there something more to this?" she asked, all innocence as she instructed herself in the body of a man and the art of loving.

"You're making progress," he informed her wryly as he felt his body shift.

"I think you may be right," she agreed, reaching down to touch his shaft jutting against her thigh.

David grabbed her hand quickly. "A mistake," he growled.

"Turning serious on me, Mr. Hartwell?" Ellen smiled, her lips searing a path across his rough, bearded jaw, mindful to steer clear of his scars. That would come later, when he didn't care, if she could make him not care! Still, whatever chord she touched, she didn't know, but she began to sense a change, because slowly he began to respond.

How could he not? She was the best thing David ever tasted and he was sure a lifetime couldn't satisfy him, much less a single night. He explored her mouth slowly, and if she seemed a little awkward, he didn't dwell on it, because this newfound tenderness was unfamiliar to them both. Kissing her breathless, his hands roamed her body, feeling her heat. Her skin was gossamer beneath his calloused fingers as he traced a path across her hip. When his mouth covered her breast, he heard her sigh with pleasure and tried to capture the sound with his mouth. But it was gone, replaced with a kittenish smile.

"Why are you laughing?"

"I'm not laughing," she said indignantly. "I'm smiling. There's a difference. And I'm smiling at you. You make me happy, so I smile."

David was so shocked, he didn't know what to say. No one had ever said anything like that to him before. But here was this young beauty throwing herself at him, and he wanted her so much he ached, but all he could suddenly focus on was the misery that lay ahead for both of them. In a month or so, after she'd had her operation, got her sight back, he'd be history. It wasn't anybody's fault, and it wasn't anything they could stop, but how could he make her understand that? Perhaps he could not.

Ellen's sensitive fingers felt his sudden hesitation, even in the midst of his passion. He was holding back. She could almost guess what he was thinking. "You don't want me?" she cried hoarsely.

"Ellen, for chrissake!"

"*For chrissake,* yourself, David Hartwell! It's a yes or no question."

"It's not even a question!" His decision made, David rose up, tumbling her back, a giant looming over her body as he nudged her legs wide and gently rocked between her thighs. With one, firm thrust, he pushed his way inside. Ellen couldn't see the anger behind the heat in his eyes, and beyond that, his ineffable sadness as he came up against her barrier. His grief was crystalline.

"Oh, Ellen, tell me *no*. I never would have touched a virgin. Never! Why didn't you say?"

"I love you, David," she whispered, her eyes swimming with tears. "Isn't that reason enough?"

"So help me, Ellen, I don't deserve you. I'll try to go easy, but I can't leave you like this." Slowly he eased from her, then returned with gentler thrusts. With every effort, he tried to help her adjust to his presence.

"Try to relax," he ordered gruffly as she squirmed beneath him, his endurance precarious at best. She tried to obey, but it was too late, nature won out. Swept away by ungovernable passion, David took her, and Ellen went willingly.

They lay spoon position, and that was just fine with David. It gave him license to curl 'round her drowsy body. Sleep for him was impossible, in any case. Not wishing to disturb her, though, he distracted himself by trying to digest what had happened.

It went far beyond sex, that much he knew. She had said things—*I love you*—the chemistry of the moment, of course, but he savored her words nonetheless. His scars were imprints on a soul that would never seriously entertain such fiction, but for the first time in his life, *a woman had told him she loved him!* He'd heard her. If that didn't count for something, nothing ever would! It made him want to weep for joy at the same time that it sent a shaft of grief through his heart thinking what *might have been.* He had no weapons with which to fight, circumstance had rendered him powerless, but the knowledge hurt nevertheless. What *could be* never crossed his mind.

She must be having a wonderful dream, he thought as he watched her smile in her sleep. But not possibly dreaming of him. Surely by now she must know the secret of his disfigurement. Did she wonder what he looked like, or had she a preconceived image? Suitably tasteful scars or the monstrous reality? But how would she know?

Perversity begged him to ask her how his scars felt—
if she'd tracked them with her fingertips or felt them
abrade her when he nestled against the tender skin of her
white thighs. Or had she perhaps noticed them when his
cheek brushed the delicate underside of her breast. Or had
her soft lips been chafed by his pitted skin as she roamed
his body? Had she thought about them when they made
love? Or after? Or before? Did she counsel herself to ignore his deformity in the name of passion? What basis of
reality did blind people have, anyway? Perhaps she was
setting the whole matter aside until after her operation,
when she could see. Did she have his banishment already
planned? Not that he wasn't going to save her the trouble.

David was so good at torturing himself, telling himself
so many dismal things, that he was primed for battle when
Ellen stirred a little while later. It was time for a reckoning. "Well, good, you're finally awake," he growled,
forcing himself to resist the pull of her seductive body.

But Ellen wouldn't allow it. She only laughed. "David!
For a minute there, I forgot."

"I should have known."

She reached to lay a hand against his unscarred cheek.
"Oh, no, David, never that."

"Ellen, I want to know why."

"Why what? I don't want to talk," she protested. "This
is no time for conversation."

"Ellen—"

"David, no words!" She kissed him soundly and soon
they had a reckoning of another sort to meet. Her hands
exploring, he surrendered to her seduction. This time she
welcomed him into her body.

He tried to question her again, over dinner, but Ellen
refused to talk about anything serious when they finally
dragged themselves down to the hotel restaurant later that

evening. She was too busy enjoying her meal. How could she not, he teased, as he watched her polish off her steak, when she ordered nothing less than filet mignon?

"And you? Are you enjoying your fish?" she asked politely in between bites of her steak.

David looked down at his dinner plate, his salmon broiled to perfection, but left untouched, the champagne chilling in its silver chalice, his own glass full. "Everything's perfect," he lied.

"Perfectly expensive, too, I'll bet!"

"Well, money isn't something we have to worry about, is it?"

"*But?* I can tell there's a *but* in there somewhere."

"Yeah, well, I guess I'm just more comfortable in the Longacre Diner."

"A regular meat-and-potatoes guy, huh?"

"It's Mary's pie, if you want to know the truth."

In a better frame of mind when they returned to their suite, they made love again, long and languid, but all their lovemaking couldn't make Ellen forget what lay ahead. David pulled her into a sleepy embrace, instinctively knowing that wherever she drifted, there was no longer any place for him. He could only guard her sleep.

In the morning he would have liked to make love again, his appetite for her was insatiable, but she was so tense, he didn't dare ask. She was scheduled be admitted at eleven o'clock for a battery of tests, so there was just enough time to shower and breakfast. Her toast became a plate of crumbs fit for birds, her nervousness palpable, but there was nothing David could do except lend her moral support. She was going somewhere he couldn't follow.

They were sucked into an alien world the moment they crossed the threshold of Johns Hopkins Hospital. State-of-the-art, it was a well-oiled machine ready to test, probe, suture, laser—anything your heart desired, even if it was a new heart! Minutes after Ellen was settled in her room, she was whisked down to X-ray, leaving David to his own devices. Finding his way to the cafeteria, he lingered over some surprisingly decent coffee, then returned to her room to wait. He was glad she didn't have a roommate, because he wasn't up to small talk. He didn't want to think, even, because all he would think about were the number of days they had left together. Because as sure as shooting, he wasn't going to be there when she had her bandages removed. He wasn't going to be the first thing she saw when she regained her sight!

But he was there when she returned, subdued by the higher authority of the hospital. Ellen had left him in spirit, had crossed the line from person to patient. As she must, David realized sadly, if she were going to survive the hospital experience. They needed her full cooperation to succeed. He was an outsider, now, of the process that was stealing her away. He didn't say a word, though, it wasn't his right.

Sharing dinner at Ellen's bedside, David noticed how she picked at her food. He had, too, he recalled, the night before such major surgery. She was such a bundle of nerves that the staff offered her a sedative, but she declined, opting for a walk around the floor instead. Sensing the couples' closeness, the head nurse allowed David to stay beyond visiting hours, but eventually she insisted that he leave. Ms. Candler had to get her rest. Ellen protested tearfully but the head nurse only smiled and pointed David toward the elevators. Ellen wanted to walk him to the elevator bank, but he insisted she return to bed. Not knowing the layout of the floor, she would be more trouble than she was worth. She didn't like that remark, or any other joke he attempted.

"All right, just go!" Ellen ordered him, flouncing back on her pillows. "Go!"

Oh, sweetheart, he wanted to say, but words like that were unfamiliar to his lips, and anyway, he did want to go, he couldn't stand dragging out their separation. So he chucked her under the chin, promising to be there in the morning before she left for the operating room.

"Promise?"

"I swear it!"

"With chocolate ice cream?"

"French vanilla, didn't you say?"

David walked the streets of Baltimore until he was exhausted, coming to terms with the pain of loving Ellen Candler now that he was about to lose her. Her innate goodness and gentleness had managed to tear down barriers no one else had ever surmounted. She was beautiful, yes, but it was her innocence that had burrowed into his cold heart.

No mean feat, that. Fifteen years after a car accident that had left him disfigured, David was still battle-scarred. Hospitalized for months as a child, and unable to share his misery with his father, young David had languished. After he'd been discharged he had refused to return to school or to run around with his friends. When he'd realized that what had happened to his face was permanent, he'd refused to see them. The ensuing five years of painful surgery to reconstruct his features had only made him lonelier. In and out of hospitals the entire time, surrounded by strangers—an endless parade of doctors and nurses, anesthetists, physical therapists, tutors, orderlies—no one noticed his childhood disappear. He'd slipped into an early adulthood, lonely and bitter, his scars so deeply gouged that he'd come to believe they were a part of his person. He'd thought he was monstrous—and imagined that everyone else had thought so. It had never occurred to him that people could see beyond his scars, and no one had thought to tell him otherwise.

Extremely bright and loving to learn, the one thing David had forced himself to publicly suffer was college. But he'd learned quickly to keep to himself, shunting from class to class in low-brimmed hats and oversized coats with high collars. He'd chosen his career as carefully as his hats. Loving nature and science equally, as a forester, the career combination was a natural. Graduating from Yale with honors—he would have been valedictorian except that he'd refused to give the requisite speech at graduation—and picking up a masters or two, he'd eventually landed on an obscure mountain in the Adirondack Park. Ten years later, hard work had earned him the respect of his colleagues, and his foray into forestry research had done much to improve New York State's timberland.

But his past continued to haunt him. Injured in more ways than one, he was unable to respond to overtures of friendship from his fellow rangers, or any of the other residents of the nearby town of Longacre. He shopped at Patty Carmichael's mercantile store for provisions because it was small and dimly lit, but he shied away from her bubbliness. He suffered Chuck's insistent handshake but declined all invitations to stop by for a beer. He allowed Rafe Tellerman to winnow into his life because, well, there was just no stopping Rafe. And besides, David secretly enjoyed Rafe's glib and irreverent conversation, although he'd die before he ever admitted it. Every Tuesday found him at the Longacre Diner because every Tuesday they served homemade brisket. And every Saturday, they made extra fried chicken because they knew David Hartwell would be asking for a doggie bag. And it was no bad thing to let Mary coddle him with an extra serving of pie.

Then one night, a fire on the Carmichael farm necessitated volunteers. Hearing the ear-piercing alarm all the way up his mountain, David had run. Sharing a case of beer at dawn with fifteen other exhausted men from the area, he'd begun to thaw. Although he'd refused to believe they didn't pity him on some level, David had nonetheless been able, for the first time in his life, to ignore his unusual appearance for the warmth of friendship that suddenly enveloped him. How good it felt. Perhaps his face didn't matter all that much to these hardy men. After all, if the town really had been founded in 1691, it must have seen its share of oddities. What was one more, then? So did David make his peace with Longacre, uneasy, but of some substance.

Only since Ellen's arrival had he come to realize how limited his hospitality was, how unsociable he must appear, how narrow his life. In his heart, he had remained an outsider.

Watching the town take Ellen under their wing these past few months, something had stirred in him. He thought it was envy, and it was, but not only of their affection for Ellen. The more he'd ventured off the mountain, the more he'd begun to notice what he was missing, hiding away in the hills. He'd begun to observe more closely the people who came to camp out in his territory, young couples with eyes only for each other, proud parents harried by their exuberant kids, senior citizens enjoying their golden years. And if it suddenly dawned on him that he was never going to have a family, he was also beginning to realize that he wasn't going to have many friends, *either,* was going to grow old known as the town hermit, if he didn't change his ways. It was a wonder Patty and Chuck and everyone else put up with him, the way he behaved. Rafe Tellerman probably wasn't feeling too kindly toward him lately. Hank Collins, either, now that he thought about it.

He had forgotten how to be kind.

Then came Ellen.

Descending on him unwillingly, a fireball of passion with the patience of a saint, she had endured his outrageous temper and jealous fits, and unmanned him with a single tear. Forced to open his home for her, he hadn't suspected that his heart would be part of the deal, though any fool could have read the situation rightly—except the dumb fool who'd fallen for her right from the first! Unbelievable. Inexcusable. That she forgave him was a mystery.

And his father! Wasn't John the picture of a saint, now, having taken Ellen under his wing! Assuming that Ellen had been with him since she was about twelve, basically John had adopted her. God, how could John have kept her existence a secret? Had he, David, been so self-absorbed that he'd missed her?

Yes!

Even if he hadn't been home in a decade, surely a whisper of her presence should have reached his ears!

Surely!

Had John been trying to make up to David by offering Ellen his home? Harry Gold hadn't mentioned that specifically, but now David began to wonder if that hadn't been the case. Pretty decent of John, if he had, and boy, wasn't he having the last laugh? Just as he'd promised in his letter. But it still didn't explain the secrecy. Surely that wasn't *all* David's fault. His father had always played things so close to the breast that David was at a loss to explain half the things he'd done. Perhaps it was the lawyer in John. One more thing David was never going to know.

But always, it came back to Ellen. Recalling the curious looks Patty and Chuck had been giving him all summer, his jealousy of Rafe, that foolishness in the diner with Hank Collins, any one of his friends had probably guessed how he felt about Ellen way before he did! It didn't matter. He was now her slave for life.

Losing himself in the crowd, David mingled with tourists who came to browse and shop in the fancy stores of Inner Harbor. Or as David eventually did, came to rest against an iron railing and gaze across Chesapeake Bay, mesmerized by the blinking lights that beckoned from the other side of Baltimore. Until his brain told him to think about tomorrow, to go get some rest. When he arrived back at the hotel and collapsed on his bed, it was 4:00 a.m.

The next morning, when David got to the hospital, he looked like death warmed over, and was glad Ellen couldn't tell. Already sedated, she wore a silly smile on her face while her jovial, obnoxious doctor perched on the edge of the bed. Holding her hand, for Pete's sake!

David stood by the door and glared until Dr. Gleason noticed. "Ah, your friend is here, my dear."

How cleverly Gleason skirted their relationship. Probably hedging his bets, the bastard!

Ellen sat up so quickly, she collapsed back on her pillows in a dizzy heap. "Wow! That's some stuff you sell here."

Dr. Gleason laughed. "I've heard it's rather taking."

David's goodwill was stretched thin, but when Ellen called out to him, he promptly walked over to the bed. "How you doing, sweetheart?"

"Ellen is doing just fine," Dr. Gleason answered for her. "Well, now your guardian angel is here, my dear, I'll go scrub and then we'll see about this miracle we're going to perform."

Wow, this guy didn't think small! He watched the white coat leave—good riddance!—and turned to Ellen. Her small hand trembled, but the smile pasted on her face was brave.

"Aren't you going to kiss me hello?" she asked softly.

"Oh, sure." When he leaned down to plant a tender kiss on her lips, he felt her hands wind around his neck, but now they were alone, he didn't know how to behave. Twenty-four hours ago they were making love. Now he was planning to leave her. When they wheeled her away, the countdown would begin.

"I know I'm acting stupid," she giggled, "and I know it's the drugs, but, I'm so glad to see you! I wouldn't have gone until you came."

David's throat was so tight, he had to swallow twice before he could speak. "I'm here now," he said softly and watched as she struggled to stay conscious, battling the sedative to finish her thoughts, even though her eyes grew heavier and her speech slurred.

"I have something…to tell you. I want you to know…I know everything. I…wanted you…it…didn't…matter… wanted you…"

Accepting that Ellen was speaking through a haze of drugs, and he wouldn't hold her to anything she said, David didn't try to stop her. But Ellen had nothing else to say. She just held fast to his neck, her eyes closing until he felt her resistance ebb.

"Well, princess, thank you for telling me," he whispered sadly, but he didn't think she'd heard. When two aides arrived with a gurney, he helped with her transfer and held her hand all the way to the elevator.

"Last stop," he told her weakly, pressing a light kiss to her forehead. "I'll be waiting with the ice cream—" he smiled as he brushed a dark red curl from her forehead "—so hurry up." But Ellen was at the point where she couldn't even manage a smile as the elevator closed on her pale face.

Six hours later they wheeled her into recovery, where David had been waiting every minute. When he saw what she looked like, he was sick to his stomach. Her eyes bandaged like a mummy's, she looked as though she was in some sort of horror movie, except that this was for real. The only good part was that she was still sedated and didn't seem too near to surfacing.

"How you doing, lady?" he whispered as he groped for her hand through his tears, although he knew she couldn't hear him.

The orderly wheeling Ellen's gurney laughed. "Hey, miss, looks fine compared to hubby. He looks a little green, don't he, Ritchie?"

"Shoot, it's always like that." Ritchie grinned. "Remember that guy who fainted when we brought his wife back from gallstones? And hey, that poor schnook whose wife had triplets. Now *that* I could understand!"

David glared. "You guys are a regular comedy team."

"Yup," Ritchie agreed with a broad, toothy smile. "We're the A-team of Recovery."

His friend chuckled as he tucked the blankets around Ellen's inert form. "Okay, sweetie, you're all set. Good luck, and take good care of your old man, you hear? I think he needs a doctor." He laughed as he wheeled the gurney out, his partner following behind.

David pressed Ellen's hand and bent to kiss her under the watchful eye of the gray-haired nurse supervising Ellen's return from surgery. "So nice to see young love," she said with a smile. "But you must take yourself off, now you've seen your wife, my dear. I've got to get her vitals and my patient needs her sleep. Why don't *you* go get some rest? It will be some time before she comes out of it, but she's going to be just fine, I promise. You can see that for yourself."

David *couldn't* see that for himself, but he didn't want to make a scene. She was right about one thing, though. Ellen's hand was limp in his.

"Go on," the nursed ordered him gently. "I'll take good care of her. Quite frankly, Mr. Candler, you look awful. Get some food in you, why don't you, and come back later, around five. She should be coming out of it by then. I'll sneak you in, I promise."

David looked at her doubtfully.

"I promise! Now, go!"

Bowing to authority, David left, although he could only bear to go as far as the basement cafeteria. But she was right. A couple of eggs, a stack of toast, and three cups of coffee made him feel infinitely better. He nursed his last cup till five o'clock, when he returned to the information desk and insisted the security guard call the ward nurse.

True to her word, the nurse came and got him. Right

on time, she praised him, and looking a whole lot better. And so was his wife, she added cheerfully.

David liked the sound of the word *wife*. He hadn't bothered to correct the day-shift nurses who had made the same mistake, and he didn't bother to correct this night nurse now. It was a little bit more fantasy to feast on. But he was glad to see his *wife* stirring when he entered her room minutes later. She was glad he was there, too, she told him weakly. Beyond that, she could hardly move. So he sat murmuring sweet nothings, pretending that he *was* her husband. And, for the moment, he was.

Chapter Nine

"Isn't he here yet?" Ellen asked, unable to hide her nervousness. This was it, the long-awaited day her bandages were removed.

The day nurse who had just come on duty shook her head as she checked Ellen's blood pressure. Everyone knew to whom Ellen referred, David had become such a fixture at the hospital. "I just passed the waiting room and there wasn't a soul there. But it's only nine-thirty. Could be he got caught in traffic."

Ellen was incredulous. "Today, of all days? I don't know. He could have, I suppose, but somehow, after all this time…"

"Ah, my favorite patient is awake. Good morning."

Ellen turned her head in the direction of Dr. Gleason's voice. "You're late, too," she grumbled.

"Well, hello to you, too!" Dragging a chair to Ellen's bedside, Dr. Gleason eyed a nearby tray of sterilized supplies, automatically tallying up the implements while he pulled on a set of surgical gloves. "Whom else were you expecting, Miss Candler? I thought I was the only man in your life," he teased.

"Who said anything about a man?"

"If you weren't referring to the stern and unforgiving Mr. Hartwell, I'll eat my forceps," Dr. Gleason protested archly.

"I don't think you're suffering his presence half so much as you complain, judging by the heated arguments you've both been *enjoying* the last week and a half."

"*Enjoying,* did you say? Well, perhaps you're right," Dr. Gleason admitted cheerfully as he began to choose a scissor. "I don't think he'd snarl half so keenly without my elevating presence."

Ellen smiled. "You may have something there. But there are some of us who seem to enjoy provoking others a little bit too much!"

"Ah, my dear Miss Candler, the boy positively asks for it!"

"Don't you dare call him a boy, Dr. G.! David is older than you by two months!"

"Perhaps, but I'm cuter!"

"Oh, my, aren't we in top form this morning!"

"It's true, as you'll soon see for yourself." But Dr. Gleason paused as a sudden thought occurred. "Oh, for goodness' sake, Ellen, are you referring to his scars? That was the last thing on my mind. I was only joking. Isn't anybody allowed to joke around Hartwell? For goodness' sake, he should be able to take a little ribbing now and then."

"Perhaps," she agreed, "but I don't think he *can* take it."

"I don't think so, either. Too bad. He's extremely intelligent and so well-educated, it's a pleasure to spar with him. But if I can't seem to relax around him, he can't feel too easy about me, either.''

"No," Ellen mused, "I don't think he is too easy about you."

"Can't stand the competition, hmm?"

"Perhaps."

"*Perhaps?* How diplomatic you are this morning, my dear. Well, where is the redoubtable Mr. Hartwell? I have to start the show." Grinning, Dr. Gleason was yet all business as he began to inspect Ellen's bandages, trying to decide where to begin to cut the gauze.

"That's what I was worrying about when you walked in. David's very late this morning."

"Well, I'm sorry Ellen, but I've got to begin. I've got a full day ahead of me."

"I know. Go ahead and start. He'll probably turn up any minute."

"Like a bad penny? Just kidding, just kidding." But even with his teasing, Dr. Gleason was all business as he began to snip away at the bandages. "Now, remember, Ellen, no expectations, today, tomorrow or even next week. The adjustment is going to take some time. Your eyes are going to need to adapt to light, and your lens and retina have to correct themselves at their own pace. It's a very slow process, as you recollect we discussed."

"I know, I know. *Don't expect anything but a few shadows and a darned good shampoo.*"

"Precisely." Dr. Gleason laughed as he began to gently strip away the bandages that covered Ellen's eyes.

David was one-third of the way back to New York, and halfway to hell, when Dr. Gleason began to remove Ellen's bandages. By the time the doctor had finished, David was entering Philadelphia. Ellen was being shampooed as he crossed the New York border. She received his telegram while she was dozing. A nurse read it to her. It was carefully impersonal.

"'Emergency on the mountain. Gleason seems capable. Good Luck. David.'"

Ellen thanked her and tucked the telegram under her pillow.

Gleason seems capable...

A few terse words and it was over. Unhappily she knew why. David had panicked. He hadn't wanted his face to be the first thing she saw when finally Dr. Gleason—urbane, young and intelligent Dr. Gleason—wrought his miracle and returned to her the gift of sight. Dr. Gleason—everything David wasn't and couldn't ever be—because David had too high regard for his scars. Dr. Gleason, here each day to unwittingly remind David of his imperfections. To be compared with, the moment Ellen could see. Her vision returned, at the expense of David's dreams—hallucinations that must seem to him the most painful mirage, nervous fantasies that couldn't be allowed to go any further without inevitable humiliation.

Ellen's heart went out to him. How lonely he must be, slouched down in the truck, windows closed to the world, his face shielded by oversize sunglasses. Returning to his forest without apology, not even a backward glance, assuming that Ellen would let him go, expecting her to understand that he refused to engage in a battle he could never hope to win.

In fact, she *didn't* understand. Fool that she was, she thought their night of lovemaking was an *event,* not a one-night stand. After all, he'd spent every day at her bedside since that momentous night—talking, reading, helping her to eat and bathe, holding her hand, gently stroking her cheek, taking her for walks down the hospital corridors, keeping her spirits up. So that when he'd been late this morning, she'd known on the instant that he hadn't been caught in traffic, or any other such nonsense; that he was gone.

And didn't let on—the flip side of heartbreak—that she was furious. David's departure was a betrayal of her trust, their short-lived affair apparently a one-sided arrangement. Believing he was made of sterner stuff, she'd allowed herself to be deluded. If there wasn't a signpost initially, she should have paid attention to the warning signs along the away. But because there had been moments—glimmers of true nobility in David—that had captivated her, she'd ignored those warning signs, preferring instead to believe that it was possible to help him set his bitterness aside. Having risen above her own handicap, Ellen thought she was equipped to help him. *The love of a good woman and all that rot!* At every turn she'd forgiven him his anger, even when it was turned on her. She'd been tolerant—oh, so tolerant, all too tolerant—wanting to tell him, *It's okay, I've been there, let it go.* Believing with all her heart that he could.

Wrong!

She saw now that she should have been a little less compassionate, and he a whole lot less self-absorbed!

And if she had allowed David to bring her east, well, she had only herself to blame. It was a reflection of her own loneliness. Even if she had been constrained by John Hartwell's will, she needn't have entered into the arrangement so…enthusiastically. Truthfully, her resistance had been very short-lived! It had been all too tempting to become a part of David's life, to adopt his friends as hers, and finally, to believe that *he* was hers. In a way, she had borrowed his life. The question now was, should she pursue him? Oh, he loved her, that much she knew. But was that reason enough to demand he take her back, insist that he had a moral responsibility that went beyond John Hartwell's will?

Force him to love her?

Ellen knew the answer to that question as quickly as it formed in her head. She would go home, to *her* home, to Montana. It was a healing time for her, and Montana was the place to do it. David didn't want her or he'd be here, plain and simple, and since she had no one else, it was the only answer, really. Patty and Chuck Carmichael were absolute saints but they had their own lives to lead. They were also a part of the borrowing she'd done from David. Rafe Tellerman would take her in, but he was a complication she couldn't handle, just now. She needed medical care, not the importunities of a lover. Yes, she would return to Montana and regain her health. There would be plenty of time to sort things out there, plenty of time to mourn what might have been and to figure out what was.

Matters were not so simple for David. Everyone who saw him drive through Longacre that day spread the word that David had come home—alone. And everyone wanted to know why. *How was Ellen? Where was Ellen? What was David doing back without her?* The calls came fast and furious. In a fit of pique, David disconnected the telephone, but that didn't stop Patty Carmichael from making the drive up the mountain to hound him for answers that he didn't want to give. His friends had had enough, watching him destroy his happiness for nothing more than the sake of pride, and Patty was pretty blunt about that. She took one look at him and started cursing a brown streak.

"You left her alone?" she shrieked, absolutely livid.

"I thought she sounded a bit off key when we spoke this morning, but I had no idea you'd abandoned her!"

"I did not abandon her," David retorted. "She has the whole hospital at her beck and call. Besides, I hired a woman to act as her duenna. She'll be accompanying Ellen to Montana when she's discharged. It's all arranged."

"You abandoned her!"

"For chrissake, Patty, they're falling all over their feet for her. She's got that hospital wrapped around her finger. Did she ask for me?"

"She never mentioned your name. That's how I *know* she's so sad."

No matter what he said, David's stomach churned at the thought of Ellen alone in the huge hospital. He'd been in one too many himself. But there was nothing he could do. Now that she had vision, he couldn't bear it if she saw his face.

"Oh, David, how could you leave her to a stranger? I mean, how's that poor girl gonna make it without you?"

"She's rich," David replied curtly. "She'll hire herself a few gofers."

"David, that's not what I mean! I was talkin' about the light in her eyes—the good Lord only knows why!—whenever you're around. The way she had of talking to a body and still be listening for your footsteps!"

"Patty, you exaggerate."

"David Hartwell, don't bother to deny what we both know for a fact! My patience is getting mighty low!"

David raised his brow but said nothing. Patty wasn't leaving until she'd said her piece, so he might as well let her get it all out.

"I wished you had told her about your face. *You* should have, right from the first."

The look he sent Patty was raw. "Ellen knows about my face, if that's what you're getting at."

Patty was incredulous. "She knows about your scars?"

"It would be different if she *saw.*"

"David Hartwell, you stubborn old mule. If it doesn't matter to the entire town of Longacre what you look like, what the hell difference is it going to make to the woman who loves you?" She made sure to slam the door as loudly as possible when she left.

In the end, it was Patty who brought Ellen home. It was a long drive, but she drove to Baltimore the very next day to make sure Ellen was all right. She listened patiently to how her friend was planning to move back to Montana, and when Ellen was done, read her the riot act. Ellen's home was in New York, no matter what she said. Patty insisted it was so. There was nothing for Ellen out west. Wasn't the Hartwell mansion up for sale? Had she any really close friends there? Not like Patty! She, *Patty,* was her best friend now, and Ellen should accept her best friend's help. Chuck had become mighty attached to her, too! Why, all of Longacre loved her! They were waiting for her to come home. Yes, that's exactly how the whole town saw it. Who did she think had sent all these flowers stinkin' up the place? Miss Callie herself was just dying to nurse Ellen back to health, the chicken soup was waiting, and Rafe, well, ahem, Rafe was waiting, too. And some really obnoxious guy calling himself Hank kept telephoning. Did she happen to know who he was?

David? Why, let that old mule stew in his own mess. Why should *his* problems create problems for *Ellen?* Come home to Longacre, Patty begged.

In the end Ellen listened. A week later, wearing dark sunglasses to protect her tender eyes and a floppy hat to shield her face from the early autumn sun, Ellen found herself being chauffeured through Albany. She couldn't help but remember the last time she'd been here. Things were very different, now. For one thing, she could see the city—sort of—as they drove by. Oh, it wasn't perfect, but she *could* see gray shadows that were slowly developing into faint colors of dimension.

Colors! How spectacular to witness even the palest of rainbows everywhere she turned! To relearn a shape with everything she touched. How wonderful to be able to determine her path, to avoid obstacles not because she felt them but because she saw them. And how wonderful to find the eyes of the person she was talking to, even if she couldn't divine their features. If she wasn't quite ready to set her cane aside, Dr. Gleason promised that as her vision developed, clarity would follow.

From Albany, Patty drove straight to the Carmichael house up in Longacre, where Chuck had put a room together for Ellen. "Took myself up to David's cabin last weekend and removed all your stuff. Your clothes are hanging in the closet, your laptop is on the desk, and your toothbrush is even hanging in the bathroom over yonder. I know it's not much to look at, but I figured you would fix it up nice with girly stuff and all. But it's yours," Chuck told her, "for as long as you want."

Ellen looked around her, able for the first time in years to visually distinguish the shape of a dresser, a bed in relation to the rest of the room, the vague red of the blanket that covered it, the outline of a fluttering curtain. Drawn to the window, she spread the curtain wide and allowed the sun to dance across her face. It was early days to be able to delineate trees with exactitude, but she was still able to detect their outline.

"Oh, Chuck!" she sighed, her eyes welling with tears.

"Ellen, if you refuse us, I'll just sit down on this here

staircase and bawl like a baby—a very loud baby! The whole damned town will hear!''

"Please, Ellen, do as he says. My ears couldn't stand it and neither could yours.''

"But—''

"No *buts,* sweetie!'' Patty cried as she dashed from the room. "Sorry. I wish I could stay and continue this discussion but I do believe I just heard the doorbell.''

Ellen had heard the bell, also, and her heart had dropped at the sound. It would, too, she knew, for a long time to come, wondering whether the person on the other side of many a door was David Hartwell. Whether the voice at the other end of the telephone would be his rough growl. Whether the tall lumberjack walking down the road was *her* lumberjack.

It wasn't David at the door, but it was—over the next two hours—practically the entire town of Longacre, or as many could fit through the Carmichael door to fill Patty and Chuck's tiny living room. Neighbors with flowers, neighbors with casseroles and pies, neighbors with candy, neighbors just wanting to stop by to say hello and to wish Ellen the best. So many hugs to show her their love. Ellen's eyes filled with tears so many times that Patty finally had to insist that the party could go on, but Ellen Candler had had a very long day and had to go lie down. All this crying couldn't possibly be good for her eyes. Proudly did the town of Longacre applaud as Ellen ascended the stairs without her familiar cane. Only when her head touched the pillow did she permit herself to feel the sting of David's absence from the well-wishers.

Exhausted by her ordeal, Ellen knew she must nurse her strength over the next weeks. Her eyes would be black and blue and swollen for the next month or so, and more importantly, were still terribly sensitive to light, so she declined to leave the house. It gave her plenty of time to daydream, but when she found herself getting maudlin, she roused herself, determined not to fall into depression. Struggling to combat her apathy, she fiddled with her laptop. But she still could not make out all the letters. Patty calmly reminded her of Dr. Gleason's warning that her sight would take time to regenerate. Rafe bought her a box of large-tipped markers and drawing paper and encouraged her to try her hand at drawing. She drew pages and pages of free-formed shapes and filled them with vibrant, primary colors. Patty secretly took possession of the first drawing and had it framed. When she presented it to Ellen a few days later, Ellen could hardly speak. Patty herself was in tears.

"Look at the two of us actin' like a bunch of weepin' willows," Patty sniffed. "This calls for a celebration! Chuckeeeee! We're going out tonight. Dinner at the diner! For three! And no excuses." She frowned when she saw Ellen open her mouth. "You can't say the light's too strong 'cause it's sundown. I ain't cookin', and that's that!"

"I was only going to say that a hamburger and fries sounded real good," Ellen said with a laugh and went in search of a sweater.

The diner was filled to capacity but there was always room for one more, or two, or three, at the Longacre Diner. It took ten minutes to get seated, everyone wanting to say hello to the trio. Ellen could not yet distinguish features, but her memory for voice was so fine-tuned that she had no trouble identifying people, and she didn't correct the townsfolk who thought she was using her eyes to sight them. Only Patty and Chuck knew her limitations and they didn't say a word.

Not a word to David, either, who soon sauntered in and

landed himself at the counter. Who forced himself to spin 'round on his stool when he heard their familiar voices. Who had been waiting weeks for the moment when he next saw Ellen, knowing that eventually he would, having scoured 'round for every bit of gossip he could, foremost the fact that she had returned to Longacre and that she was living at Patty's. He only wished this first sighting of his beloved wasn't such a public venue.

Busy as they all were having a good time, no one seemed to notice his entrance. And lady luck was more than generous because Ellen faced his way and he was able to drink in the sight of her. God, but she was every bit as lovely as he'd remembered. How was he going to live the rest of his life never to see the teasing smile in her eyes, the way it hovered on her lips, just short of laughter? How was he going to live without ever again feeling the twist of her red curls between his fingers, much less her soft skin beneath his palm?

But she didn't seem to notice him. Through those sunglasses, Ellen probably couldn't even make him out. He'd heard her sight was coming 'round, but faulty. Well, that was to be expected. But perhaps this was a blessing. Maybe he should leave quietly before she made him out in all his miserable glory. Maybe he should be careful not to slam the screen door as he left the restaurant. Maybe he should head home as quickly as possible.

A week later Chuck went in search of David, driving forty miles early one morning to beard the lion in his den. The den was the Adirondack Preserve Greenhouse in Newcomb Center where timberland research and botanical experiments were conducted on behalf of the forestry service. David regretted not bringing Ellen to the beautiful greenhouse where he carried out his research. She would have enjoyed the misty warmth and piney scent that accumulated beneath the hothouse roof and permeated the air. He had always felt this was the best part of his job, where he got to play scientist, instead of fireman to sloppy tourists and careless hunters.

"How you doing, David?" Chuck greeted his old friend. "Long time, no see."

His eyes wide with surprise, David smiled from across the manmade forest. "Hey, Chuck, how's it going?" Setting aside his plants, he grabbed a cloth and rubbed away the mud before he walked around the workstation and held out his hand. Less formal, Chuck ignored David's outstretched hand and replaced it with a bear hug.

"So this is where you've been hiding out."

"I haven't been hiding!"

Chuck's brows rose. "No? Well, I haven't seen much of you around, buddy."

"Maybe we've been missing each other. It happens. Hey, nothing's wrong, is it?" David asked, suddenly alarmed at Chuck's unexpected appearance.

"No, no, nothing's wrong. I was just in the neighborhood. Well, not that far off," he said to David's suspicious look. "Just thought I'd stop by and say hello, is all. See why you went to ground."

David shrugged. "I've been busy. Lost so much time the last month that I'm totally behindhand. Worked till midnight twice last week, nursing along a crop of seedlings for an early planting in Tupper Lake. And did you notice those fields on the ride up, those baby evergreens hungry for a good feeding? Hell, my database is so overdue to be updated, I'd even let *you* have a go at my computer! I wouldn't call all that going underground."

Chuck laughed, but he wasn't fooled. "David, you went underground the day Ellen came out of surgery, that's a fact."

"Untrue!"

Chuck ignored the denial for what it was worth. He could be as forthright as his wife when he wanted. "She loves you David, so why are you doing this?"

David's answer was to march down the narrow greenhouse aisle as Chuck trailed behind, flicking an occasional leaf. The greenhouse was a wonderland of flora and fauna and any other time, Chuck would have been entranced by the selection, being a farmer himself. The humid greenhouse replicated the outdoors of the countryside, a laboratory where answers were sometimes found to combat disease and drought, where new species were identified and, once in a great while, even created. Right now, though, the only thing that had his attention was David. And his frustration was apparent. It was in his voice, just short of a bark.

"I told you, I'm not hiding."

"This whole thing, it isn't going to win you any medals, David, that's for sure. Just the opposite. You've got a long stretch of life ahead of you. You aiming to hide here the rest of your life?"

"If I were, it would be my business."

"Yes, it would. But what about that poor girl?"

"If you're talking about Ellen Candler, she'll find someone else."

"What if she doesn't want anybody else?"

"Come on, Chuck." David frowned impatiently. "She wouldn't want me, once she saw the beautiful picture I made."

"Seems to me she ought to have some say in the matter."

David shrugged, but underneath Chuck was ripping him apart. Hell, didn't anybody know how his heart was breaking? Did they have to torture him, too?

"She's doing fine, if you want to know."

"Is she? I'm glad. She deserves to, what she went through."

"Yeah, her life hasn't been a bowl full of Jell-O, has it? But then, whose has?" Chuck clapped him on the shoulder, suddenly expansive. "Well, think it over, David. I know you've got your ideas, but Ellen is allowed hers, too. She's a mighty fine woman, spunky, and not hard on the eyes, either. I'd like to have her as a neighbor. And Rafe thinks so, too, by the way," Chuck added casually. "Just a rumor, mind, but he *has* been spending a lot of time at my house. Hank Collins has been sniffin' around some, too, now I come to think of it."

"What does Ellen say? About these guys, I mean."

"Oh, Ellen doesn't say anything. The soul of discretion, that one, but I think she's not so happy."

"It's probably post-operative depression."

"I thought that was for new mamas."

"No, no, anyone can get it."

"Well, perhaps you're right," Chuck conceded, "but I wouldn't bet the farm. She moons about a lot. She thinks we don't see, me and Patty, but we do. Something's on her mind, but hey—" he grinned, clapping David on the back one last time "—maybe you're right! Maybe she *is* thinking about making a choice between those two local yokels. Never thought of that! Thanks, David, that was pretty insightful. Glad I stopped by, old buddy. Always could depend on you to help me see the way." Almost, he could see the steam coming out of David's ears. Satisfied, he hurried back to work.

Chapter Ten

Something was wrong.

The minute she thought it, Ellen knew she was right. Her sight was not returning. The bruising was all but gone, her eyes were no longer sensitive to light, but still she only saw shadows. If the surgery had taken, she should be seeing more than she was. She'd tried to tamp down her sense of apprehension and not transmit her worries to her friends, but in the weeks that had passed, she'd even felt a visible *decline* in her vision. The shadows were becoming lighter and fainter. According to Dr. Gleason, she should be seeing more. He said so every time she spoke to him, until she'd put it to him bluntly last week and he'd admitted she might be right. It could be that her sight was failing, that the surgery had been less successful than anticipated. A trip to the ophthalmologist in Albany who was overseeing her recovery confirmed the bad news.

Shaken, she contemplated the implications. The main

thing she decided—without question—was that before her vision went completely, she wanted to secure her freedom. She wanted to break loose of the silken ties that bound her to everyone who'd ever helped her—bless them—and didn't understand that help wasn't what she needed, that silken ties could bind and even choke.

She wanted a home of her own.

One night, over a cup of tea with the Carmichaels, she said so. She was very grateful to Chuck and Patty, but if they would please be so kind as to understand…she wanted to find an apartment…or a house—that would do just fine—but she wanted to live alone.

Patty became hysterical. She marched around the kitchen, slamming pots, whipping the counter with her dish towel as she conjured up every argument she could find against the idea. But Ellen stood her ground.

"Patty, I want to stay in Longacre. This is my home now, I understand that. I love it here. I love you guys and I want to be near you. I love the whole town."

"Well, thanks a lot!" Patty groused.

"Cut slack, Patricia," Chuck ordered her, a thing so rare that Patty stopped in her tracks. "Ellen's a grown woman entitled to her own life."

"Thank you, Chuck," Ellen said softly as she watched Patty—a shadowy Patty—prowl around the bright kitchen. "Patty, it's time for me—not to go, no—but to begin. You and Chuck have been all that good friends should be and I will never forget it, but I have to get on with my life. I'm not an invalid, anymore. I can see better than ever, and now that I can, I want to stand on my own two feet."

"Let her go, Patty."

"O-oh, are you chasing away my friend?"

"That's unkind, Patricia. You know that's not how I feel, and Ellen knows it, don't you, Ellen?"

"Of course I do," Ellen promised instantly. "Patty's just upset. We both know she doesn't really believe that."

But Patty was not mollified. "What if something happens, you'd be so alone."

"What if something happened to *you* when you were alone?" Ellen argued lightly.

"But what will you do, wandering around all alone in a big old house?"

"I'm a writer. Did you forget that I actually made a living writing, once upon a time?" Ellen teased.

"And don't forget that fancy inheritance." Chuck smiled. "You won't want for help, if you should need it. A housekeeper, and all, I'm thinking."

"Well, actually, I was thinking of returning most of it to…um…David," Ellen revealed weakly.

"Are you crazy?" Patty shrieked. "That scoundrel? After the way he treated you, don't you dare! Besides, he doesn't need it, you do! If you returned that money, I'd think you were hell-bent on suicide."

"Patty's right, there, Ellen. David doesn't need your money, and he has the rest of his father's estate to spend, too, not that he ever buys anything. Remember, he'll be seeing the proceeds from the sale of the house and its contents. Besides that, he makes an excellent salary."

Her face troubled, Ellen pursed her lips. "Well, I'll think about it. I suppose you're right. John Hartwell meant my share of the money to be used this way."

"Yes, he did, and you should respect his wisdom."

As casually as she could, Ellen threw caution to the wind. "Patty? Chuck? I have a question. Why didn't I know about David's scarred face? How come he never told me? How come no one else ever mentioned it?"

"Whoa! That's three questions, sugar." Chuck laughed over his coffee. "Might be we don't have all the answers."

"Then give me the ones you do have. In confidence, of course," she added wryly.

"Naturally." He grinned. "Well, first off, maybe nobody mentions David scars 'cause they're used to them. He's been living here about ten years, you know, and if they were a shock way back when, well, I honestly don't think anybody hardly notices them anymore. And then, maybe we take our cue from David. It's only right, you know. Hereabouts, we respect a man's privacy."

"Are his scars all that bad?"

"Pretty bad. But they're worse to him."

"How did he get them?"

"A car accident is all we know, Ellen. He was fourteen years old, maybe closer to fifteen. The crash almost took his life, you understand."

"No, I don't understand. Tell me."

"It's not all that difficult. A nasty car accident ruined his face. Lots of glass breaking, David practically through the windshield, the usual blood and gore. And lots and lots of operations afterward, near as we can figure. But they didn't help much in the long run. Then, losing his mother so young, and his father too busy to fill in, I'd guess David figures he's got a corner on loneliness. No one else took up the slack, not that I know of. That's the story, in the main, or as much as Patty and I have put together from stuff he's said over the years. Keeps to himself, our David does, so a body can't be sure how things went *exactly*. How many girls do you think he's dated, a smart guy like him, and with a good job, to boot? He should have 'em knockin' down the door, and maybe they would, too, if he'd give them half a chance, but he won't.

He's all pent-up, raging mad about his face, thinks he's the phantom of the opera—which he ain't, by the way. Why, the kids around here are crazy about him. It's practically a national holiday when he goes around the schools and does his Smokey Bear routine. Unfortunately he sees it differently. If I looked like him, maybe I would, too. Must have been mighty hard on David, living with such a pretty thing like you.'' Chuck smiled.

''I don't think I seemed to affect him either way, except to rile up his temper.''

''That's not what Patty says.''

''Patty's got too many opinions.'' Ellen grimaced at her friend.

''Too true.'' Chuck laughed. ''Still, she says my buddy David Hartwell is head-over-heels crazy about you!''

''Excuse me?''

''Patty says that my buddy—''

''I heard you!''

''Well, is it true?''

''Your *good buddy David Hartwell* is the most uncivilized buffoon I have ever had the misfortune to meet!''

''So it *is* love, huh?'' Chuck laughed loudly.

Ellen almost started to cry but Patty quickly stepped in. ''Hey, come on, girl, don't do that!''

Ellen brushed away her tears and smiled. ''I don't know what's got into me lately. I *never* used to cry, but since I've met David, I'm on an emotional roller coaster.''

''You have been through a lot yourself, don't forget,'' Patty pointed out.

''I suppose so. Maybe that's it. John Hartwell dying, leaving Montana so abruptly, coming to New York, the surgery. And even if David is John's son, he's still a stranger to me. Oh, I miss John dreadfully. Maybe I haven't properly grieved. John Hartwell was like a father to me, you know.''

Patty didn't know anything about John Hartwell, but she was damned sure she knew what the problem was with his son. A knowing glance at her husband told her he thought so, too.

The first hurdle leaped, that of persuading her friends to let her go, Ellen and Patty went house hunting. There was only one rule, Patty decided, and it was not negotiable: Ellen must live in town. She would not hear of her best friend living out in the boondocks with raccoons and wolves and snakes. No question, Ellen readily agreed, shuddering at the thought of snakes. That agreed upon, since Longacre was not a big city, or even a big town, and four houses was what was available, they were able to see all four dwellings in one day. The choice made itself. Ellen selected an adorable wood frame with blue trim and a white picket fence. It contained a small living room, a big kitchen and a parlor that would suit admirably for Ellen's office. The upstairs floor contained three bedrooms and a huge bathroom, a bit old-fashioned and in need of an upgrade, but doable. If it was a bit far from Main Street, the fact was, she didn't really want to live on Main Street.

Ellen was installed in her new house just after New Year's Eve. Though her vision was blurrier than ever, she was able to tell everyone exactly where she wanted things placed—without revealing her diminishing sight. No one gave it a second thought that she was squinting more than ever and made a few false moves that badly bruised her knees. It was accepted by everyone that her fierce squinting was a part of her recovery, not the problem.

Ellen's main concern had been that if she said anything

about her decreasing vision, Patty would have made the move difficult, if not impossible—with the best intentions in the world, of course. But Patty could have become an immovable force that even Chuck might not have been able to budge. She might even have gone as far as to convince Rafe and Hank not to move her. Thus, Ellen had been close-mouthed. And now, sitting around her spanking new kitchen table with her closest friends at the end of moving day, devouring the shepherd's pie that Miss Callie had thoughtfully brought by, Ellen knew she'd done the right thing.

David, on the other hand, sat alone on his mountain the longest winter of his life. The moment hunting season had opened, in September, the male of the species had seemed to crawl out of the woodwork, shooting up white-tailed deer, black bear, wild turkey and whatever else happened to pass their way, including themselves. Now it was January, the same hunters were on the lookout for snow geese and ruffed grouse. David accounted himself lucky there had been no fatalities in his district.

When snow fell in record heights, it seemed he was digging out every other morning to get to work, but he was glad of the labor, it utilized his pent-up energy. If he had ever had visions of showing Ellen the pristine elegance of New York's mountainside, now that she could see, or tumble in the snowdrifts with her—definitely share a kiss or two in the snow—he dismissed them as soon as they materialized. Every day, a hundred times a day.

Mid-February, when Pansy gave birth to a mysterious batch of puppies, he finally had the excuse he was looking for. When they were six-weeks-old to the minute, he took the best of the litter, tied a red ribbon around its neck and headed down to Longacre.

His first stop was at Patty's store. When he walked in, Patty nearly fainted.

"As I live and breathe! It's himself!"

David smiled but it was sheepish. "Yes."

Patty grinned broadly and rounded the counter to bury him in a huge hug. "I've missed you, soldier."

"I've missed you, too. And Chuck."

"Anybody else you miss?"

David blushed like a schoolboy, not even pretending to miss Patty's meaning. "Is she here? I was passing by and thought I'd say hello."

Passing by, my foot, Patty thought with a smile. "Ellen doesn't live with us anymore."

David blanched and swallowed hard but Patty saved him the trouble of speaking. "She lives on Cowan Road. Moved out on us a week or so ago."

"No!"

"Yes!" Patty grinned. "Believe me when I say I fought the whole idea, but she insisted, and Chuck backed her up. So did Rafe and Hank Collins, that young ranger you hired a ways back. In fact, they both helped her move. Seein' as how she's doing real good, I guess it was the right thing to do."

"Does that mean her sight's back?"

"Not completely. I see her run into stuff, chairs and things. And the other day, I noticed she couldn't find the light switch right off. But she manages. Dr. Gleason warned us that her recovery would take a long time."

"Yes, I remember."

"Do you?" she said, her eyes fixed on his. "I don't remember your sticking around long enough to hear."

Shifting uncomfortably, David sighed. "Let's not go there, Patty."

"Are you joking, David? The whole town has *gone there!* Like, *where'd that Hartwell guy disappear to?*"

"I didn't disappear, I've been busy, as I've told your husband," he said brusquely. "People shouldn't gossip when they don't know the situation."

"Oh, David, get down off your cloud. Everyone knows *the situation,* as you call it. And we're all pretty angry at the way you've treated that poor girl."

"Does *she* say so?"

"Ellen? She never mentions your name. And if I or anybody else happens to do so, she turns away or changes the subject. That's how I know she's eaten up inside. And it's all your fault!"

David didn't know what to say. His words were casual, but the fear in his eyes was sincere. "Patty, I want to see her. What do you think?"

Patty was unmoved. "What do *I* think? I think you'd better ask her what *she* thinks!"

"I'm asking you."

"And you don't like my answer? What kind of answer do you want, lover-boy? You have fair to broke that poor girl's heart. Do you honestly think she would want to see you after what you did? Leadin' her on, then abandoning her so…so…heartlessly!" Patty fumbled for the dramatic, and succeeded, her arms stretched wide. "Leaving her alone at the hospital, not a word when she came home, not even a lousy telephone call asking how she was doing? Would *you* want to see *you?*"

Home truths hurt.

"Oh, David," she said softly, her soft heart abruptly switching gears. "Didn't you love her just a little bit? Was she so hard to trust?"

She watched as David leaned over the counter, his long

fingers tunneling through his thick, black hair. "Patty, my life is living hell, I love her so much."

"Then why?"

"My face…"

"Not good enough, David. Your face was never an issue for Ellen."

"Perhaps it wasn't for her," he said grimly, "but it was for me."

"Then get over it, David, or it will be the ruin of two lives."

"It's already the ruin of mine."

"Well, buddy, if I know Ellen, that girl's probably willing to give you a second chance. You gonna take it, or you goin' to hell in a handbasket?"

The silence was weighty. Patty watched him, his face a grim study as he wrestled with his demons. "I care about you, David," she said softly, her hands clasping his in earnest. "Chuck cares about you. The whole bloody town adores you! Doesn't that tell you *anything?*"

Slowly lifting his head, David took a long hard look at Patty. "Longacre is the best thing to ever happen to me, after you and Chuck."

"Speak of the devil, he appears." She smiled, looking past David's shoulder to watch her husband throw open the store door.

"Whoa there, mister, you foolin' with my woman? Hey, fella, don't I know you from somewhere?" Chuck smiled as he dusted the snow from his boots.

"Chucky, close the door. You're letting in all the cold air."

"Hello, Chuck." David smiled faintly.

"Ah, me, yes, my eyes are not deceiving. It's David Hartwell, all right! I thought you looked familiar. What's up? Hey, is something wrong?"

"No, nothing is wrong, Chuck. I just stopped by to say hello."

"That's all?"

"That's all."

"Well, not quite," Patty said softly as she filled a bag with gumdrops. "Seems his sweet tooth was botherin' him." Slowly she pushed the bag toward David. "Go on, take it, it's on the house."

David looked at the bag, then at Patty, and smiled faintly. But he took the bag, shoved it in his pocket and headed for the door.

"Hey, wait a minute! You're leaving already? Set a spell! We've got some catching up to do."

David clasped Chuck's shoulder as he passed him. "Got to make a delivery. But it was good to see you."

"Well, hey guy, can't it wait five minutes?"

"*I* can't wait five minutes." David smiled and closed the door quietly as he left.

Ten minutes later David pulled up in front of Ellen's house, turned off the ignition to his car and wondered whether he really intended to get out of the truck. His feet didn't seem to want to cooperate. No matter what he'd told Patty minutes before, now he was here, the whole idea of seeing Ellen again seem crazy. It would take a mighty forgiving woman to overlook what had happened in Baltimore, abandoning her the way he had. And he hadn't been much of a prize before that.

And as for now, he hadn't seen her in months, hadn't called once or lifted a helping hand in her direction. Not that a day didn't pass when he didn't discreetly inquire about her or drive by Patty's to see if he could get a glimpse of her, or sit in the Longacre Diner long after his coffee had gone cold, in hopes she might pass by. Once, spotting her on Main Street, he'd almost climbed from his truck to say hello, but his nerve had deserted him at the last minute. Now here he was staring up at her curtained windows, unsure which was going to be worse, her reaction to his face or the repercussions of her temper.

Ah, jeez, David groaned to himself, how could life treat him so badly? The most beautiful woman in the world sitting in that house, and all he could do was admire the view. He'd never dreamed that the pleasure of a real woman would ever be his. Ellen had been a harmless fantasy, her blindness a safety zone that he'd enjoyed all too briefly. Then she had started making inroads on the desert of his heart. Who knew what he'd been thinking, letting his guard down, that night in the Harbor Hotel? The wall he'd so carefully constructed was rebuilt soon enough, but the damage had been done, or why else was he sitting here like a fool?

Turning on the ignition, he put the truck in drive. A fool, yes! This was ridiculous. Ellen would faint when she saw him, scream her head off.

David turned off the ignition. Patty swore that Ellen loved him, but Patty said many things. Ellen had even claimed it was so, in a moment of passion. A notoriously unreliable moment. Still, if he didn't take that short walk up those steps, he'd never know.

A squirming puppy in hand, David Hartwell pushed past the gate of Ellen Candler's white picket fence. "Hush, little one, or you'll ruin your pretty red ribbon," he admonished the pup gently as he rang the bell. Shifting nervously, he waited for Ellen to answer the door, his heart beating fit to burst. The memory of their first meeting couldn't help but come to mind, the first time he had ever seen her, when she had opened another door, the door to his father's house in Montana. He was unprepared then, he was unprepared now. Both times did the sight of her take his breath away. Only now, as she stood in the doorway, her hair still damp from a shower, he had more at stake. Sporting a long green sweater reaching to her knees, the informal style suited her, but so would a paper bag to his lovelorn eyes.

"Hello, Ellen."

Ellen was so surprised that she couldn't say a thing.

"I was in the neighborhood," David explained lamely as his heart fell. Look how she stared, repulsed, just as all the other women he had ever known. Her silence was damning to his ears. But he wouldn't back down.

"I suppose I should have told you a long time ago."

Ellen looked at him blankly. It took a moment for her to understand his meaning, to realize that David was referring to his face. She must be better at faking sight than even she knew.

"I don't mean to scare you," he said softly.

How ironic, she thought with a sad smile, that his biggest fear was an unnecessary worry, because her vision was all but gone, that she couldn't see a scratch on him, and never would. So she pretended to scan his face, because she could *just* discern the outline of his head, and besides, it was what he expected her to do. With the little time she had left to see, she would memorize its shape, the dark shadow that hid his brow and told he wore his hair long. She would trace the outline of his ears and know they lay flat, capture the vague outline of his eyes and see that they were dark, that his beautiful mouth was wide, that his beard was heavy. But his scars were impossible to discern, charted on a cheek that was smooth. "You don't frighten me, if you are referring to your scars."

"Well, yes, I was."

"The things that scare me about you are not sketched on your face."

David paled at her blunt words. "You don't have to tell me what a bastard I've been."

"Actually, I do. It's part of your redemption, isn't it?" she asked with a faint smile. "Why else are you here?"

"You're right. I have come to apologize."

"And you assumed I would accept one?"

"No, I didn't. But there was only one way to find out, without the use of go-betweens."

"And you would have hated that. So public!"

"Ellen, will you at least talk to me?"

"I am doing that," she snapped, "so I think perhaps you are asking me for something else."

"I came here with good intentions!"

"You should not have!"

David hung his head, not wanting to fight with her but not knowing what else to say. "I...um...Pansy had puppies. I thought—I was wondering—you don't have to say yes, of course—but I thought that since she'd had a litter of four, that perhaps you would like to have one." Rummaging through his pocket, he found the bag of candy Patty had filled for him. "And gumdrops, I brought you some gumdrops," he added shyly as he held them aloft.

Ellen looked at the pup, then to David, and opted for the candy. "Gumdrops, yes, thanks. The dog...I'll have to think about it. I'll let you know."

Before he had time to think, Ellen closed the door on his face, leaving him nose-to-nose with an ornamental brass knocker. She wasn't letting him in. Chagrined, he strode back to his truck and gently placed the pup back in her carrier. He should have known it would not be easy. Nothing had been, up till now, in their relationship, so why should things have changed?

Had he changed? Perhaps the answer was yes. *Had she?* Oh, most definitely. But did they ever do things on the same timetable?

David came back every day the long week that followed, and each time that Ellen closed the door on his face, he shouted that he would be back. He was, too, until the day she finally relented and invited him in. Relief swept through David as he stomped the snow from his boots on her tiny porch. She probably would have let the pup in the first day, he thought wryly, if he hadn't been part of the package.

It was awkward removing his jacket as he clutched the squirming dog, but Ellen ignored him when he tried to hand her the puppy. Following her lead into the living room, he took the seat she offered him, not daring to put the dog on her fancy new carpet.

"Nice place you got here," he said, looking around the room.

"Thank you. I love it."

"Nice and homey. A far cry from Montana."

"How do you mean?"

"No antiques."

She understood his reference and smiled. "That was your father's domain, not mine. Personally, I prefer rustic and overstuffed. Patty took me to Albany a few times to shop."

"Yeah, she does that real well, I know."

The silence was awkward. David took the path tried and true. "Oh, hey, I nearly forgot, I brought you more gumdrops."

Ellen held out her hand. "Yes, you can bribe me with candy. I'm easy." Grinning hugely, she thrust her fingers in the bag and scooped out a handful. "Want some?"

"Thanks. Green is my favorite, if you don't mind."

She handed him a yellow and a red. He relied on the puppy to get him through the next few minutes. "Well, what do you think? You want to hold her?"

"Her?" Ellen repeated.

"The dog. This little lady needs a home, remember? I was hoping you'd like to give her one."

Leaning forward, Ellen stared hard at the pup trying to get free of David's arms. She could just make him out. "I'm not too sure. I don't know if I want a dog. It's such a responsibility."

"Why don't you try her out? Hey, little miss," he said, holding the dog aloft, "you stop that squirming or you'll give the lady the wrong impression. Got to show her who's boss." He grinned past the pup. "But she really is the gentlest of the litter and a beauty, don't you think?"

"Yes, um, she's very pretty. What do you call her?"

"I didn't give her a name. I thought if you kept her, you would want to do that yourself. Do you like her colors?"

"Er…yes, very delicate."

"Yes, the gold in her coat complements the copper highlights in your hair."

"How fanciful of you."

David looked down at the dog in his arms, a black mutt with nary a glimmer of yellow, and cast a flinty look Ellen's way. He'd known the moment she'd declined to hold the dog, back in the hallway, that something was not quite right. The gumdrops were another alarm.

"The way the little devil keeps scratching at my new blue shirt, here, it's not going to be worth the effort to wash. I wore it especially for today," he explained with a laugh.

Ellen was noncommittal. "It's a very nice shirt."

Actually, it was red. As red as his face was with anger.

The joke was on him. She hadn't seen his scars, and she never would. It was all pretense and he couldn't say a word. Or maybe she couldn't distinguish colors yet. Yes, that could be it. He wondered who to ask, though, because the mood she was in, she sure wasn't going to answer any of *his* questions! Not that he dared ask any.

"Here," he said softly as he slid across the couch to sit beside her. "Why don't you try holding her? She squirms around a lot only because she's a baby."

Gingerly, Ellen took the puppy in her arms and cuddled the downy fur against her cheek. "She's adorable."

As the pup began to lick her chin, she laughed that special laugh that always made David feel right. He was so entranced that he almost didn't hear when she said she'd keep the pup for a trial period. "Good. I brought one of those retractable leashes, and enough dog food for a month."

"That sure of yourself, were you?" Ellen asked archly, glancing his way.

"Just in case," David returned, impressed that she could find his eyes. She must be able to see something. "I was hedging my bets."

"A gambling man. That's something I never knew about you." There, she'd done it, alluded to their past. Did he really think she was going to make things easy for him, strutting back into her life without so much as a by-your-leave?

"Talking about gambling—how did your operation go?" There, he'd done it, thrown his cards on the table!

Tilting her head, Ellen gave him a long look. "It went well."

"How well?"

"My sight is very limited but promises to improve."

"What does *very limited* mean?" David dared to insist.

"Vague outlines, very little color, not much clarity."

"Can you see me?"

"Do you really mean *you* or do you mean your scars?"

David blushed. "Both, I suppose."

"Both—you may suppose."

What was that supposed to mean? It didn't sound like yes or no to him. "Ellen, about Baltimore—"

Ellen scrambled to her feet, the puppy still in her arms. "Hey, what say we take this little lady for a walk?"

"Ellen!"

"No, David, you may *not* talk to me about Baltimore. The subject is closed and if you wish to stay, you must play by my rules."

"But why?"

"I don't have to give you a reason any more than you have to give me a reason for why you left. Do you hear me asking?"

"No, but I want to tell you."

"I don't want to hear. I did once, but I don't any longer. Do you understand?"

David rubbed his eyes and thought for a minute, then shuffled to his feet, feeling defeated. Still, he reminded himself that he was lucky to be within two feet of her. He had patience. He could wait. "I'll go get the stuff from my truck."

He returned holding a case of puppy chow and a long, red leash. "Here we go. Would you like to put on her collar?"

"Um, no, you do it. I'll watch."

"No problem," he said, not minding one bit as he crouched beside her and fumbled with the collar. "Maybe if you put your hands over mine and feel what I'm doing, it will help you to learn the maneuver."

He was charmed by the way she turned pink. Her cool

hand fluttering on his was the most wonderful thing he'd felt in ages, aside from her knee brushing his. It was all he could do not to curl his arm around her waist and pull her body to his. Her lips would part, they'd be so soft beneath his, her taste so sweet after his long drought.

"Here's the hook, it connects to the leash. Do you feel it, how it slides apart when you press this metal clasp?" His hand covering hers, he pressed Ellen's thumb along the hasp and showed her how to slide the hook apart.

"Well done," he said, ignoring the way his face burned. "Sit, doggie." The pooch surprised them both and sat. "Good girl! She's a smart dog, Ellen. It's almost like she's made for you. Okay, now give me your other hand, here, that's right." He felt her fingers flutter in his palm and for a brief moment he almost forgot his purpose. "You must find poochie's collar, slide your fingers around to locate the metal loop—excellent—and slide the hook into the loop."

"Well done! You two are ready to go." But when he held the leash to her left hand, Ellen didn't notice. Wordlessly he dropped it into her lap. "I'll go get our coats."

From the hall, he watched as Ellen searched with her fingertips for the leash, instead of using her eyes. Old habits died hard, but it was just as well, wasn't it? he thought, his eyes welling as the implications of Ellen's fumbling bore down upon him. Still, he gave her time to complete the act, then took a deep breath and returned to the living room with their coats.

"All set?"

Ellen smiled as she rose to her feet. "This is going to be an adventure!"

"You always were up for an adventure," David said absently.

Ellen froze, but what had she expected? The past would

always be there. If he would be so daring as to brave a visit, shouldn't she be strong enough to ignore the past? She'd known when she made the decision to return to Longacre that David would be a part of the background and would eventually surface. Of course, it was different to theorize. Now that he was actually here, sitting in her living room, *now that it was happening,* she must make the best of it. She must forgive him, to some extent. Perhaps she had, the day she returned to Longacre. This visit was *his* peace offering. Perhaps she should treat it as such.

"I'm almost ready," she said as she searched for her gloves.

"You're not the only one." He smiled as the pup scratched at the door. David handed her the leash. "She's all yours."

The whole of Longacre heard about their walk, quite nearly before they arrived back at Ellen's house. Perhaps they would not have, but the couple walked almost the entire length and breadth of Longacre, losing track of time so that their *short walk* took almost two hours. They didn't say much, but who relished the company of the other more was up for debate. Small talk, doggie talk, Longacre talk. The safe stuff, and there was wisdom in that. In the end, in companionable silence, they dragged home a very tired pup. David said he would give them a few days to be alone, then return to see if she was going to keep the dog. If she did, he would help Ellen to train the puppy, an offer she didn't refuse.

Chapter Eleven

She named the dog Candy, because when she woke the next morning, her gumdrops were gone and the brown bag lay in shreds on the living room rug.

"Lesson number one," she said with a small shake of her finger at the unrepentant pup, "anything containing sugar is not on my diet or yours!"

After breakfast they made their first excursion out into the world together. Candy was a true lady. She never pulled or started, and when she needed to stop, she tugged gently, as if some sixth sense told her that her new mistress needed extra special care. A sneaking suspicion made Ellen wonder if David had already been working with the dog. After all, if the past was any indication, he would never give her anything wild, not even a parakeet.

The truth was—and it would stay a secret for as long as possible—her vision all but gone was a major reason she had decided to accept the dog. Once she made a few calls to obedience schools to be assured that kind of dog was trainable, she'd made up her mind to keep her. The way she saw it, she'd been given the gift of sight for two months, but it had never been that considerable in the first place. Gravely disappointed, she'd quickly come to terms with it, determined not to fall to pieces. The blessing in her life, as she saw it, was that she had been given just enough time to set up her own household before anyone discovered her secret. Her freedom was worth every little white lie she had told her friends, to get herself installed on Cowan Road. Soon, though, she would have to tell everyone the truth. It was only a matter of time before they noticed. David, too. Silly man, worrying all this time that she would despise him for scars she'd never see! Sometimes she wanted to ask him if he'd prefer to be blind! She'd love to hear what he said to that!

The silly man returned one evening, a few days later—just to see how they were doing, mind!—to find Rafe Tellerman puttering around Ellen's pretty yellow kitchen, making dinner.

Making Ellen dinner!

David was enraged, and worse, there wasn't a thing he could do about it! And Rafe knew, too, the way he was making himself at home, wandering around the kitchen, a wide grin on his face as he fooled around with pots and pans.

"Care to join us, David? There's more than enough to go around. Spaghetti sauce has a way of proliferating, and there's plenty of meatballs, here. In the pot, I do mean." He broke into a loud guffaw that made David want to take a swing at his friend.

"It's Ellen's home, not yours," David said tersely.

"Meaning?"

"Meaning it's her place to invite me, not yours."

"You're absolutely right!" Rafe mocked. "I take back my invitation. Do please leave."

Sweetly, Ellen vanquished Rafe. "Of course you're welcome to stay, David."

But was that hesitancy in her voice? This must be a tryst. He'd interrupted a lover's tryst! He was about to decline when the doorbell rang. Moments later, she was leading Hank Collins into the kitchen.

"More meatballs!" Rafe cried when he saw Hank.

Taking no offense, Hank sniffed the air. "Man, do I love spaghetti and meatballs!"

"I take it you're staying?" Ellen laughed.

"As a matter of fact…" He raised the string bag he was holding. "Well, what have we here? A bottle of Chianti!"

"It's my sauce!" Rafe cried indignantly. "I should have a say who eats my tomato sauce!"

"But it's Ellen's table!" Hank retorted with a laugh. "And it's my wine! Hey, David, how you doing? Would you mind opening the wine while I find us some glasses?"

The free-and-easy banter of Ellen and Rafe and Hank cut through David as he fooled with the wine cork. Why couldn't he be like that? Why did he carry the weight of the world on his shoulders? No one thanked him for it, certainly not Ellen, so cool about her uninvited guests, so affable, so friendly-like, fooling around the way they did.

Did they know she was blind? Would they be so cheerful, if they knew she was blind? Obviously they knew something he didn't. Or did they? He couldn't tell. Was it possible that it didn't matter, that they didn't care if she was blind? Could they love her nearly half as much as he, so that her blindness was a non issue? He plunked down the bottle of opened Chianti and began—unasked—to slice the bread for the table. He was staying.

The sauce was hot, the pasta al dente, and the meal a raucous delight. The bottle of wine was big but the drinking slight. They all knew they were driving home. The only thing that astonished David more than the fact that he was having a good time, was the fact that Hank and Rafe didn't seem to have a clue that Ellen couldn't see. God, but she was good! Making eye contact, but fleeting, careful to keep her eyes on her plate, asking someone to pour her wine, to pass her the cheese, oh, and could you please send the bread her way? She was real good. David did everything possible to help keep her secret, serving her food, filling that wineglass, discreetly replenishing it. And when cleanup time came, they refused to let her help, that part accomplished with such finesse that David wondered if they were all coconspirators. Accomplished with more finesse than their good-nights.

Rafe bestowed the requisite goodnight kiss and drove away.

"Good night, Ellen," Hank called, "and don't forget next Thursday, honey."

Next Thursday? David was livid.

Standing six feet two in his bare feet, it would be no easy thing for Ellen to give David a quick hug good-night. And on this night, his legs just didn't seem to bend. He took her hand instead. "I didn't mean to crash your party, Ellen. I was only stopping by to see about the dog."

"Candy."

"Candy?"

"That's the name I gave her." She laughed. "It has its own meaning."

"Uh-oh. As in gumdrops?"

"Got it in one!" she said dryly. "And a bit of a sore belly, the next day."

"Where has she been tonight?"

"I left her upstairs. I didn't want her overwhelmed by strangers."

And you didn't dare have her underfoot, either, I'll bet. "Well, like I said, I didn't mean to crash your party. I was only stopping by to see if you were keeping her."

"I named her, guess I'm going to keep her. She's a lovely present, David, and I adore her. Thank you."

"I'm relieved to hear that, no kidding, being as how I still have three more pups to find homes for. Well then, I guess I'd better come around and help you train her."

"I guess you can, for a while, but I've enrolled her in a training program. It just doesn't start for a while."

"What kind of training?"

Ellen stammered, realizing what she'd said. "Oh, all the regular stuff. I didn't want to bother you too much."

David fooled with his hat, unable to think of another thing to say. "I guess that's a good idea. Then I guess I'll say good-night."

"Good night, then."

Coward, no kiss!

Although they began to be comfortable with each other, Ellen refused to let David get personal. If he ever referred to their past, she would pretend she hadn't heard. And he was dying to get personal. He wanted to explain his awful behavior, why he'd abandoned her in Baltimore and refused to make contact until now. He wanted to apologize. He wanted to be forgiven. But it was as if she had a sixth sense. She made sure that their association was limited to training Candy. She kept their conversation light. She never invited him to coffee when she was alone, or lingered at the door when he was leaving. And more often than not, someone was there when he arrived, either a neighbor or Patty or Rafe or Hank. Even the cleaning lady chaperoned them on one occasion. David had no idea how to get past the barrier that Ellen had set up.

Ellen didn't want him to. She knew what he wanted: absolution. And she wasn't going to give it to him. He'd made his choice back in Baltimore, and if he didn't like it, that was just too bad. She had her own problems too, and had no energy to help him with his. She was carving out a life for herself that didn't include him. Not in the way it would have three months ago.

It didn't include Rafe or Hank Collins, either, not in the way they wanted, in any case. Ellen made that abundantly clear to them both, privately, when they both asked her, privately, if they had any chance with her. She didn't want them to be under any misconceptions about their friendships. They took it well, and remained her staunch allies.

There was a limit to how long Ellen could keep her encroaching blindness a secret, though, and that limit was finally met the following week during Sunday dinner at the Carmichael house. They were all there, including David, who surprised everybody by accepting Chuck's invitation, and Rafe, who arrived late.

"Got a last-minute phone call from the university," Rafe apologized as he found himself a seat. "Seems the English department has run a little short-staffed this term. Some guy from L.A. was a no-show, so they're looking for someone to fill in for a grad class. Creative writing. Twice a week. Nothing too complicated. Wanted to know if I had any suggestions." A twinkle in his eye, he stared hard at Ellen as he made his announcement. "I took the liberty of mentioning your name, Miss Candler."

The table went silent as all eyes turned her way, watching as she came to attention, surprise scrawled all over her face. "Me?" Ellen gasped.

"Yes, you," Rafe repeated as he helped himself to some roast beef.

Ellen rolled her eyes. "You must be joking."

But Rafe was in earnest. Looking around the table at his friends' faces, he knew they were waiting for an explanation. "Although my reputation precedes me, this time I am not joking! I meant every word, and I would not have gone to bat for you—and risked my reputation, such as it is—if I didn't think you could do it."

"Oh, come on, Rafe," Ellen argued as she toyed with her food, "there are so many obstacles it's not even worth talking about."

"Oh, I don't know," Patty said as she set a bowl of mashed potatoes on the table. "Rafe might have something here. Let's hear him out."

"Patty!"

"Rafe doesn't usually go off half-cocked, Ellen," Chuck argued as he served himself up a large helping from the bowl.

"Why, thank you, Mr. and Mrs. Carmichael!" Rafe smiled as he poured himself a glass of water.

"Well, I think he's gone off the deep end, now," Ellen retorted, her face troubled. "First of all, I've never taught. And then there's the logistics of getting there—and back. And marking papers. How does a blind person mark papers?"

The silence was leaden.

Quietly, her face a mask of guilt, Ellen spoke into the silence. "I was going to tell you…I was just waiting for the right moment…I guess it's come," she said ruefully. "The thing is…the truth is…my vision has not returned. It never will."

No one knew what to say, until Rafe brought them all back to earth.

"First of all, my dear Ellen, it's grad school, so one hopes that these overeducated scholars have mastered the rudiments of composition. What they really need is the finesse and polish of a published author to get them more focused. That's you," he said, pointing a forkful of salad Ellen's way. "Secondly, everyone here can alternate driving you. It's only for ten weeks and the drive is under two hours. Or you can hire yourself a driver. Or take the bus down to Albany yourself, if that's the way you want it. It stops right at the campus gate. And thirdly, nobody marks papers anymore, darling, they *critique* them, and since it's a seminar, it's a round table, so everybody gets to criticize everybody else. The kids love that part, let me tell you."

Ellen leaned forward, her hands clenched. "Doesn't anybody have anything to say to what I just told you, that I've lost my sight, what little I had? That I'm never going to see? Doesn't it mean *anything* to any of you?"

Everybody looked at each other and sighed communally.

"It means you won't care when I have a bad hair day." Patty smiled.

"Hey, I liked you when I met you, and you couldn't see then," Chuck reminded her.

"I won't have to worry about shaving just to please you," Hank piped up.

Only David remained silent, but in the rush to comfort Ellen, no one seemed to notice. Patty swung 'round the table to hug her friend fiercely, while, at Rafe's urging, the rest scrambled to fill their glasses.

"A toast," he cried, "to the prettiest blind teacher in the state university firmament."

Tears brimmed over Ellen's cheeks as she leaned into Patty's embrace. "But I'm blind!" she said bitterly.

"Yes, you're blind. We heard you the first time," Rafe chuckled. "Did you really think we didn't know? Did you really think you could keep that from us, that we wouldn't notice? We're polite, you see. It's the Yankee in us, darling. If you didn't want to speak about it, we weren't going to pry. Now, you have ten minutes to deal with it or we will all be on the floor crying with you!"

"Oh, Rafe." Ellen hiccuped through her tears, a smile forcing its way forward. "I love you."

"Then our wedding's still on? Hope springs eternal!"

"Over my dead body," Hank swore over his glass.

"Easily arranged," Rafe snorted. "Ranger Hartwell, do send Mr. Collins on bear patrol tomorrow. Young Henry here is beginning to have a detrimental affect on my love life."

David smiled faintly but his eyes were fastened on Ellen. When the joking stopped—

But it would not. No one took her blindness more seriously than her five best friends, they all promised, but it was their duty to see to it—if she could not!—that her handicap did not become just that. That's why she should give Rafe's offer her utmost consideration. It was all fine and well to have set up house on Cowan Road and resume her writing career, but getting out into the world was also a part of life, and it was missing from hers. Walking her new dog was not sufficient. It only counted for an airing. She needed to become a part of the world beyond her front steps and this teaching job was a good way to wet her toes.

David drove her home. Ignoring everyone else's offer, he handed her into the passenger seat of his truck and sped off before they could protest. They were at her door in a very few minutes. "Who shoveled the snow?" he asked as she searched for her house keys.

"Mrs. Louis's boy, Jonah. He's a great kid, he runs all sorts of errands for me, too. Did he do a good job? He must have—" she smiled "—because I haven't tripped yet."

"Seems pretty clean to me," David said as she unlocked her front door.

"He even salted it. For free, as he solemnly informed me. But I secretly added it into the price of the shoveling."

"Ellen, I'd like to come in a few minutes, if it's all right with you."

Taken off guard, Ellen hesitated. "Well…"

But David was determined. "Thanks. Don't mind if I do," he said, a shade acerbic. Once inside he took his coat and hung it alongside hers. But anything he'd planned to say was put to the wayside with the vociferous greeting of the pup.

"Candy!" Ellen scooped up the little dog. "Did you think I'd never come home, you silly?"

David smiled while they cooed like long-lost friends. "I guess this is a success story," he observed as he followed them into the kitchen.

"Most definitely." Ellen smiled as she doled out some kibbles and placed Candy's bowl on the floor. "She's a treasure I shall always be grateful for, David." Uncertain what to do next, she filled the teakettle. David's presence was unnerving. She had been careful up until now never to be alone with him if she could help it. Training the dog didn't count. That was all business. But now, something was different, electric, she could feel it in the air, in its heat, in his scent, even if she couldn't see him.

"Would you like to join me? I always have tea in the evening…it's becoming a ritual…I drank more coffee in Montana, but somehow tea suits the climate up here." She replaced the teakettle on the stove and lit the gas. "I'm babbling, aren't I?" she said with a sheepish smile.

David leaned across the counter and curled a stray lock behind her ear. "I *would* like some tea, if it's not too much trouble."

It was a pleasure to watch as she put together tea. She was so lovely, a slender reed of auburn curls and creamy skin that held just the hint of a blush. Maybe more than a hint. He could tell she was nervous, the way she was fiddling around, but she had mastered her kitchen, for sure. She knew exactly where the yellow ceramic tea jar was, placed blue mugs alongside a matching blue sugar bowl, found spoons and the tea strainer in the correct counter drawers, and bade him sit at her table as she handed him napkins. Watching how smoothly she went about setting out the tea, it occurred to him that she had known far earlier than she'd let on—of course she had!— that she was going blind. If he had known the month before, she had known twice as long. Now that he thought of it, she'd probably rushed to get this house in order before she lost all vision.

They sat sipping tea while Candy scampered around their feet until she grew tired of her game and found her bed.

"Patty picked it up at a flea market," Ellen explained the wicker crate. "It wasn't meant for pooch here, but she has a way of making her needs known."

"Dogs do."

"How is Pansy? I miss her."

"Fine, she's fine. Taking to motherhood like a champ."

"Lucky girl," Ellen sighed.

David's brow rose. "You planning on any for yourself?"

"I don't understand."

"Having kids. When I see those two buffoons prowling around you like you were the last woman on earth, I figure it's on someone's list."

"Oh, much ado about nothing there." Ellen grinned. "They're just being boys."

"Boys?" David snorted. "I don't think so!"

"Well, it's nothing for you to worry about, is it?" she said quietly, but David heard the trace of humor in her voice.

"What are you going to do about Rafe's job offer, Ellen?"

"I don't know," she said irritably. "Must we talk about it now?"

"Yes, we must."

"Why?"

"Because you have to decide soon. And because you're afraid."

"Well, I have good reason to be, don't I?"

"I'm not too sure. Are we talking about the actual job, or coming down from the mountain?"

"Oh, that old saw!" Ellen mimicked David. "Are we going down memory lane tonight?" The moment the words were out of her mouth, she regretted them. She sounded waspish even to her own ears. But she didn't want to talk about the job offer because, yes, she was terrified of taking the post, and she hated that David knew.

Setting his cup aside, David knelt beside her. Her hands sheltered in his, he smiled. "Listen, lady, I know that even though you're scared, something about that job offer excites you. I saw it in your eyes back at Patty's. I think you should take it. It's a step forward. *Another* step forward. I see what you've done here and it's a damned miracle. Make another miracle, Ellen. Take the job. Work out the details later. Like Rafe said, we'll all pitch in."

"That wouldn't be standing on my own two feet!"

"No, it would be standing on half a dozen feet, but you'd be standing, all the same."

Her shoulders slumped, Ellen sighed elaborately. "I'll think about it."

"Promise?"

"I promise."

"Good. I'll be going, then. Give you some time to think." He smiled.

She walked him to the door, listening carefully while David shrugged into his heavy sheepskin jacket. She imagined that it doubled his size, he was so big to begin with. His hand on the knob, she heard it turn, then heard it stop.

"Oh, yeah, and one more thing to think about."

Before she knew it, David swept her into his arms, his sheepskin coat a cloak around her shoulders. Her hands splayed across his chest, she could feel his heart beating, his breath tickling her cheek as his mouth hovered near hers. Although she knew a moment's panic even through the excitement that surged through her body, he seemed to know no such thing. His lips were warm as they pressed against hers, a gentle taking, but the passion of a man intent.

She did not protest. It was a homecoming, of sorts. She almost sobbed at the remembrance of his taste. She'd missed him, more than words could say.

Then it was over. He set her on her feet and left.

Ellen started her job eight days later. But she refused to let anyone accompany her, insisting that she must begin as she meant to go on. Since she already knew the route to Patty's, had counted every step to her door, she wanted to do the same to the university. So they all pitched in to do dry runs with her, to the bus stop, which stopped on

Main Street—count fifty steps and make a right, count eighty-seven more and make a left—while Rafe arranged to have one of her new students meet her at the other end and escort her to class. Her independence was heady. David had been right. This was the thing to do.

Her students loved her, two of them literally, the moment they saw all that flaming hair flowing down her back, her green eyes glowing with excitement and her wide, beguiling smile. The class of twelve sat at a round table just as Rafe had promised, and spent the first day getting to know each other. During the second session, they each read brief samples of their own work, and then jointly critiqued them. She was such a success that word about her spread around the campus, and the class size mysteriously began to grow. Grad students, and undergrads, too, began sitting in just to hear the pretty blind teacher lecture and listen to the spirited round-table discussions that began to be more the norm than the exception. When the English department heard what was happening, they secured a guard at the door to limit the entrants to seventy-five.

All this she told David at the end of her third week of teaching. He'd arrived early Saturday morning, one of Candy's training days, as they began to call it. "Rafe was so right," Ellen admitted as David watched her leash Candy for her daily walk. Even though she had been attending obedience school, the dog was a natural and needed very little discipline. Early on, she learned to stand out of the way of Ellen's cane, and quickly learned to walk *beside* her as she tapped, so that tripping was not a worry for Ellen. They also noticed that Candy knew how to hone in on the correct house, when it was time to return home. Almost, Ellen didn't need to count steps.

"I was thinking that I'd like to get Rafe a little something as a sort of thank-you for getting me the job," Ellen said as they were walking back to the house. "I'd better ask Patty when she's going to the mall, so I can go with her and pick something out."

"I'll take you," David offered.

"You?" Ellen laughed. "But you hate..." She was going to say, *You hate to be seen in public,* but something held her back. "You hate shopping," she finished instead.

"I'll take you," David repeated firmly. "Today. Now. This afternoon, if you want. I have no plans."

"Not the social butterfly?" Ellen grinned.

"They ain't exactly knockin' down my door," David joked.

They went to the mall, America's home away from home, David teased as he adjusted his hat, then threw it on the back seat at the last minute.

"What was that noise?" Ellen asked as she scooted from the truck, ever sensitive to sound.

"Freedom," declared David, and said no more.

Together they entered Crossgates, Ellen's cane a light click upon the tiles, David's scarred face exposed for all to see. He rather liked not wearing a hat and brushed his hair from his forehead, suddenly not caring what people made of his face. As the day went on, he was surprised to note that no one even stared at that much. What they did stare at, with broad smiles, was Ellen, but he was sure that was because she was so beautiful. Her hair cascading past her shoulders, her skin glowing with health, her smile reflected in her pretty eyes, how could anyone resist a peek at her? Wearing a frilly dress, a deep blue paisley that accentuated her slender figure admirably, more than once he'd wanted to stop and kiss her. But of course, that would have been too outrageous. Besides, he reminded himself, he was waging a campaign to win back her affection. That kiss the week before, which he could not get out of his mind, was his opening gambit. If she'd missed it—no flag could have been redder—she was more than blind, he told himself, she was obtuse.

If there was one thing about Ellen, she was not obtuse! On the contrary, she was a lightening rod of other people's emotions. Too much so, she sometimes thought. But that kiss had never left her mind, either. The problem was that although she wanted more, she was not going to let herself go down that road again. David had hurt her badly. When the stakes had got too high, David had folded. Though she sympathized, she could not forgive.

She told herself she should not criticize him. She knew what it was to be handicapped, the mountains she had to climb, and didn't there seem to be a new one every day? Well, David had his own mountains to conquer. Did he understand that? She didn't know, he didn't say; they were careful not to stray from the formalities.

One thing she knew, though, was that he hadn't wanted her help the first time around and she had no reason to expect things were different now. That was not to say she wasn't aware of his unfolding generosity at this difficult time in her life. She recognized his heroic efforts on her behalf. But something in the back of her mind insisted it was due to the influence of his—their—friends, whose efforts on her behalf were also generous beyond belief. That was big stuff for him, she knew, but he had a long way to go. And of paramount importance, she didn't want him to change for her sake, but for his own. Until she was absolutely sure of his motivation, she would limit her approbation.

And then there was her sight, or the lack of it. When they had been lovers, and even before that, there had been the keen hope that her sight would return, and it had col-

ored her world. Now that hope was gone. There would be
no more operations—and no miracle—and the optimism
she'd clung to had faded. In the face of her defeat, she
must get on with the business of creating a new path for
herself, and it did not support the distraction of a man like
David, who came encumbered with his own emotional
baggage. So, okay, she might dwell on his kiss, and even
hope for a few more, but she didn't dare look past those
moments to any future with him. Protecting herself in this
way made it easier for her to enjoy the day, to stroll
through the mall with her arm linked in his, to listen to
the symphony of sound that teased her ears—pleasing,
jarring, exciting—and to smell the people, the perfume,
and the plastic that filled the air.

"Well, what shall I get him?" Ellen asked after they'd
been wandering a full hour.

"Him?" David had completely forgotten their errand
in the face of spending an entire day with Ellen.

"Rafe, silly."

"Oh, *Rafe,* right." David inwardly groaned. "How
about we stop window-shopping and actually go into
some of these stores? Then I can describe some of the
junk—sorry, the stuff—they sell. Look, there's a pet store.
How about a ferret? It would suit him, what do you
think?"

"I think," said Ellen with a slow smile, "you'd better
take this more seriously or you'll find yourself back here
tomorrow."

Looking down at the tiny redhead by his side, David
couldn't help but smile. "I think I could handle that. Yes,
I think I could."

Ellen shook her head with a laugh. "Don't push your
luck, David. A mall, two days in a row? You'd give yourself a nervous breakdown."

In the end, Ellen settled on a paperweight, the snowy kind with a minuscule schoolhouse on the inside of the globe, *I Love My Teacher* engraved on the base. She knew it was silly, David told her so, but she liked the idea and thought that Rafe would appreciate the corny humor it inspired. And a bottle of champagne. He would appreciate that, too.

"Wasted on Rafe, if you ask me," David said as they browsed the aisle and he read her the labels and prices. "And you know we're only all going to drink it for him, anyway."

"Then make it a very good bottle of champagne," Ellen warned.

She wasn't finished yet, but David was brave. Stifling a sigh, he led her to the bakery where she bought a pound of cookies for their next potluck dinner. Then she *really* got into shopping!

For Hank, she decided on a shaving kit, the old-fashioned kind with a soap brush made of real boar's hair. Chuck was hard, but in the end, she decided on a book, a British murder mystery in the classic mold.

And perfume for Patty, *that* was a must. They stood at a kiosk and David swore they must have smelled a hundred bottles before Ellen narrowed it down to Je Reviens and Angel.

"So, you like that French stuff, huh?" David observed, and bought her a bottle of Angel on the sly.

"And lest you think I've forgotten you," she teased when they finally called it a day, "I'm saving your gift for when I come back with Patty and do a serious shop!"

"A serious shop? My God!" David laughed as they headed for the truck, "What do you call this outing?"

"Oh, this was just fine, but it wasn't down and dirty. Why, we didn't even begin to look at clothes!"

"Hey, but I would have," David protested. "You just didn't mention it."

"I didn't dare," Ellen teased. "But you did outdo my expectations and I sincerely thank you." Reaching high to find his face, she planted a kiss on his raw cheek, then pulled back, slightly embarrassed.

"I can live with that." He grinned, straightening his shoulders.

They went home very tired, but Ellen was enormously satisfied with her purchases. She looked so beat, though, that David insisted he be allowed to walk Candy, and Ellen let him. When he returned half an hour later, she was asleep on the couch, so he fed the dog and quietly left. But it was a scene that made him daydream, and when he arrived home, the cabin suddenly didn't seem so inviting.

Chapter Twelve

Ellen's birthday was fast approaching, and when the group found out, they voted to celebrate the occasion in the grand manner. They decided to dress up—really dress up—and drive to a local nightclub just outside of Saratoga Springs. Dining and dancing in great style was the order of the day.

To which end, Patty and Ellen drove to Lake Placid one morning to buy fancy dresses and shoes and, oh, a few pair of pants, a sweater or two, definitely a few pullovers for the new teacher. And how about some sexy lingerie, Patty insisted. After all, a girl never knew.

Ellen knew. She'd never need that kind of stuff in Longacre. It was too darned cold! Oh, heck, Patty argued, not all her nights were destined to be frosty. Sooner or later, there was bound to be a hot spell, she joked, and it never hurt to be ready. Ellen shook her head, but allowed herself to be persuaded. It wasn't hard, either, silky teddies like gossamer on her fingers, delicate lace a feminine reminder that she did like pretty things, after all.

They made it their last stop, before they left the mall— the gift for David that Ellen had not forgotten. She knew exactly what it was she wanted. Patty's brow rose at Ellen's choice, but when Ellen didn't explain, she didn't ask questions.

In the interest of keeping David at arm's length, Ellen asked Hank to pick her up for the drive to the nightclub. David would be annoyed, but he'd been hanging around way too much lately and she wanted to reestablish some distance. So Hank had the honor of escorting Ellen, and was bursting with pride when they made their entrance to the club an hour later.

In a chiffon gown of pale green, a thin strand of gold resting on her creamy breast, Ellen was a vision that stopped even the maître d' in his tracks, and he'd seen many beautiful women in his time. Her red hair coiled at her nape to allow only a few stray curls to frame her face, while long, gold earrings brushed her shoulders. Patty had taught her to apply only the tiniest hint of makeup, and to use the lightest hand applying clear mascara. Putting on blush was a piece of cake. Using the discreet color palette that Patty had chose for her, Ellen could make very few mistakes. Lipstick? The redder the better, Patty swore. Fire-engine red, it was!

"My Lord, Ellen Candler, you are a seriously lovely woman," Hank had said when he'd picked her up.

Everyone else was equally well-dressed, when they gathered together an hour later. Patty was dressed in turquoise and gold, and the men in suits freshly pressed. Heads turned at the handsome party they made, David not the least, so striking in black, but he hadn't the wit to notice. He only had eyes for Ellen.

To die and go to heaven with her in my arms like this, that would be my last wish before I died, David thought as he held her tightly and led her 'round the dance floor. "Happy birthday," he whispered.

"Thank you, David. And it is! I'm having a wonderful time!" Ellen promised, her cheek resting lightly on his chest. "Everyone has been so kind. My new dress, this lovely dinner, dancing with my friends. Who would have thought a year ago—" She left off, feeling awkward talking about Montana, and chose a safer route. "Do you like my dress?" she asked, searching for a safe topic.

"You mean, that scarf you're wearing?" David said, biting out the words. "Be careful not to sneeze!"

"David, what on earth—" Surprised, she tipped her face to his, and David almost had to kiss her.

"Damned if you're near to spilling out of it, Ellen! If you know what I mean!"

"No, I don't know what you mean!"

"It's… You know, the top part…the front. It's cut way too low, *okay?* And it's too damned tight, if you must know! You can see every…every…everything!"

"Everything?" Ellen laughed, knowing it couldn't possibly be true, that Patty would never expose her so.

"Well, damned near everything!" David insisted angrily as he led her back to their table.

No matter his temper, David was no competition for a steak dinner! Ellen sat back and enjoyed her party, determined not to let him spoil the night.

Saving the best for last, the group had secretly arranged for a huge birthday cake, replete with sparklers, to be brought out toward the end of the evening. Tears filling her eyes, Ellen just managed to blow out the candles while everyone in the restaurant rose to their feet and applauded.

She received so many presents, she didn't know which

one to open first. But when they were done, she took the opportunity to give out her own gifts. They couldn't believe she'd bought all that stuff, and with such an unlikely chaperon as David.

"Oh, but he was so patient," Ellen promised them with a twinkle in her eye as she pushed a gaily wrapped box his way.

"For me?" David asked with surprise as he began to unwrap the box. They all leaned forward to read the title of the book he held aloft. *The Return of the Native*. David's mind flashed back to his first evening in Montana when he'd stumbled across Ellen in the library, reading the very same book.

When he'd walked into the library and fallen in love.

He was deeply moved. "You remembered all this time?"

"I did," Ellen said smugly. "And look, there's something more."

David dug down into the box and removed something delicately wrapped in tissue paper. "A paperweight?" He smiled faintly.

"A little more than that," Ellen warned him, "so do be careful unwrapping it."

The entire table gasped as David gently tore apart the tissue paper to hold in his palm the most exquisite figurine they'd ever seen outside a museum. Standing eight inches tall, it was the windswept figurine of a woman, one hand stretched high to keep hold of her huge beribboned hat, the other hand delicately held aloft in greeting. Sculpted to perfection from the purest white marble, her every feature was an elegant line, from her gay smile to her solemn Gypsy eyes. David knew the worth of what he held.

"It's from my father's collection, isn't it?" he guessed, his voice a heavy rasp.

Ellen nodded, her eyes glistening. "I knew you would like it. It was his favorite piece of his whole collection. He kept it by his bedside."

"Thank you, Ellen," he whispered. "Thank you for saving me from my own silly pride."

The table watched. Something was going on but they weren't quite sure what. No matter. It was time to go. Rafe was given the honor of escorting Ellen home. But when Rafe arrived at Ellen's house, David was standing in the shadows, and minutes later, after Rafe drove away, David was ringing Ellen's doorbell.

When she opened the door, he swung her into his arms and kicked the door closed behind him. He kissed her hard, not letting up until he felt her relax in his arms. Then he marched with her in his arms into the living room and sank to the sofa, taking her with him.

"That was my mother. Did you know?"

Her reply was tender, but her astonishment could not have been greater. "The figurine was of your *mother?*"

"Yes. I had forgotten its existence. But somehow you honed in on the one thing that would mean something to me. It boggles the mind. Do you think it's karmic?" he teased lightly as he raised his eyes to hers.

"I don't even know how to spell it!"

"Well, spell this."

But there were no words to his verse. It was a kiss, its sublime gentleness whose meaning didn't need a fancy turn of phrase, but spoke to Ellen nonetheless. Flowing through her body, his kiss awakened her senses, stirring her so deeply there was no turning back. Crushing her against the cushions, David's lips trilled down her slender neck, then stole back to tease the corners of her mouth. Soon he was demanding entry of the most exquisite kind, at the seam her soft lips made. Slowly she let him taste her, the tip of her tongue shyly meeting his, but they were soon engaged in a duel that left her panting.

Looking down at the tousled heap she'd become, David saw that he had overcome Ellen's resistance. Her eyes focused on his, seeing and yet not, her answer was clear. Desire was in her eyes, and he understood that she was his for the asking, and he would have her. Slowly, so that she clearly understood, David eased the straps of her gown past her shoulders, and tugged at the bodice till it was a puddle at her waist. Magically, his hands roamed her body, almost prayerful as he brought her smooth, pink breasts to rosy peaks. He could feel coils of desire spin through her body, feel her arch toward him as his tongue caressed a tender, beaded nipple. Her hands aflutter, they slid around his neck to urge him closer, eager for more of his touch.

Warm thighs. Soft thighs. What a divine creation she was, David thought as he rucked her dress to slide his hand beneath the hem. But his greedy palm wanted more than soft, tensile skin, it wanted the wet warmth of her vulnerability. Slowly his fingers trailed the silky skin of her thighs to find purchase at the juncture of her legs. Slipping beneath the thin, trim border of her pantie, he found her most secret spot and began to stroke her lightly. Her pleasure was pure and explosive. Unzipping his trousers, he slid into her warm center before she could think to protest. He watched as, astonished, her eyes opened wide. She tried to rise, confused and unsure of her passion.

"David!"

Rearing up, he began long, strong stokes of penetration. "Tell me that you want this. Your body says yes, but I need to hear it in your voice."

"Oh, yes, I want this!" Ellen cried, falling back into

the silky cushions, her hands digging desperately into his forearms. "I want this so much! Don't stop. Don't stop."

He could have stopped, and he would have, if she'd said any differently. But she'd said yes, and David was satisfied that she understood her commitment. His own voice was a low growl, foreign to his ears, as he continued to love her, but he was fiercely determined to maintain his control solely for the pleasure of pleasing her again. Looking down, watching her struggle to prove her own desire, he was overwhelmed by love. Every stroke he made, languorous and deep, was an avowal of that love. This time it would be different. He would never leave her again. God forgive him, but he even hoped he made her pregnant.

He returned to her mouth, to her breast, breathed his hot breath upon her shell-like ears, urging her on to a burning sweetness. She went willingly, screamed when the moment came, arched her back and wrapped her legs around his heavy thighs. He almost laughed with relief, what it did to his sanity to maintain such tight control. But, Lord, it was worth the effort. He rose along with her to heights he'd never known and collapsed on top of her, careful where he landed in his passionate expense. It took him a while to catch his breath.

"I love you, Ellen."

But his princess was asleep. Tenderly he moved them into her bedroom, lay his head upon her breast and fell asleep, too. Sleeping heavily, they didn't stir until the rising sun alerted David to the time. He was on duty in an hour. The clock told him so.

"I've got to go, Ellen," he whispered in her ear.

"Hmm."

"I'll be back later, sweetheart, right after work," he

promised, running his palm along her shoulder. "Give me a kiss. It has to last me all day."

Half asleep, Ellen fluttered her pale lids and felt an alien hand on her breast. David saw her smile and stole a kiss from her sleepy mouth, then crept from the room, his shoes in hand.

Ellen turned over and crawled beneath her covers, never once opening her eyes. It had all been a delightful dream, she was sure. But she was confused when she woke later that morning and felt a strange soreness between her thighs. Perhaps her monthly—

The night came back in a lightening surge of memory. Before regret could blossom, her remorse was covered in a mantle of anger. She had been trying so hard to lengthen the distance between her and David, and now this! He had been getting too close, insinuating himself into the fabric of her life, every chance he got. Through Patty and Chuck, and Rafe and Hank, he didn't care. Even giving her that puppy—no matter that a dog and its companionship was precisely what she had needed. Buying her perfume— never mind it was her favorite. Lending her the emotional support she needed to become a teacher—humph! She had been going to do it, anyway!

Nothing was going to win David any points. When Ellen thought about what they'd done the night before, she burned with shame. He'd been artful, he knew his way beneath the sheets far too well for her to put up a decent fight. Not that she'd wanted him to stop, he'd made her feel so good. *That* was the problem. He'd taken advantage of her, rekindled old, forgotten feelings, created new ones, too, with his skillful hands. O-oh, if he were here, she would strangle him!

It was quite a morning for poor Candy, barely noticed in all the stomping her mistress did around the house.

Instinct told her to hide away under the couch, and she didn't dare show her nose until Ellen called her for a walk. Her *very short walk,* for immediately they were out, they seemed to be back in the house. And she didn't get breakfast till way past noon, for goodness' sake, her mistress was so distracted.

In the state she was in, Ellen gave David no credit for what it cost him to love her. To appear in public, to socialize, to concern himself with her well-being. To reveal his face. To work past the pain and humiliation he had lived with most of his life. To tamp down his defenses when someone glanced his way. To believe—at least *try* to believe—that people were looking past his scars to the person he was. Not quite believing it, but hoping it might be true. These things he'd done for her sake, as much as for his, for the sake of being with her. They were giant steps for David Hartwell, and could not be discounted, but Ellen didn't want to think about these things. She didn't want to be moved to a certain tolerance. It meant she would have to take responsibility for a whole lot more than what had happened the night before, and she wasn't going to do that. She wasn't ready to do that. Hence, it was far more convenient—and less risky—to dwell upon his flaws. After all, look what happened in Baltimore. He'd made love to her there, too, then abandoned her. How could she be sure he wouldn't do it again? Hadn't she woke this morning to another empty bed, one he'd occupied only hours before?

And another thing. What part did love have in all this for David? He'd never even mentioned the word. After all, she loved him!

She *still* loved him! Oh, Lordy, where had that come from? That was good for one smashed cup in the kitchen sink.

No, no, this was a mistake, a thought out of nowhere, histrionics taking over. She couldn't possibly still love him! Okay, maybe she had thought so, once, but certainly not now! He'd been careless with her heart, and her heart was not that forgiving. Or was it? Did she have no governance over her emotions? Was she so foolish as to let them take precedence over her head? Hadn't stories— tragedies, to be sure—been written over and over about the folly of misplaced affection? Where were the lessons to be learned from the past?

If Ellen were bent on making herself miserable, David was not far behind. For all that he accomplished that day at work, he might as well have stayed home. He began the day by spilling coffee all over his shirt, and no one in the office had a clean shirt that fit past his broad shoulders. This meant he had to spend the day looking like a slob, which did not lend itself to the figure of authority he was supposed to be. Later, on morning patrol, his truck took a turn so wide, he ended up in a ditch. It turned out that he had bent the front axle and had to be towed. Back at the office, he found himself reading his mail three times before the content penetrated. By four o'clock, he'd crashed his computer twice and was snapping at everyone so much that his supervisor got disgusted and told David to go home. David agreed it was a good idea. He borrowed a car and left.

Back at his cabin, he attended to Pansy and her pups. Got to get you guys a new home, he thought as he fed them. Can't afford to feed all these Pansys. He made a mental note to post a notice at the Longacre Diner. They had a bulletin board for posting just that sort of thing, for announcing community events, Help Wanted, Pups For Sale…Free To A Good Home.

He showered and shaved, taking a long time with his

razor, twitching his lips every which way to get it just right. He sure didn't want to abrade Ellen's tender skin, he thought with a wry smile. Combing his hair, he made another mental note to get a haircut, long overdue. He wouldn't want Ellen to think he was unkempt. She might not be able to see, but she sure could feel its length. Picture perfect, he thought, checking himself out one last time in the bathroom mirror. Even his scars didn't seem as obvious. Who you kidding? He smiled into the mirror. They just weren't that important anymore. His priorities had shifted. Other things had become more important— like Ellen.

Tossing down the comb, David hurried to his bedroom to throw on some clean clothes. Maybe he should iron his shirt, though. It was looking awfully creased. Jeez, he laughed to himself as the iron heated, he was acting just like a schoolboy on his first date. Why, he'd even polished his shoes.

He was so nervous going down the mountain to Ellen's, he maintained a speed of ten miles, just to be sure he arrived in one piece. By the time he knocked at the door to her house, the sky was dark. Hank Collins answered with a smile.

"Hi, David, come on in. Although it can't be a long stay. Ellen and I are on our way out."

"Hello, David," Ellen said as she came into sight, rummaging around in her pocketbook. Cool as a cucumber, no inflection in her voice, not a hint of what had gone on between them.

David swallowed hard, forcing down the bad feeling rising. "Hello, Ellen. I came to…" The way Hank was all ears, David didn't want to get too personal, and the way Ellen was behaving, he could see she wasn't going to help him out. In fact, she seemed kind of annoyed that he was even there.

Puzzled, David said the first thing that came to mind. "I thought we had...um...plans."

Ellen frowned, a mocking smile on her lips. "Plans?"

All right, he would play it her way. "To work on Candy's training. *You know.*"

"Oh, that." Ellen smiled, but it was filled with pained tolerance. "David, I really think that Candy's doing so well that we can dispense with her training. She's such a smarty, aren't you, pup?" she crooned as Candy nibbled at her feet. "I know the effort you made to help me, and all that running down here to town for our sake, I feel so guilty. I don't want to put you out anymore. Candy and I are a team now. Anyway, she's enrolled in obedience school, if you remember. They'll take care of anything else she needs to know."

"It was no trouble. I never minded."

Ellen laughed, and if Hank could not detect the hollow ring, David could. "No, I insist. There's really no need, and you could be putting your time to better use."

"Ellen—"

Her eyes were cold and her voice was firm. "I insist."

David was stunned. He watched as Ellen shrugged on her coat and headed for the door. "Hank?"

"Yes, ma'am." Hank held the door as they all exited, but Ellen was calling the shots. He was there because she had summoned him an hour earlier, saying she was dying for a hamburger, and would he like to take her out to eat? If things seemed more complicated than she'd made out, that was not his concern.

There was nothing for David to do but to watch them drive away. He called Ellen the next day and left five messages warning her that he would be there that night, straight from work.

She left one for him. Don't bother to come, she wouldn't be there. She had plans and would be sleeping at a friend's house that night. Not to worry about Candy, either. Candy was spending the night at the Louis home and Jonah was thrilled.

David searched high and low for his old whiskey bottle and spent the night wondering who Ellen's friend was. He'd already called Patty's, but Chuck said she was out playing poker with her girlfriends. When Chuck asked how Ellen was, David knew he'd struck out. At Hank's, there was no answer, and no one answered the telephone at Rafe's, either.

He had a helluva headache in the morning.

But he was spitting nails as he drove to work, and he was still angry when he pulled up to Ellen's that evening, determined to have it out with her. What the hell was she doing shutting him out like this, after everything that had gone under?

Alas, Patty and Chuck were visiting, looking as though they were settled in for a long evening, listening to some old records they'd picked up at a church bazaar. As a matter of fact, Ellen told him coldly, Patty was sleeping over so she could drive Ellen to an early doctor's appointment down in Kingston.

"I can do that," David said in a clipped, furious voice.

Patty gave him a flinty look.

"Well, don't you have a store to open?" he said gruffly.

"I can open late, it's no problem," Patty explained lightly. "I'll drop Ellen at her class afterward and head straight home."

"I'll pick you up from work, then," he told Ellen.

"No need, thank you. Some of my students and I are going out for drinks. I may even stay overnight in Albany. One of them invited me to stay over."

"Is that ethical?"

Ellen laughed. "Jeezus, David, her mother said it would be fine!"

Beet red, David turned on his heel and left, not caring what his friends thought of his surly behavior.

He left their confrontation for the weekend. Confrontation was the only word that he could apply to the situation, now. It was clear that Ellen was avoiding him, punishing him for a sin he didn't know he'd committed. Unless making love to her was a sin, and he couldn't believe that, not the way she'd responded so passionately. Not when he remembered how she'd clung to him. Just the thought of that night made him head out back to split logs for an hour.

Jonah Louis was on the street corner, walking Candy, when David arrived at eight Saturday morning.

"Hey, Jonah, how you doing?" David called from the cab of his truck. Everyone knew everyone in a small town, and Longacre was no exception.

Jonah looked up at him with the all the wisdom of a fourteen-year-old boy, as he lightly tugged on Candy's leash. Beautifully obedient, Candy immediately sat and looked up at David, her tail wagging fondly. "Hello, Mr. Hartwell. Ellen's not home."

Was he so transparent? David grimaced. "Okay, Jonah, you know so much, where is Miss Candler?"

"She said I should call her Ellen. She said her friends called her *Ellen*."

David tried not to roll his eyes. "Okay, kid. *Ellen*. Do you know where *Ellen* is?"

"How come you don't call her *Ellen?*"

"I do call her *Ellen.*"

"No, you didn't."

"I'm telling you I do," David said, his jaw muscle working furiously. "I was just being polite."

"Are you her friend?"

"I'm trying to be."

"Oh, then you're not, not yet."

"Ah, jeez, kid, is this the Spanish Inquisition?"

"This isn't 1480 and we're not in Spain."

"Say what?"

"The year of the Spanish Inquisition. The first one, anyhow."

"Jonah, where is Ellen? Please!"

"She's away."

Lord have mercy, David thought. "Where to?"

"Don't know."

"Whom did she go with?"

"Professor Rafe."

"Okay, last question, son—"

"I'm not your son, you know."

"This I know to be a fact, kid!"

Jonah stared up at him with the most unreadable face David had ever seen on a child. "You going to be a lawyer, kid?"

"That'd be two questions, Mr. Hartwell."

"Call me *David.*"

"Why, are we friends?"

"You called Mr. Tellerman *Rafe.*"

"Yeah, but he's my friend. *He* brings me Twizzlers."

Good Lord! That was bribery, sheer bribery! Rafe was buying the goodwill of this fourteen-year-old Einstein!

"Jonah, do you really know where they went?" David asked, suddenly suspicious.

"No, actually I don't. They're frolicking somewhere."

"Frolicking?"

"It means—"

"I know what it means!"

Jonah ignored him in the interest of exactitude. "It means laughing, having a good time."

David was nauseous. "Do you by any chance know when they're coming home?"

"Now, *there* I can help you, Mr. Hartwell," Jonah announced proudly. "Ellen asked me to keep Candy overnight, so I think it's going to be tomorrow. I love Candy, she's a beautiful dog, don't you think?"

"Yes, she is," David agreed, chewing on his lip thoughtfully. "You like dogs, huh?"

"I love them!" Jonah said, scratching Candy's head while Candy closed her eyes in ecstasy.

"Tell you something, guy. I have a whole litter where that came from. You ask your mom if you can have a dog, I'll let you pick one out."

Jonah's eyes grew wide. "You mean it?"

David smiled. "I mean it."

"Gee, David, could you wait here and I'll go ask my mom, right now?"

"Not now. I've got to run an errand. Just ask her, and if she says it's all right, we'll arrange it."

"Wow! Thanks!"

"No problem, Jonah. See you around." David turned on the ignition and started to drive away, but put the car in reverse and carefully backed up. "Hey, Jonah."

"Sir?"

"What kind of candy do you like *besides* Twizzlers?"

Chapter Thirteen

David called all day, but Jonah Louis had the right of it. Rafe and Ellen were making a night of it. The next day, too, it seemed, because he still got no answer on Sunday. He knocked around his cabin, doing laundry, cleaning out all the strange and unidentifiable food that had seemed to have sprouted overnight in his refrigerator, but when he saw the sun setting, and still got no answer at Ellen's, he'd had quite enough. He would go down to Longacre and sit in his truck until she arrived home.

The house was dark when he arrived, but luckily, he only had to sit ten minutes before Rafe Tellerman pulled up to Ellen's house. Ellen jumped out, but apparently Rafe wasn't invited in, because he saw her to her door, got right back in his car and drove away. David was knocking hard on the door as soon as Rafe had turned the corner.

Ellen answered almost immediately, shaking her head. ''Come on, Rafe, I told you it was late.''

"And what are you going to tell *me?*" David snarled.

"David?"

"In the flesh! And I'm not leaving till we talk."

"But it's late and I have a class to teach tomorrow."

"Too bad. I don't feel too sprightly myself. I haven't had a decent night's sleep since—" David barged past her and shut the door. "Where were you with that Romeo? Don't bother to deny it, I just saw him drive off. You were with him all weekend! If he laid a hand on you—"

Disgusted, Ellen stomped away. "Oh, for heaven's sake, David, we drove down to a concert in Woodstock, all right?"

"No, it's not all right! Where did you sleep?"

"Boy, do you ever have a nerve, forcing your way in here like Attila the Hun, for no reason I can see, wanting—no, demanding!—to know where I slept! And I'll just bet you'd love to know with whom," she added with a sweet smile.

David was furious. Clasping her shoulders, he gave her a small shake. "I'm warning you, Ellen, don't fool with me. I'm at the end of my rope."

Hands on her hips, she faced him squarely. "David Hartwell, are you threatening me?"

David's hands fell at once. "No, of course not. I just wanted to know if you and— Never mind, don't answer that!"

"My, my, don't you have a high opinion of me!"

"That's not what I meant!"

"What exactly did you mean, then?" she asked, her voice dangerously low.

"I just meant...I was wondering where you were, is all. Come on, Ellen, I think have a right to ask, for chrissake!"

"Why you need to know my whereabouts is beyond me. It's certainly no concern of yours! But if you must know something, then know this, I can well afford my own hotel room!"

David's relief was almost palpable. "Dammit, Ellen, everything you do concerns me! And dammit, why is it so dark in here? Could you please turn on some lights? Didn't you pay your bills?"

"Stop!" Ellen commanded. "Leave the lights off!"

"But I can't see."

"Neither can I," she said curtly. With unerring accuracy, she walked into the living room while David stumbled after her. Sitting on the sofa, she folded her hands in her lap and listened to him curse when he banged his shin on the coffee table. "There's an armchair to your right. You may sit there."

David found it, rubbing his leg as he sat. "What's this all about, Ellen, sitting here in the dark?"

"I always sit in the dark."

"But *I'm* not blind!"

"You are now," she said cheerfully. "How do you like it?"

David swore softly. Was this some kind of test?

"Tsk, tsk, such language! Well, I hate it, too, the eternal dark, but this is the way it is for me all the time, so I think you can humor me, this one night. Now, say whatever you wish to say, and then I'd appreciate it if you left."

Sitting here in the dark, listening to Ellen's silence, David wondered where to begin. It was too weird sitting in the gloomy living room, hardly able to discern any outlines. Unnatural, too, not to be able see her face and to take his cues from her expressions. Was this what she was driving at? Was it only the turn of phrase that counted for her, and the quality of emotion behind it? He'd never thought about that before. She was asking him to rely on senses he hardly used, *to see with his ears*. Well, fair enough, he would play it the way she wanted and as honestly as he could.

"So that's what you call it, *the eternal dark?* I never heard you say that before, or that you hated being blind."

Ellen laughed, disbelieving. "Did you think I liked it?"

"I never thought about it. I guess I thought you were…um…philosophical about it."

"Well, you were wrong, but don't worry, most people think the same thing. It just isn't something I can do anything about, is it? My being blind, I mean. I trained myself early on to be…*philosophical*…did you say? Your word, not mine."

"But you never said."

"You never asked! You've done a lot of things for me—good things and bad—but the one thing you never once did was ask me how I felt about being blind! Or how I felt about the operation failing. Not that it makes any difference now. I mean, what would I say? Should I beat my breast in anger? Where would it get me?"

"I can't believe you've been holding all this inside you and never said a word."

"Oh, my, look who's talking! I lived with you for almost four months and you never said a word to me about your car accident, much less your sacred scars! I might as well have been a doll sitting on a shelf, for all you ever confided in me, so please don't go scolding me for not confiding in you!"

Ellen was right. He'd treated her like a pretty doll and never given her the opportunity to share her emotions. Or revealed his—aside from his temper! Perhaps that was why he had run away, back in Baltimore. Not because she might have hated his face, but because she might have made him learn to live with it.

"Do you hate them so much?" she asked quietly into the silence.

He didn't even pretend to misunderstand her. "My scars? No, not anymore. Not since you. You taught me not to. I thought...I thought if you could be so brave, I could be, too."

"Well, guess what? I'm not so brave, and now you know."

David made a slight movement that Ellen sensed immediately and made her sit up swiftly. "Please, don't come near me. Please don't use your body as a weapon."

Quickly, David sank back down on the armchair. "I guess I really screwed up in Baltimore, leaving you like that."

"Leaving me like that hurt."

"Ellen, for what it's worth, I'm sorry. If I knew then what I know now, I never would have left you."

"And what is it that you know now?"

"That my scars didn't matter. That you wouldn't have cared."

"No, I would not have," Ellen agreed coldly.

"Oh, Ellen, it was a hard won lesson that took time to learn. I've lived this way most of my life. Looking in the mirror every day, watching people stare at me like I was some sort of freak. You don't know—"

"I don't know?" Ellen repeated, incredulous. "Haven't you heard a word I've said the last few minutes? After all I've said, you still think I don't know what it's like to be treated like some sort of freak?"

"But you couldn't *see* my scars, not the way I did," David protested sadly. "Not in the hundreds of mirrors that told no lies."

"No, I didn't have to look in any mirror, but, oh, David, I had ears! Ears so keen they couldn't avoid hearing how people talked behind my back, cringing to hear how they pitied me, enduring the way they talked to me like I was an invalid, or worse, an idiot. Your father, bless him, tried to protect me, but the cage he built was gilded. The way *you* treated me, on the other hand, when you arrived in Montana, was a breath of fresh air. Bursting in unannounced, shaking that silly mountain up, bossing everyone about, unafraid to voice your opinions. Dragging me down from my ivory tower! Even if I hated it at the time, I knew something exciting was about to happen. *Some of us have to work,* you said, and I took that as a challenge. At last, someone was treating me as an adult!"

David was shaken. "I didn't realize."

Suddenly, as quickly as it sparked, the fight left Ellen. "I'm sitting here today, an independent woman in my own home, because of *you,* David. You said you were taking me down the mountain, and you did. You kept your word and I'll bless you for it for the rest of my life."

"If I remember correctly, I thought it was time for *both* of us to come down the mountain. I went with you, Ellen. If it weren't for you, I wouldn't be walking down Main Street the way I do nowadays, or dancing in fancy nightclubs. Why, I haven't seen my felt hat in weeks. Remember that letter my father left me, after he died?"

"I never read it, but yes, I remember."

"I'll show it to you sometime, but there are two lines he wrote that I know by heart. *I know you will protect her with your life. In return, she will give you back yours.* He was talking about you, and he was right, you have given me sight—yes, you have—your sight! To see the world the way you see it, even if you are blind. You taught me that to share a glass of wine with friends was a fine thing to do, and that to buy a woman a bottle of perfume was a rare treasure."

This time David did move, to settle beside Ellen, though he was careful not to touch her. "Ellen, no matter what, I can never go back to the man I was before I met you, and I don't want to. You gave me back my life, just as my father promised, and now I want to do something for you."

"Can you help me to see the sun rise?"

"No, but I can walk with you out into the sunshine and share its warmth."

"I would rather walk myself."

"Then I would follow behind you. I love you, Ellen."

Ellen jumped to her feet. "Please don't say such a thing!"

David felt for her hand and grasped it tightly. "I *will* say such a thing because it's the truth. I want to marry you."

"Marry me?" she scorned. "Where on earth did you come up with that idea?"

"From the idea that I love you?"

Ellen dismissed his declaration without a qualm. "There's a whole lot more to marriage than love."

"Whoa, hold on there, lady!" David laughed. "It has to be worth something! At least, that's the rumor, these last five hundred years."

"David, I give you a great deal of credit, but that doesn't mean you're ready for such a big step."

"Come on, Ellen, I'm thirty-five and then some. Gray hair is even starting to show. I'm more than ready, so what are we *really* talking about here?"

"All right, David, I'll be honest. I'm not too sure I want to marry *anyone*. Just because *you* think you're ready to settle down doesn't mean that I am. I'm...I'm just beginning to find my feet and I'm not sure I want the distraction of a relationship."

"There's a lot of stuff about *you* in that, but what about *me?*"

"You asked me to marry you, not figure out your life."

"So I did," David agreed quietly. "That said, who's the coward now?"

"Coward?" Ellen rejected that, out of hand. "Have you really considered how difficult it would be, married to a woman who is blind?"

"Gee, Ellen, I think I hear you whining!" Reaching toward the lamp on the end table, David turned the switch. "Sorry, but if this is going to work, one of us has to see, and I'm it."

"Couldn't take being blind for even an hour!" Ellen scoffed.

"No, I couldn't. But since I've been living with my ugly mug for fifteen years, you'll forgive me the lapse. Come on, sweetheart, come sit down." Gently but firmly, David pulled Ellen down to the sofa. "Now, when are we getting married, sweetheart? Is tomorrow too soon?"

Ellen folded her arms across her chest, her lips pursed, a picture of mutiny. "Something tells me you're not listening."

"What did you say?" David teased. "God, but you're beautiful, even when you're angry!"

"Oh, David, looks are *so* unimportant. You always did assign too much importance to them."

David laughed. "Okay, fine. But you are beautiful, and it's my ace in the hole, honey. I have to live with a shrew the rest of my life, it's okay with me if she's easy on the eyes."

Lifting her small hand, David placed it on his scarred face and rubbed it across his right cheek. From the top of his black brow to his jawline, he made Ellen touch every grotesque pit and furrow. "Feel my face, Ellen. Feel my scars. Feel what a hundred pieces of glass did to me, and don't tell me that I put too much emphasis on beauty. It's been a battle to come to terms with how I look, and no one knows that better than you. If I've been rewarded with the exquisite splendor of your face, let me enjoy it. It's a gift I think I've earned."

Gently, David wiped away Ellen's tears. "And another thing..."

"There's more?" she sniffed.

"Yes. Remember this part?"

His hand cupping her cheek, his lips feather-like but persuasive, his mouth covered hers. "What are we going to do about this part?" he asked softly.

"Oh, David," Ellen whispered, "it's just sex. It will die a natural death."

"Yeah, me, too, eventually. But in the meantime, even if it is *just sex,* will you let me kiss you? God, Ellen, but I've been aching for you."

"I missed you, too."

"Good, that's real good, Ellen. I'm glad to know we were both miserable apart." Pulling her close, he brushed her mouth with his, danced a slow waltz around its softness, then a tango to declare his possession.

Ellen couldn't find the strength to stop him. Her brain might be appalled at his heavy-handed seduction, but her body was enthralled. But David could always have her with a kiss. Sliding an arm around her waist, she let him pull her into his arms. His scent, his heat, was intoxicating, and she went willingly, her cry of frustration at her unruly body all the permission David needed to pursue her.

Impressions of honeysuckle and sun-kissed strawberries

swirled through his head, the taste of her always more than David expected. He felt light-headed, and at the same time, curiously grounded. Unable to stop kissing her, he paused only for the slightest moment, to see if he could find the same response in her. But dear God, wasn't she the sweetest thing he'd ever seen, lying there in his arms, her cheeks flushed, her mouth moist and swollen, because of him!

"What's the problem, Ellen?" he whispered, his fingertips registering her tension as they stroked her pale cheek. "Why do you keep me at arm's length? I love you!"

"I love you, too, David. There was never anybody but you. Last week, when we made love, all the old feelings I had for you came back. But you left me once and I couldn't bear it if you did it again. I can hardly stand this."

"Let me get this straight," he said softly, his lips nibbling at her earlobe. "You don't trust me, and you won't marry me, but you'll let me make love to you?"

Ellen shrugged. "When you kiss me, I have no strength to fight you."

"Then I'll kiss you a lot." He kissed every part of her until she had no will to protest.

"Think we'll ever make it to a bed, sometime?"

Ellen hardly heard, she was so dizzy with want, but David was in full control. "Like it, do you? How much, Ellen? Tell me how much you want me to keep kissing you."

"Oh, David, I love you so much! I never said I didn't."

"Then marry me, Ellen. Say you'll marry me, or I swear I'll walk!"

"David!

"Dammit, Ellen, say *yes.* I don't want a damned mistress, I want a wife!"

"I can't!" she wailed.

"Why? For chrissake, why? *Tell me why, really why!*"

"Because I'm blind!"

Stunned, David abruptly pulled away and looked at Ellen as if he'd never seen her before. "What on earth? But I told you—"

Slowly, Ellen sat up and straightened her clothes with the little dignity she had left. "You love me, now," she told him wistfully. "But I'm young, now, and pretty—that's what you keep telling me, anyway—and you are young and in the throes of passion. But when I grow old, when my body is not so soft, when my hair isn't so red, and the loving doesn't come so easy, what happens then? How will you feel about carrying a blind old lady on your back?"

"Ah, jeezus, Ellen, tell me that you're joking."

Ellen's silence was her answer and David's brow clouded in anger. "I can't believe you're really doing this, destroying us like this!" The hands that held her so tenderly moments before dug deep into her shoulders.

"Well, have it your way, darling. But when you're sitting here alone at night—enjoying the damned *eternal dark*—the thing you might want to think about most carefully is, who is the one who is really handicapped now?"

David allowed Ellen plenty of time to think. But he took to hibernating again. He refused to attend Patty's Sunday dinners, declined to escort Ellen on her errands, did not answer Chuck's phone calls, and barely spoke to Rafe or Hank. He was just too distraught and didn't have the kind of temperament that withstood the agony of small talk.

He bided his time until late spring, when the crocuses were fully established and the roses were in bud, until school was out. Then, on the best of days, when his preparations were in place, David knocked on Ellen's door. She was astonished to hear him say hello, and she really tried to stop her heart from thumping, but she'd missed him so much that she almost cried. He couldn't know that all he had to do was to take her in his arms and she'd capitulate, he was that intent on his plan. So he took the long road, but in the end, he had much pleasure. It just didn't seem so promising at the time.

"I thought you'd like to go for a ride," he said coldly.

Used to David's surly gracelessness, Ellen agreed. She didn't even ask where they were going, she had missed him that desperately. Since her heart was leading the way, his bad manners counted for nothing. Her safety was a nonissue. Full well she knew that David would never hurt her in any way.

He drove without speaking, his blue eyes thoughtful slits. He didn't explain anything, and she didn't ask, not for the entire hour it took to arrive at their destination. The last few miles, he drove along a road that was fairly rough and somewhere in her memory was the vague recollection of a similar ride, but the distractions of the moment obscured it. Then he braked.

"Wait up and I'll help you out."

Ellen listened as he jumped from the truck and opened her door a moment later. "Where are we?"

"We're at a site I found so many years ago, I can't remember."

"We're in the forest, though, aren't we? I can smell it."

"Well, your senses are still operating. I guess it's just your common sense that's lacking," he said obliquely as he sat her at a picnic table. "Not too cold, are you? I have extra clothing, if you are. No? Good. Sandwiches all right for dinner? It's a little late for me to start cooking."

Puzzled, Ellen nodded.

"Good, then let's eat."

He sorted provisions and they ate in silence. To every word Ellen spoke David was noncommittal, so she dropped all pretence to conversation to wait out his game. He was leisurely coming to the point.

"It's bedtime."

Now, *that* was attention getting. "Excuse me?"

"You ever camp out before?"

"Before what?"

"Before now."

Ellen's answer was slow and careful. "No. Is that what we're doing? Tents and bonfires and marshmallows?"

"That's right, except that I forgot the marshmallows." He led her to the tent, explained its configuration and pulled her inside.

"It's one of those walk-in types, and I put a little chair in here for you. I didn't think you'd appreciate a pup tent, just yet. But don't look for a cot, it's sleeping bags all the way."

"All the way?"

"I padded them below with pine needles," he told her, adroitly skirting her question, "so we should be pretty comfortable." After helping her to remove her shoes, he handed Ellen a pair of pajamas. "You have five minutes to change."

"But—" But he was gone, and when he returned, she was still dressed.

"What's the problem?"

"I think—"

David just grunted, lifted her in his arms and stuffed

her into a sleeping bag. "Think in the morning. Right now I'm pretty tired, if you don't mind." Then he crawled in beside her, gave her his back and was sleeping in thirty seconds. They lay in the darkness together, her temper rising as his snoring gathered momentum.

"Excuse me," she whispered.

"Excuse me," she said more loudly, and added a tiny poke to his shoulder blades.

"Excuse me!" she shouted, and David turned over.

"Humph?"

"Don't mind me. Sorry to disturb you, but would you mind telling me what's going on?"

"Nothing. Don't worry, nothing is going to happen to you. You're perfectly safe. No bears up here in years." David turned away and tried to go back to sleep but Ellen wasn't satisfied.

"That's not what I meant, and you know it."

"I've had a very long day, you know. What with running back and forth preparing all this, I really could use some sleep."

"David, what's going on?"

"Can't you figure it out?"

"If I could figure it out, I wouldn't be asking!"

"Well, let's see, how should I put it? *Would you like to consider yourself camping out or kidnapped?*"

Ellen considered, rising up on her elbows. "Do you mean I can't go home if I want to? You wouldn't take me home if I asked?"

"Of course I would," David said indignantly. "You just have to ask."

"Even if it's the middle of the night?"

"Just as soon as possible."

"So there's a catch?"

"No catch."

"Then would you please take me home in the morning?"

"It's not possible."

"You said—"

"I said *as soon as possible.*"

"What constitutes possible?"

"Our getting married!"

It was Ellen's turn to get indignant. "Our getting married? But that's blackmail!"

"No, it's common sense, sweetheart. I love you. You love me. People in love get married. I gave you all of May to think about it."

"I did think about it. A lot."

"And?"

"Nothing's changed."

"That's too bad because I hear it's gonna rain tomorrow." He was snoring again in about a minute.

Ellen was wrathful, but the fresh air proved too much and she, too, was soon sleeping. When she woke in the morning, it was to find David's leg flung over her hip, his arm coiled heavily around her waist. Still snoring loudly. And beneath it all, it was lovely. She felt warm and protected. But was it enough to commit? She didn't know. It was tempting, but the fears she had expressed in April still worried her. On the other hand, the way his hand lay across her belly was beguiling, and she wasn't thinking in terms of sex. It would be very pleasant to wake every morning for the rest of her life with a husband whose large hand covered hers.

Then suddenly the hand was gone and David was sitting up and rubbing the sleep from his eyes. "'Morning, princess."

"Humph."

"That all you have to say?"

"Yes."

"Too bad. I was hoping you'd say something romantic like *I do.*"

"Not a chance!"

David was philosophical. "No problem, we've got all the time in the world. I brought a CD player and tons of batteries."

After what Ellen considered to be the worst breakfast in history—dry cheese sandwiches and tepid coffee—and lunch promising to be no better, she was ready to go home. She told David so in no uncertain terms.

David smiled. "Does that mean you're ready to get married?"

"No! I told you *no!*"

"Okay, so do you want to go wash up and listen to some Beethoven, then?"

"I want to go home!"

"Marry me!"

"David, this is an insane game you're playing. My friends will worry."

"Actually, I told them we were eloping, and Jonah Louis is dog-sitting Candy and Pansy and her pups in exchange for one of the pups and a case of Dove Bars, so like I said, we have all the time in the world. You know, nothing personal but you could do with a wash, honey."

Lips pursed, Ellen allowed David to lead her to a small stream. The brisk water felt great but the rumble of thunder made them head back for the tent sooner than they liked. Still, it was warm and snug crawling back into the sleeping bag and Ellen was napping within minutes.

When she woke, it was to feel David's fingers stroking her breast and his mouth following the trail they made.

"I thought you said I would be safe." She frowned

through her sleepiness. She could feel him smile against her skin.

"You are safe. I would protect you with my life," he promised as he wrapped his arms around her hips and buried his face between her breasts.

Resting her cheek on his head, Ellen believed him.

They said very little to each other the rest of the afternoon. David's intention was never to persuade Ellen—they had talked enough in the past—only to let her natural instinct dictate her decision—her decision to marry him, of course. To wait her out, as it were. He had enough vacation time to do it, too. He would have liked to shake her and say, *For goodness' sake, woman, you love me!* but he knew that wasn't going to hurry her along. And he wasn't a man of profound cunning. This was as complicated as things got for him. So he settled in for the long haul and tantalized her instead—never quite making love to her—but teasing her with soft, sweet kisses, gentle tugs and artful caresses.

It was she who seduced him, in the end. Waking him the next morning with kisses so well placed that he woke with a shock. "Jeez, Ellen what the hell are you doing, for Pete's sake?"

Stretching her bare body for the delight his eyes would find, she smiled. "Aren't you pleased?"

"Very!" he gasped, his eyes wide.

"But this is not part of your scheme?"

"It could be!"

Quickly she flung herself across his chest, her mouth hot against his neck. "Take me home," she whispered, "and I'll make you a happy man. A *very* happy man."

"Are you going to marry me?" David asked suspiciously. "I have the license right here in my backpack."

Frustrated, Ellen flung herself onto her back, all hope

of seduction gone. Her arms stretched wide, she took a deep breath and exhaled the longest sigh. "Oh, David!"

"I'd like children, lots of children, and the sooner the better."

"I wouldn't mind waiting a little bit myself."

"A year suit you?"

"Just so we could get to know each other a little better."

"I love you, Ellen. I promise, I'll spend the rest of my life making you happy."

"Oh, David, loving you was never the issue."

"I know that. That's the thing that will get us through all the rest. Even when your hair turns gray—and mine is gone!"

"Ugh!" But Ellen laughed. "Now can we go home?"

"No problem," David smiled as he scooped her up into his arms and walked outside.

"Done!" He took the steps to his cabin in a flash.

Ellen smiled, her arms wrapped around his neck. "You know, I kind of thought that ride up the mountain was familiar."

"You know," David laughed, "I kind of thought you did."

* * * * *

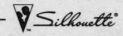

If you enjoyed what you just read,
then we've got an offer you can't resist!

Take 2 bestselling love stories FREE!

Plus get a FREE surprise gift!

▗▚▚▚▚▚▚▚▚▚▚▚▚▚▚▚▚▚▚▚▚▖

Clip this page and mail it to Silhouette Reader Service™

IN U.S.A.	IN CANADA
3010 Walden Ave.	P.O. Box 609
P.O. Box 1867	Fort Erie, Ontario
Buffalo, N.Y. 14240-1867	L2A 5X3

YES! Please send me 2 free Silhouette Special Edition® novels and my free surprise gift. After receiving them, if I don't wish to receive anymore, I can return the shipping statement marked cancel. If I don't cancel, I will receive 6 brand-new novels every month, before they're available in stores! In the U.S.A., bill me at the bargain price of $3.99 plus 25¢ shipping and handling per book and applicable sales tax, if any*. In Canada, bill me at the bargain price of $4.74 plus 25¢ shipping and handling per book and applicable taxes**. That's the complete price and a savings of at least 10% off the cover prices—what a great deal! I understand that accepting the 2 free books and gift places me under no obligation ever to buy any books. I can always return a shipment and cancel at any time. Even if I never buy another book from Silhouette, the 2 free books and gift are mine to keep forever.

235 SDN DNUR
335 SDN DNUS

Name	(PLEASE PRINT)	
Address	Apt.#	
City	State/Prov.	Zip/Postal Code

* Terms and prices subject to change without notice. Sales tax applicable in N.Y.
** Canadian residents will be charged applicable provincial taxes and GST.
All orders subject to approval. Offer limited to one per household and not valid to current Silhouette Special Edition® subscribers.
® are registered trademarks of Harlequin Books S.A., used under license.

SPED02   ©1998 Harlequin Enterprises Limited

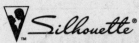

COMING NEXT MONTH

#1597 ISN'T IT RICH?—Sherryl Woods
Million Dollar Destinies
Single and happy-that-way Richard Carlton refused to act on the foolish feelings that PR consultant Melanie Hart inspired. Melanie brought passion to his too-organized, too-*empty* life. But soon her bundles of energy were no longer giving Richard a headache as much as a whole new outlook on life…and love!

#1598 BLUEGRASS BABY—Judy Duarte
Merlyn County Midwives
Dedicated midwife Milla Johnson was unfairly accused of malpractice…and only bad-boy doctor Kyle Bingham could save her. But what would the jury think if they discovered Milla and Kyle had shared a night of passion? And what would Kyle do when he learned Milla now carried their child?

#1599 TAKE A CHANCE ON ME—Karen Rose Smith
Logan's Legacy
A childhood tragedy had pitted CEO Adam Bartlett against all things medical. But when he learned his blood could save a little boy's life, Adam turned to nurse Leigh Peters—his first love—to help see him through the emotional procedure. Were the sparks that flew between them just an echo from the past…or the promise of a future?

#1600 WHERE YOU LEAST EXPECT IT—Tori Carrington
No one in Old Orchard knew that teacher Aidan Kendall was a man on the run. Aidan hadn't intended to stay in the small town…until he met Penelope Moon. The mystical beauty made Aidan believe in magic and miracles. But would their love survive when the danger on his heels caught up with him?

#1601 TYCOON MEETS TEXAN!—Arlene James
The Richest Gals in Texas
Avis Lorimer wanted a no-strings affair to go with her London vacation. Wealthy businessman Lucien "Luc" Tyrone was only too happy to oblige the soft-spoken Texas beauty. It was the perfect fling—until Luc decided he wanted Avis not just for the moment, but forever. Convincing Avis, however, was another matter!

#1602 DETECTIVE DADDY—Jane Toombs
A Michigan storm had landed a very pregnant—very much in labor—Fay Merriweather on the doorstop of police detective Dan Sorenson's cabin. After a tricky delivery, Dan was duty-bound to see that Fay and her baby got the care they needed. He never intended to actually fall for this instant family.…

SSECNM0204